PRAISE FOR *THE VATI*

"Michael Balter masterfully crafts a high-stakes thriller that plunges readers deep into the shadowy corridors of power, crime, and deception." —Gary McAvoy, author of the *Vatican Secret Archive Thrillers*

"We can't remember the last time we read a mafia thriller that was this fun." —BestThrillers.com

"Emotionally compelling, astute in its logic, delightfully unexpected ... hard to predict or put down." —D. Donovan, Senior Reviewer, *Midwest Book Review*

"A fast-paced, action-packed crime thriller that will have readers on the edge of their seats until the very end." —The Feathered Quill

"A must-read for lovers of gripping high-stakes crime thrillers with a touch of adventure, action, and drama ... I loved it." —Keith Mbuya for Readers' Favorite

"An intricate, masterfully crafted plot peppered with twists, authentic detail, and smart dialogue" —Warren C. Easley, author of the *Cal Claxton Mysteries*

"Addictive and compelling ... Marty and Bo are under the gun again in this explosive follow-up to the award-winning Chasing Money" —Michael Lindley, author of the *Hanna* and *Alex Low Country* mystery series

"A brilliant mix of danger, deception, and intrigue ... with complex characters, unpredictable twists, and high-stakes action" —Al Warren, House of Mystery Radio Show

PRAISE FOR *CHASING MONEY*

Winner – 2024 Crime Thriller of the Year – BestThrillers Book Awards

Winner – 2024 Feathered Quill Award – Mystery, Thriller, Suspense

Winner – 2023 Best Indie Book Award – Crime Thriller

"A strong voice paired with authentic dialogue … Packed with action" —The BookLife Prize

"Grows funnier and more surprising every step of the way. Balter's gift for pacing and dialogue make this a series to watch."

—Publisher's Weekly

"Gritty descriptions, simmering threats, and a wry sense of humor contribute to a countdown to disaster. Exceptionally clever and compelling." —*Midwest Book Review*

"A heart-pounding thriller that grabs you from the first page and won't let you get away." —Michael Lindley, author of the Amazon #1 *Hanna* and *Alex Low Country* mystery series.

"The DaVinci Code for grownups. Tinged with noir and ringing with authenticity. Don't miss this impressive debut novel!" —Warren C. Easley, author of the award-winning *Cal Claxton Mysteries*.

"Chasing Money is a roller coaster of a ride. It's wildly inventive and incredibly entertaining. I couldn't put it down." —Charles Cutter, author of the acclaimed *Burr Lafayette* legal thrillers

"Balter's acerbic wit, clear writing style and extensive knowledge of art history make this a captivating read!" —John Wemlinger, author of *The Cut*, a 2022 Michigan Notable Book

"A simple but satisfying crime novel that will keep readers hooked." —Kirkus Reviews

"Chasing Money is an impressive debut novel by a gifted author." — Awarded 5 Stars, Essian Asian, Reader's Favorite.

THE
VATICAN
DEAL

Mission Point Press
2554 Chandler Road
Traverse City, Michigan 49696
www.MissionPointPress.com
231-421-9513

Design by Sarah Meiers

Printed in the United States of America

ISBN softcover: 978-1-965278-44-4
Library of Congress Control Number: 2025903508

THE
VATICAN
DEAL

A MARTY AND BO THRILLER

MICHAEL BALTER

M·P·P
www.MissionPointPress.com

To my wife, Suzanne,

the love of my life.

CHAPTER ONE

Rome — Monday, January 19, 2004

BO LOVES TO TALK ABOUT MONEY.

How to make it, how to lose it, and most importantly, how to spend it.

"I think I can get a Cessna Citation for twenty million, give or take," he said, staring at the Egyptian obelisk rising from the fountain before us. "The fastest jet on the market. Cruises at about five hundred knots. From New York to London in six hours."

We sat on the terrace at Caffè Domiziano in the Piazza Navona, soaking up the warm winter sun and spooning *affogatos*—vanilla ice cream drowned in espresso. I wanted decaf, but when the *cameriere* kept repeating, "Sanka," I surrendered and ordered what Bo had.

A stove cart piled high with hot walnuts stood near our table, facing Bernini's Fountain of the Four Rivers. The vendor shoveled and stacked bags with practiced ease, sending up a warm, smoky aroma that mingled with the sweet scent of pastries from the café. The vibrant elliptical plaza was less crowded than in the summer months but still bustling with off-season tourists and street artists.

"We're up to our eyebrows in shit, and you want to talk about buying a plane," I said, gazing blankly at the massive statue of the god of the Danube.

"I need to talk about something else," said Bo, rubbing his side. "My ribs hurt, my face hurts, everything hurts. I need to stay positive. Let's talk about buying something."

1

"We're here to buy an Italian foundry," I reminded him.

"I'd rather buy a plane."

"I'm not sure Natalya will approve."

"Natalya has her own plane."

We fell into silence, each of us submerged in our own swirling anxieties, avoiding the obvious—how in hell did we get caught between the mafia and the Vatican?

We waited for Natalya.

She was late.

"This is fucked up," I finally said, and it was. A four-alarm trainwreck of a fuck up.

Bo winced. His face was so bruised from the beating that I couldn't tell if he was agreeing with me or just in pain.

I was about to say something cynical when a large man, as large as Bo, filled our space, casting us in shadow as he loomed over our table. He looked disheveled, as if he'd just fallen out of bed, his shabby work clothes hanging heavily over his substantial frame. He didn't look at us, his eyes fixed on the cheap grocery bag in his hand.

"*Ciao*," he grumbled.

Before we could react, he flipped the flimsy *sacchetto* upside down, and a dark blue Birkin fell out.

"From Natalya," he muttered before turning away, his broad form blending into the sparse crowd dotting the piazza.

"Italian UPS?" Bo wisecracked, his brain running a full beat behind.

"That's Natalya's purse," I said, and the joke turned cold.

Bo's pain either subsided or adrenaline kicked in, because he quickly reached for the tote without flinching. Inside was nothing but a plastic sandwich bag and a Polaroid. He pulled out the photo, showing Natalya's contorted face as she held up her right hand. In the white area below the image were the scrawled words *Lascia Italia. Stai lontano da Chiurazzi.*

"I think it says: 'Leave Italy. Stay away from the Chiurazzi,'" he said, leaning close to the photograph.

I plucked out the Ziploc bag and held it up to the sun. Inside was a silver and blue sapphire ring, which I recognized immediately, and a small red fragment I didn't. Bo shut his swollen eye, pressed his open eye closer, and recoiled.

"It's a goddamn fingernail," he said.

I yanked the bag closer to my face.

What looked like shrapnel was a bone-white shard, rough and ridged, splashed in blood, and severed at the proximal fold. The amputated nail was still attached to a delicate strip of skin and flesh; raw finger pulp clung to the ridges of its grooved bed and the smooth, manicured outer edge.

Nausea rolled through me. The sour bile of coffee burned my throat. I swallowed hard and forced my eyes back to the photo. Natalya's hand was splayed out, showing all her fingers. The end of her ring finger, missing the blue sapphire, was grisly and wet. I stood up and looked out over the piazza, feeling my skin dampen.

"This is some sick mob shit," said Bo, shoving the bag and photo back in the purse in case the waiter walked by.

"It is," I replied. My heart rate accelerated, and I looked past Fontana del Moro, the far fountain in the piazza, where the man had disappeared.

I suddenly felt cold.

"We need to get out of here," said Bo in a dry growl. He scanned the crowd and tossed some euros on the table. We got up and looped back through the restaurant to the street side, where the taxis waited.

As we stuffed ourselves into a small white Fiat, I seethed through gritted teeth, "What is it with mafia assholes and fingers?"

CHAPTER TWO

Three days earlier — Friday, January 16th

THERE'S AN OLD RUSSIAN SAYING—*Yesli boish'sya volkov, derzhis' podal'she ot lesa*—if you're afraid of wolves, stay out of the forest. When Bo and I arrived in Italy, we discovered that the forest was Rome, and the wolves were hungry.

Rome was to be a short trip. A quick in and out. Tour the asset, meet the muckety-mucks, shake hands, nod soberly, look like we know what we're doing, and seal the deal.

All the critical decisions had been made. Negotiations were over. The only thing left was to sign the papers, taste the tiramisu at Caffè Greco, and, time permitting, visit the Pope's Garage.

At least, that was Bo's plan.

Mine was a bit more ambitious.

//////////////////////////////////

We arrived at Fiumicino International at 7:30 a.m., a half hour after we'd departed Portland International the previous day. Winter weather in the Eternal City was surprisingly pleasant, with temperatures in the mid-fifties and a brilliant sun that made it feel warmer. We took a taxi to the Michelangelo Hotel on *Via Crescenzio*, located so close to the Vatican that our travel agent boasted we would hear Gregorian chants from the Sistine Chapel Choir if we kept our balcony doors open.

The entropy of Rome's traffic was chaotic and exhausting, with little regard for rules or order. The taxi's closed windows didn't shield us from the frenetic score of horns, engines, motorbikes, and screaming pedestrians. Our driver, a surly man of few words, attacked the maelstrom like a gladiator looking for another victory: lane weaving, tailgating, horn blasting, and passing legions of four, three, and two-wheeled vehicles with bullying determination. Other than the backseat jouncing and shoulder collisions, I wasn't bothered because I'd driven hundreds of times with Bo, a former race car driver with a permanent case of road rage.

After checking into the Michelangelo, Bo and I freshened up and changed from our airplane clothes to business attire. We were scheduled to arrive in Naples in the early afternoon for the foundry walk-through.

We met up with our host and emissary, Leo Giacobbe, in the hotel restaurant, 'Dome.'

"Welcome to Rome," he said. "I bring gifts."

He reached into his briefcase and handed us each a Nokia phone. "Everyone on the team has one. Names are all preprogrammed, and you can reach each other instantly; no more problems connecting your American phones to the Italian network." I was relieved. The last time we traveled overseas, Bo and I hadn't been able to communicate with anyone locally.

After a brief lesson in essential Italian phrases and courtesies, we grabbed a continental breakfast, choked on the coffee, and reviewed our five-day itinerary, which was as dense and relentless as a drum solo.

The restaurant was empty, except for two other men hunched against a far wall, their black clothes seeming to swallow the light. They looked bored and misplaced. I noticed them only because Leo kept glancing at them. He gulped his steaming coffee as though his tongue was dead, and after finishing his *fette biscottate* topped with ricotta cheese, he pushed his plate aside.

Then, darting his eyes between us, he said with a feigned gravity, "On your behalf, I spoke with His Eminence, Cardinal Bertolini, who talked to Ambassador Nicholson and Prime Minister Silvio Berlusconi, and they all agreed that Paladin is the right company to own the Chiurazzi."

Bo and I exchanged glances. Leo's dramatic flair was starting to grate on us. His relentless persuasion sparked my suspicion that the entire venture might be a carefully orchestrated ruse in which he played the roper, luring us into a far chancier scheme than we'd anticipated.

"Stop closing, Leo, we're sold," I said.

"Your commission is safe," added Bo.

A smug smile spread across Leo's face, lifting not just the corners of his lips but also the tension in his shoulders. "My daughter thanks you," he said.

"Does she live with you here in Rome?" I asked.

"I don't live in Rome," he replied. "It's too big, too crowded. I live in Orvieto, a town about seventy miles north of here. When I have business in Rome, I stay here, in the Michelangelo. The church helped me negotiate a ridiculously low room rate."

"Your daughter lives with you?" I asked.

"No. She was accepted to Berkeley shortly after we lost my wife. I moved to Italy on my own. She's a senior now, but let me tell you, out-of-state tuition is a crime."

We nodded in agreement. Bo had three daughters, either in college or about to be, while my son and daughter were in high school.

I'd first learned of Leo Giacobbe several months earlier. He'd approached Dante Scava, our friend and master artist, to discuss replicating art from the Vatican Museum to raise money for charitable events. He was an odd character working for the Vatican in a vague capacity as an intermediary or chargé d'affaires between the Holy See and the secular world. During his conversations with Dante,

Leo claimed to have more than just Vatican images to offer—he had everything in the Vatican Apostolic Library for sale.

Dante nearly swallowed his tongue and quickly realized he needed to involve his mentor and benefactor, Natalya Danilenko, our company's chairperson, in the discussion. In his initial meeting with Natalya, Leo suggested an even more fantastic scheme—acquiring the world's most valuable sculpture foundry.

Stick with me—it'll all make sense soon.

CHAPTER THREE

Lake Oswego, Oregon — three months earlier

WITH THE DEAL ALREADY HALF IN HER POCKET, Natalya called me.

"Sounds like he's got a bridge for sale," I said after she told me about Leo Giacobbe and his proposal.

"Do you think I am stupid?" she shot back.

"I'm sorry, Natalya, but what would we do with an art shop in Italy?"

"It's not a shop; it is a sculpture factory. It is the famous Chiurazzi Foundry in Naples, and it comes with two incredible assets." She used the Russian slang *kruto* for incredible, which I understood because she used it often.

"Still sounds like a bridge to me," I repeated.

She ignored me and said, "I will tell you what these assets are, you understand?"

"I'm listening."

"Are you sitting down, Martin?"

"Yes," I answered.

I wasn't.

"First asset is the most valuable inventory of Renaissance sculpture molds in the world—most have never been cast."

My silence conveyed my apathy. Natalya took a deep breath. "And the second asset is—are you still sitting, Martin?"

"Yes?"

"The Vatican Seal."

I sat down.

Natalya had rendered me mute. She had to be wrong. She was Russian, after all, and English wasn't her first language. The Vatican Seal is the most potent religious symbol in the world; its triple crown tiara, resting within the crossed keys of St. Peter's, represents the gatekeeper to the kingdom of heaven.

Impossible.

///

After her jaw-dropping pronouncement, Natalya called for a power huddle at our corporate offices. Rejecting our standard conference call, she underscored the deal's significance by jetting across the country from Miami in her Hawker 800. We even had a private dinner meeting where she secured my allegiance. The following morning, we convened at our company headquarters.

Paladin Holdings occupies the first floor of the only commercial building on Lake Oswego, just outside Portland, Oregon. Bo's and my office, aptly named the glass cage, is a sizable window-walled space overlooking the lake from the ground level. Furnished with leather seating, Bauhaus lamps, and small tables, it resembles a large living room with a spectacular view.

Christine, our office manager—who we call 'Chief' because she runs the place—had coffee and a box of fresh pastries waiting. We mustered for the first few minutes, shook hands, and remarked on the typical grey Oregon weather; everyone pretended to be a meteorologist.

Natalya was impeccably dressed, looking as though she were going to a photo shoot. Her dark blonde hair framed her sharp features, creating a captivating contrast with her intense brown eyes, the aristocratic line of her nose, the angled grace of her brows, and the alluring curve of her lips. Her face had fascinated me since I first saw it two years earlier. It was extraordinary, like Natalya herself.

Bo, a big man who easily fills a doorframe, wore a new sports coat and stylish vest, clearly trying to keep pace with Natalya's polished look. An aging footballer with kind grey eyes and a brilliant smile, he moves with a purpose that seems to convert the air around him into energy. That morning he passed out empty coffee cups, then filled them individually, looking everyone in the eyes as if he were meeting them for the first time.

Despite Bo's objections, Dante also attended, looking awkward, as usual, in what was likely his only white shirt. While he didn't work for the company, Dante possessed unmatched knowledge of Renaissance art and sculpture foundries.

Having Bo and Natalya in the same room is like flying through turbulent air—safe but bumpy. Both possess alpha qualities I admire but can never quite emulate. Bo has a natural gravitas, while Natalya has an innate poise. Both absorb more than their share of oxygen, leaving the atmosphere a little thinner, so I've learned to operate in lighter air. That day, I was curious how our guest, Leo Giacobbe, would adapt to the higher altitude.

He arrived ten minutes late, likely by design, wearing a drab trench coat with its collar flipped up. I searched his hands involuntarily for the missing fedora. His appealing smile contradicted his milky eyes, which made him look older than Natalya had led me to believe. Silver threads quilted his otherwise black hair, recently cropped, and he hid his bulkiness in a dark, noirish suit.

As he mingled, he discharged charm like he had too much of it and needed to lighten his load. Bo and I were not impressed. We don't trust charm: sugar looks the same as salt. Watching him, I surmised that Leo was one of those characters who navigated the fissure between legitimacy and grift like a feral cat exploring an alley.

Although I'd been thoroughly briefed the night before, I pretended ignorance, and once everyone selected their places to settle, I invited Leo to pitch us on the foundry purchase. He read the room before gazing at the lake, where a smallmouth bass broke the surface to feed.

"The Chiurazzi is the second oldest foundry in Italy and the most important purchase you'll ever make." He contorted his mouth and enunciated the name *Kew-rat-see* as if he were teaching us Italian.

No one responded. Leo's assertion carried the awkwardness of a wet handshake. He strained a wry smile and diverted back out the window. "What an amazing view."

"Everyone says that," sighed Bo, his voice tinged with boredom.

Then, with the practiced rhetoric of a magician performing his climactic trick, Leo unpacked the history of what he deemed the most important purchase we would ever make.

I'll spare you the sales hustle and summarize.

Founded in 1870, the Chiurazzi Foundry became the world's foremost factory for casting and replicating iconic three-dimensional art. Museums like the Vatican, Louvre, and Uffizi hired the foundry to create perfect duplicates of their most prized statuary as insurance against vandals, earthquakes, war, or fire.

However, in an ironic twist of fate, while the foundry cast reproductions of world-famous sculptures from world-famous museums, it also built, unintentionally at first, then intentionally later, a cache of authentic molds capable of replicating the originals with the posthumous accuracy of its genius creators.

This incredible appropriation of treasured masterworks happened without the Chiurazzi paying a dime. Paradoxically, the museums paid the foundry for its services. Its inventory grew to more than 1650 molds, and it sold reproductions to many of the wealthiest families in history, including the Windsors, the Romanovs, the Rockefellers, the Vanderbilts, the Carnegies, and the Gettys.

Things slowed down after WWII, and the foundry lay dormant, producing only a few works on request. Then, in 1972, the Italian Parliament changed the art world forever by passing a law prohibiting any new castings from authentic Renaissance works. Creating copies directly from masterpieces became illegal, making the Chiurazzi statue collection as artistically valuable as the originals.

"That can't be true," interrupted Bo.

"Perhaps not," replied Leo. "But what do you think a posthumous copy of an original Michelangelo is worth?"

"What is a fraction of priceless?" asked Natalya buoyantly.

"Sounds like we can't afford this purchase," I injected.

"Well, that's where you're wrong," answered Leo. "No one has ever valued the Chiurazzi inventory. Sixteen hundred molds, gathering dust, with no value other than their original production cost."

"That can't be true," repeated Bo.

Leo's eyes narrowed. "Alexander Graham Bell offered to sell his patent for the telephone to Western Union for a hundred thousand dollars, but they turned him down, saying his invention lacked potential."

He grinned at us.

"Shit happens."

CHAPTER FOUR

SIDEBAR:

Bo Bishop and I are entrepreneurs. No, scratch that—we were entrepreneurs.

We chased money for years and then abruptly caught it—lots of it. Maybe too much. We'd founded Paladin Inc., a profit-sharing start-up that provided fully customized online retail stores for schools and nonprofits. Our motto was straightforward: "*We* deliver the store; *You* deliver the customers; *We* share the profits."

It sounded great on paper and captured the attention of Dmitry Chernyshevsky, Russia's sixth-richest (and climbing) oligarch. He, along with his unconventional girlfriend, Natalya Danilenko—a shrewd and savvy art dealer—bought forty percent of our company when it was on life support. Their investment resurrected us and lifted us off the ground.

For two broken and beleaguered entrepreneurs whose company was on the verge of collapse, having Dmitry Chernyshevsky as a business partner felt like winning the lottery with one crucial proviso: we were tethered to a bomb, and the consequences of failure were the stuff of nightmares.

Over time, this stark reality led me to formulate one of my many axioms: it is easier to accept money from a lethal billionaire if you concentrate more on the word *billionaire* than the word *lethal*.

Initially, things did not go well.

Schools and nonprofits did little to promote their online stores, concerned that doing so would divert resources from their more traditional fundraising efforts. Our motto sadly devolved to: "We *delivered* the store; You *didn't* deliver the customers; We had *no profits* to share."

Paladin began to fail, which, as I just said, was not an acceptable option, so we pivoted. First, we turned our existing operation into a philanthropic subsidiary (more on that later), and then we restructured Paladin into a holding company for acquisitions.

Dmitry's bottomless pockets gave us the one thing we never had before—boundless money, which "opened the aperture," as Bo liked to say. He and I understood a fundamental truth about early-stage companies: buying revenue was easier than generating revenue. In other words, when you can't sell stuff, buy stuff. In our case, "stuff'" was other companies.

We changed our name to Paladin Holdings, Inc., managed the business, and installed Natalya as our board chairperson so she could represent Dmitry's interests and, by default, her own. Natalya's primary responsibility was to shake the Chernyshevsky money tree while Bo and I searched for companies to acquire. We had no industry preference and only three criteria for our purchases: the product and production had to be simple (no high-tech), the company had been profitable for the past five years, and the owner's children were not involved in the business.

Unexpectedly, the oligarch proved to be a good partner. He did not interfere in company operations, asked few questions, communicated only through Natalya, and, most remarkably, sent money when asked. We held quarterly phone conferences during which Dmitry, accompanied by his interpreter, would conference in from his yacht (we could hear the navigational horns and whistles) and listen impassively. Natalya did most of the talking, often in Russian, using our prepared notes, occasionally calling him *milyy*, which I looked up. It means sweetheart. His comments were always supportive and insightful. And yet, despite his tranquil presence in our lives, his influence over us was as prodigious as an indulgent parent.

To say the company succeeded would be an understatement. Paladin Holdings roared to life like one of Bo's former race cars. Each new acquisition symbolized another checkered flag. In the first year, our acquisitions included a California boat builder, a Northwest sporting goods retailer, a Portland hotel with an iconic bar, and a Midwest plastics manufacturing company. The following year, we added a half dozen more, including a string of pubs, a Michigan sawmill, and a regional chain of convenience stores. Each was a standalone entity with its own management and operations.

After two years and ten companies, Paladin's value had sky-rocketed along with our personal fortunes. Because our partners were Russian, we were forced to remain a private company, but our compensation was generous, and we'd developed a good reputation and brand. Bo and I never pried into Dmitry's business and kept Natalya—as far as Bo was concerned—at arm's length.

Natalya's art business also surged. Her Boca Raton gallery was already one of the most exclusive showrooms in the country, with a client list so elite it had become a bragging right. Then she part-nered with our friend Dante Scava, who had an exceptional talent for forgery, and she went from art curator to art producer.

Legal forgeries were all the rage. Natalya's *old-money* patrons wanted replicas of their priceless paintings so they could store the originals in a vault while displaying the copies to their unwitting peers. On the other hand, her *new-money* patrons (Natalya called them "wannabes") wanted originals that looked like they'd been painted by the great and famous so they could lie about them to other "wannabes." As Natalya once explained, "It is illegal for the seller to lie about the provenance of a painting, but it is not illegal for the buyer to lie about it."

Bo and I had facilitated this fortuitous coupling of Natalya and Dante after Dante's brother Nico Scava, our previous business partner, had been murdered by Natalya's nephew Vasili Bobrov, whom I then killed in return.

It's how we all became friends.

CHAPTER FIVE

Rome, Friday, January 16th

BO AND I LEFT LEO IN THE HOTEL RESTAURANT to work on his to-do list and took a cab to Termini Station, where we boarded the train called *Frecciarossa*, the Red Arrow, to Napoli.

I'd never ridden a bullet train. The ninety-minute ride was smooth and quiet, accompanied only by the faint sound of wheels gliding on tracks like the whisper of skates on ice. The executive class compartment was separate from the rest of the train, and we were its only passengers. Wrestling with jet lag, Bo reclined his leather seat and napped. I envied him. He could fall asleep anywhere, anytime.

Looking out my window at the rolling hills covered with fields of grey olive groves and the skeletal tendrils of dormant vineyards, I caught glimpses of the Tyrrhenian Sea as photogenic villages floated by—Frascati, Marino, Anagni, Cassino.

As our train approached the outskirts of Naples, postcard scenes gave way to terracotta and brick buildings rising three to four stories tall; burrowed alleyways and shaded courtyards; laundry fluttering from metal-railed balconies; the domes and facades of tatty baroque churches, buttressed by scaffolding that clung like steel cobwebs; and the silhouette of Mount Vesuvius in the distance.

The platform at Napoli Centrale, Naples' central train station, was a spasm of frantic energy flowing into Piazza Garibaldi, where we scuffled to find a taxi to Casoria. I stayed intentionally behind

Bo, drafting in his wake, as his size, gait, and resolve cleared a path through the scrum of tourists and commuters.

Our cab, driven this time by a large, cheerful woman named Elena, wove through the city's narrow roads, passing modern and medieval structures clustered together like shuffled cards. I snapped hurried photos out the window of Castel Sant'Elmo atop Vomero and of Castel Nuovo, its massive towers standing like sentinels—a testament to seven centuries of toil and moil. I sat in the front seat of the little Fiat to give Bo some elbow room in the back, where he hunched over in the middle, looking shoehorned.

Elena knew as much English as we knew Italian, so we communicated with hand gestures. She would point at things and say "big," or "pretty," or "old." It was like getting tour commentary from an infant. Bo and I loved it.

As we neared Casoria, the hectic traffic calmed, replaced by wider roads and fields of tall grass splattered with colorfully painted homes with clay roofs. Elena dropped us in front of a large single-story brick building, old but not ancient. Bo tipped her heavily, and we waved goodbye like she was a lifelong friend.

From the outside, the Chiurazzi Foundry wasn't much to brag about. Years earlier, it had relocated to a standard warehouse next to a truck repair business. Bo and I strolled in, looking for Dante and Natalya, who had arrived the day before as the advance team. Instead, we encountered a squat but sturdy man with a face that looked like it had been punched once too often. A fine layer of industrial dust coated his head and shoulders, and his hair resembled a patch of neglected grass with dead spots.

"You are the other American buyers here to inspect our foundry," he said in excellent English.

"Yes, we are. We let ourselves in. I hope that's OK," said Bo.

"I am Alessio Rosa," he answered tersely, and we shook his gritty hand.

He explained that Natalya and Dante had gone for a late lunch, and we asked him to show us around while we waited for their return. This visibly irritated him, and after sighing loudly, he walked us through the factory.

The building reminded me of a large machine shop, with lofty ceilings, brick walls, and concrete floors. Ventilation canopies attached to large, sinuous pipes hung from the ceilings but stood idle, allowing a fine mist of soot to linger in the air. It felt like we were walking through the dust cloud kicked up by a truck on a dry dirt road, and I was glad I'd left my good suit back at the hotel.

Alessio preferred grunting to talking, asking no questions and answering ours with only grumbles and finger-pointing. The pouring basin and furnace pit, where molten metal once flowed from a glowing red crucible into ancient molds, lay dormant, yet my imagination still conjured the lingering heat.

We continued through the ashy haze past the inventory room to the foundry's cafeteria, a depressing little space with fluorescent lighting, a scuffed linoleum floor, and walls that had been white twenty years ago but were now a sallow yellow. The only furniture consisted of a few chrome chairs around a cheap folding table and a refrigerator that doubled as a bulletin board.

Alessio, who apparently didn't like our company, informed us we could inspect the mold vault when Natalya and Dante returned. Then, with the same jarring burst that punctuated most of his movements, he left—an abrupt, intimidating trait that left me feeling as if I were standing in the path of a swinging door.

"I don't like him," I said after the cafeteria door clicked shut.

"I don't think he cares," said Bo indifferently, looking into the empty refrigerator.

Within a minute of Alessio's departure, the cafeteria door bounced back open, and a man wearing jeans, a black shirt, and a tan sports coat entered, smiling broadly as he held his hands out to shake ours. He had sharp blond hair, a sharp nose, sharp eyes, and a sharp

Vandyke groomed to a point. I could tell he was a man of jagged edges, prickly—like thistle.

"You must be Lamberto Liuzzo," said Bo while taking his hand, recognizing the Italian attorney we'd been negotiating with on the phone over the past week.

"Welcome to Napoli," he said.

Lamberto held dual citizenship. He was born in Philadelphia during one of his father's US diplomatic tours and shuttled between Italy and America for most of his youth. He graduated from Villanova Law School before returning to Naples to join his father's law firm, *Studio Liuzzo*, where he practiced real estate law.

We engaged in prosaic pleasantries, and Bo asked him how he'd come to represent the Chiurazzi Foundry. Brushing dust off a chrome chair and sitting, Lamberto said, "Gennaro Chiurazzi's *testamento* specified that I am the executor of his estate. The old man never trusted his children to inherit it. He instructed the foundry to be sold in an open auction managed by my firm, debts to be paid, and the rest to be divided between his heirs. There is also art and other real estate. They will do fine."

Spying a coffee pot on a wall shelf also crammed with cups and red sacks of *Kimbo Coffee*, he poured what looked like straight espresso into a disposable cup. He waved the black pot at us, and Bo and I declined aggressively.

"I understand," he chuckled.

"We tried the coffee at the hotel this morning," said Bo. "Italians take their coffee seriously."

"It's like drinking caffeinated oil," I added.

"Yes, it's an acquired taste," said Lamberto.

"I think it's more forced than acquired," I said.

"At gunpoint," added Bo, and Lamberto laughed.

"We've never talked about the Vatican Seal," I said, changing gears. "It's not even listed in the Foundry's Asset Schedule; why is that?"

"Well, it's not *the* Vatican Seal. It's a license to use it, but nobody knows the difference. The license is why the Vatican is engaged in this sale."

"I suspect the Vatican is very vigilant regarding their emblem," I said.

"Church bells ring, even when they're not heard," answered Lamberto genially.

I heard Dante's voice before the door opened, and he and Natalya filed into the small, stale room. Natalya came in second, and I stepped past Dante to hug and greet her.

"OK, hello to you too," said Dante, stepping out of my way.

Natalya widened her eyes and leaned back from me, signaling she didn't like the overt attention. "Did you take the tour?" she asked.

"We've seen the operation but not the inventory," Bo said.

"Lamberto was just telling us about the Vatican license," I added.

"It was a very controversial program, and the Church shut it down years ago," Lamberto continued. "The only reason the Chiurazzi has a license is that they were among the first to buy one."

"They're not available anymore?" I asked.

"Oh no," injected Dante. "The Church tried to cancel all the licenses—went to court over it. But California law trumped Canon Law, and it cost the Church $10 million to settle the claims."

"The legal battle to contest all the licenses took several years," added Lamberto, "during which they unexpectedly brought in a lot of money. The Vatican, ever pragmatic, saw no shame in vulture capitalism if it worked to their benefit, so it didn't challenge the California court's ruling to continue the existing contracts."

"What are the terms of the license?" asked Bo.

"Every license is different, but the Chiurazzi Foundry owns the rights to replicate all the art in the Vatican Library. A treasure trove spanning millennia. Ancient maps, paintings, documents, and sculptures can all be duplicated with papal authority."

His revelation defied belief, and a disquieting chill struck me as I observed the stark contrast between Dante and Natalya. Her expression was placid and emotionless, almost vacant, while his radiated open excitement. I'd grown accustomed to Natalya's carefully constructed nonchalance and Dante's exuberant enthusiasm, but my intuition sensed something was amiss. Reflecting on it now, I realize I should have paid closer attention; perhaps I could have deflected the havoc headed our way and spared them both from the pain to come.

CHAPTER SIX

THE AIR IN THE FOUNDRY'S MOLD ROOM hung heavy with the metallic tang of molten bronze and the musty scent of old wood. Towering metal racks, fifteen feet tall with seven-foot shelves, lined the walls and stretched across the center of the massive room in rows. Giant hulks of pale bonded sand, resin, and plaster, encased in metal mesh and twisted like tree roots, occupied every inch of shelving. Fine silica grit layered the ledges and most of the concrete floor.

The dimly lit windowless room was such a catacomb of grime-encrusted clutter that just entering it made me feel grubby. It looked like a scrap heap. I reminded myself that what appeared to be piles of hardened and weathered lava were actually grainy shells holding the images of some of the most famous sculptures in the world, including the *Venus de Milo*, the *Winged Victory of Samothrace*, the *Pietà*, *David*, the *Laocoön Group*, and *Moses*—a gnarled but venerable stockpile of sarcophagi worth millions.

Alessio Rosa was our truculent guide, and we huddled around him to receive his insider briefing. A bulky forklift, its paint faded and chipped like a weathered fresco, lumbered down a narrow aisle behind him.

"The Chiurazzi family kept these molds safe for a hundred years," he shouted above the diesel drone of the forklift. "They made many sacrifices."

"Like?" shouted Bo.

"During the war, Naples was bombed many times, and the family was afraid a chance hit would destroy the collection, so they buried it in a secret location. It stayed buried for years even after the war, because the family feared Americans or Russians would confiscate it. The molds were in excellent condition when they finally dug them up."

A metal-on-metal screech suddenly pierced the air, and Alessio swung around, a string of Neapolitan profanity erupting from his lips. He left us standing without so much as an excuse and marched toward the groaning forklift, its driver, a wiry man with a massive tobacco-stained mustache, shouting back at him.

The sudden interruption scattered our group. Bo left for the bathroom, Lamberto took a phone call in the hallway, Dante launched into a monologue about the lost wax casting method, and Natalya strode down the opposite aisle from the forklift to escape his jabbering. I followed her, tugged as always by her impalpable pull.

The narrow passage felt claustrophobic, a gully pressed between metal walls. Natalya traced a finger along the course contour of a large plaster, its interior form unknown except for the sharpie label taped to its exterior.

"*Cavallo di Colleoni—Gamba Posteriore Destra* #2," she read aloud. "Colleoni's Horse—Right-Hind Leg #2."

"Have you made reservations at the Michelangelo?" I asked.

"I am not staying at the Michelangelo," she answered.

I cocked my head at her in confusion.

"I am not staying in Rome. I'm going to Capri."

Before I could register my protest, the forklift on the other side of the rack belched and shuddered. I could see the driver's face between the stacked molds, a cigarette jutting through his mustache, one eyelid closed against the smoke. He was attempting to shift a giant frame on the top shelf. His open eye flicked between the high mantel and his controls, his hands in a manic conversation with the gears. Alessio stood next to the lift, yelling something in Italian.

A primitive alarm ignited under my skin, and I barked to Natalya, "We need to move!"

Natalya blinked in surprise, still unaware. I kept staring at the driver, who suddenly spat out his cigarette and turned his obsidian eyes toward me—cold and flat, like those of a man about to pull a trigger. Then he pushed on the throttle pedal.

The forklift lurched forward, slamming into the rack with a convulsive thump. Without even looking up I sensed and heard the buckling of the upper ledge.

Natalya's eyes snapped wide as she bolted upright, a sharp breath escaping her lips. The shriek of tearing metal drowned my howl as I lunged into her, gripping under her arms to keep her upright while flinging myself with as much strength as I had ever marshaled down the tight aisle. I felt the rush of a massive hard-sand structure smash behind me, exploding in a deafening roar, showering us in a rain of pulverized gravel and debris.

The air crackled with static tension. Natalya and I lay sprawled on the cold concrete floor, struggling to pull in air. A parched taste filled my mouth and nostrils, and I thought I'd swallowed sand. I scrambled to my feet, fanning the air with my arms.

"Natalya!?" I coughed and rasped.

"Martin!?" she croaked at the same time.

"Merda!" shouted Alessio.

His strangled epithet wasn't aimed at Natalya or me. It wasn't aimed at the forklift driver who'd slammed into the rack. Nor was it aimed at the two-ton mold that just crashed from the top shelf, nearly killing us. Instead, his scream was aimed at Dante, who stood in the receding cloud of debris, his face bloodless, jaw slack, eyes wide with shock. A dark stain bloomed across his chest where a foot-long metal rod, as thick as a thumb, protruded obscenely, still vibrating from its residual momentum.

Chaos erupted.

Clamor and commotion filled the next fifteen seconds. Dante crumpled to the floor. Natalya scrambled to her feet, grabbing my arm for support as she shouted his name. We rushed toward him and Alessio raced past us, reaching Dante first and dropping to his knees. Lamberto and Bo charged back through the entrance doors just as Dante's mouth wrenched open, unleashing a primal scream that scraped against my insides.

"An ambulance!" shouted Bo into Lamberto's face. "Call an ambulance!"

Lamberto, his phone still in his hands, dialed 118.

Natalya knelt next to Dante's head and stroked his forehead. "You will be fine, Dante. Look at me. Look at my eyes. Look nowhere else."

Dante's face contorted in agony as he gasped for breath. His hand tried to reach for the metal rod, and I tugged it back. His shirt had turned the color of rust.

"We need to stem the blood," I told Alessio, who bolted up and out of the room to get a medical kit.

Lamberto panted a flurry of Italian into the phone. The only words I understood were the address. Bo knelt opposite Natalya and put his hands under Dante's head, cradling it from the concrete. "He's going into shock," he said to Natalya. "Keep him focused on you."

I could see the forklift driver from the corner of my eye. He babbled in rapid Italian and ran from the room, bumping into Alessio, who had just returned clutching a small plastic medical kit. They screamed at each other in Italian, and the driver shoved Alessio out of his way and disappeared.

My hands hovered over Dante as if they could heal him. Lamberto stood behind me, answering questions from the emergency operator. Natalya stroked Dante's head, forcing him to keep his glazed eyes on hers. Alessio rummaged through the kit, but its Band-Aids and gauze did little for a man impaled.

"This is a foundry," Bo snarled at Alessio, his voice suppressed with rage. "That's your goddamn medical kit?"

Alessio shot back a defensive grunt as if he anticipated the blame. "We don't have accidents here."

"Don't let the driver leave," I snapped. "I want to talk to him."

Alessio looked at me as if I'd asked him to strip naked. "He's gone," he exclaimed with a hint of defeat.

I was about to swear loudly, but Natalya's voice punched through the thick air. "Stop it!"

Seconds turned to gut-wrenching minutes before we finally heard the ambulance sirens. Two paramedics in bright yellow vests ran into the room, faces grim. Their practiced movements stood in sharp contrast to our earlier raw actions. They assessed Dante's condition, fired instructions at each other, stabilized Dante's neck, and then maneuvered him onto a stretcher.

Pain medicine, administered intravenously, began to take effect. Before the paramedics shoved his stretcher into the ambulance, Dante gripped my hand, his eyes nearly shut, and whispered, "Don't let me die in fucking Naples, Marty."

CHAPTER SEVEN

WE CHASED THE AMBULANCE.

Bo, Natalya, and I piled into Lamberto's BMW while Alessio ran to his Fiat Punto. Bo snatched the keys from Lamberto's hand.

"I'll drive," he declared, voice daring him to object. Lamberto knew enough not to.

Bo dogged the ambulance so closely I was convinced he and its driver were competing. They broke every traffic law, careening through the twisted gauntlet of Naples gridlock. Neither the ambulance driver nor the terrified Lamberto realized that Bo's racing instincts had kicked in. He wove through the Italian traffic behind the ambulance, adrenaline spiking.

"Remember that old advertisement promoting the city?" I shouted, white-knuckling the passenger handle. "See Naples and die."

Bo grunted sharply, eyes locked on the road. "Yeah—literally," he snapped, jutting his elbow as he cut a hard left into the hospital ambulance entrance.

The hospital must have been notified because nurses and EMTs stood by as we pulled up in a wailing lurch. Natalya, Bo, and I sprang out and followed the stretcher into the emergency entrance. Bo threw the keys to Lamberto, who drove away to park it. We'd lost Alessio many miles back.

Dante disappeared behind the yawning abyss of two giant swinging doors, leaving us at the reception desk. Natalya kept a calm voice while giving an older woman information, which she typed into a bulky computer. Bo and I stood to the side.

"It wasn't an accident," I whispered to Bo. "The forklift driver tried to kill us."

Bo blinked in slow confusion. "What?" he stammered, then shook his head and said, "Later."

When Lamberto arrived, Natalya summoned him to the desk and explained that she wanted Dante to have a private room.

Lamberto translated, and the reception woman shook her grey head in amusement.

"It's not possible," said Lamberto. "This is a public hospital, not a private one, and private rooms are impossible."

"Everything is possible," insisted Natalya, locking eyes with Lamberto and communicating to make it happen.

After ten minutes of energetic finagling with the head nurse, the hospital administrator, and even Alessio, who finally showed up looking agitated and angry, Natalya presented her black American Express. We knew then that Dante would get a private room and be pampered like prized veal.

The waiting room's fluorescent lights cast a cold, sterile glow over the worn, mismatched plastic and metal chairs arranged in the dull green space. A vending machine stocked with candy, pretzels, and chips stood against a wall, its outlet exposed for easy unplugging if emptied—though I imagined that was a rare occurrence. Next to it, another vending machine offered coffee, and the wastebasket beside it was half full of discarded paper cups. Clusters of people dotted the room in small groups.

A nurse with an unfortunate complexion, her name tag reading *Lucia*, came in to talk with Natalya, who was the presumed point person because her name was on the American Express.

"*Signora*," she said as she beckoned, then added in accented English, "*Dottore* Rossi will see you shortly. He speaks some English, but I can translate if needed."

"*Grazie,*" said Natalya. She then turned and walked toward the coffee machine.

I followed her and said quietly, "The forklift driver tried to kill us."

She offered a wan smile, fumbled with a cup, and said barely audibly, "Martin, you saved my life. I stood where the mold crashed down. I am still shaking. Thank you. I'll thank you properly later, I promise." Her comments were laced with a peculiar detachment, as if her mind was still grappling with the aftershock.

"Did you hear what I said? The forklift driver tried to kill us."

"I think you are seeing devils where there are none."

My head slumped in resignation. I was the only one who had seen the murderous intent in the driver's eyes. There'd be no convincing her, not here, not now. I would have to try again later.

"What's in Capri?" I asked after a heartbeat.

She arched her eyebrows. "You want to ask this question now?"

"Yes."

"It is not your business," she said irritably and checked her watch. "I will delay my transport until Dante is out of surgery."

"Are you going by ferry?" I asked.

"No."

"For how long?" I pushed.

"A few days."

I looked into her eyes and could tell she didn't want to continue the conversation. A silence hung between us, a charged particle waiting to spark an argument.

"I visit a friend in Capri," she finally said.

"Do I know this friend?"

"You are being difficult now," she said.

"Yes, I am. I was expecting you to be in Rome, and I suddenly learn you're going to Capri. That tends to make me difficult."

"We need to join the others," she said, touching my chest and pushing slightly.

"Do I *know* this friend?" I persisted.

She kept her hand on my chest and leaned into me. "Yes—but not as well as I do," she whispered harshly.

I stepped back and narrowed my eyes at her. She wasn't daunted and did the same to me.

A half hour crawled by before *Dottore* Rossi, accompanied by Nurse Lucia, entered the waiting room. Scanning the siloed groups of visitors, he approached our coven and explained Dante's condition in heavily accented English.

"You must give a police report," he stipulated. "There is good news. The steel *barra* met its match—the x-ray shows the patient's clavicle bone stopped the *barra* from going deeper, and there was no break. But the *barra* is coated with much grit and debris, so the wound is like a *melograno rotto*."

He looked at Nurse Lucia, who said, "A burst pomegranate."

"*Si*, and the wound must be cleaned *completamente e approfonditamente*."

"Completely," translated the nurse. "It should take about an hour, and Mr. Scava will heal quickly without broken bones. He can be released in two days after we are sure there are no infections."

After the doctor left, Natalya got on her phone, probably to make travel arrangements. Bo then signaled me to join him in the corridor, beyond earshot. I went out to join him. He stood next to Alessio. Turning to him as I walked up, Bo said, "Repeat what you just told me."

Alessio's face stayed frozen in its customary scowl. I wondered if he ever smiled. Perhaps at children or pretty women?

"You should not buy the Chiurazzi," he said.

"Why is that?" I asked, expecting another curmudgeon remark to come my way.

"Because it is dangerous."

"The foundry is dangerous. Yes, I just saw that." I decided to play along.

Bo's face hardened into an unreadable stillness, but I sensed his body tensing into a defensive posture.

"The foundry is not dangerous," answered Alessio. "*Buying* it—is."

"Why is *buying* the Chiurazzi dangerous?" I was still playing along.

"You are not meant to have it. It is not yours to buy. Bad things will happen."

I realized Alessio wasn't joking. The speed of his transformation from mug to thug staggered me. He used his face like a stage actor, morphing it to express hostility. I noticed his sharp yellow teeth for the first time.

"Bad things, like Dante getting speared?" asked Bo. His face stayed blank, but he'd balled his hands into fists.

"Where is the forklift driver?" I asked. "He ran out like he had a train to catch. I think he slammed the throttle intentionally."

"He's gone. You'll never see him again. He will vanish into *il sistema*."

"What in hell does that mean?" I asked, looking back into the waiting room for Natalya, who'd disappeared.

"It is a warning to you," he said, his lips contorting as though he'd bitten into a lemon.

"Then it *was* intentional," Bo pressed.

"You are in Napoli," said Alessio, taking a deliberate step closer to us. "Not in America. If *il sistema* does not want you to buy the business, then you don't—*È immutabile*."

He showed no fear and spoke in riddles. I recognized he was only the proxy, not the power. He took another step toward us, his shoulders rolling forward, a fighter coming out of his corner. The sterile corridor lighting glinted off the bare patches on his scalp. Bo leaned slightly forward, shifting his weight to the front of his feet.

"You will not buy Chiurazzi," Alessio snarled. "If you buy it, somebody will die." He kept his face close, and his breath smelled of soot like the rest of him. "Who do you want to die? The pretty woman? Dante? You?" His eyes flicked to Bo. "You?"

"You want to do this here—now—in the hospital?" flared Bo, tilting further into him.

"You are stupid." His voice dropped to a threatening rasp. "You have no idea what you're facing. In Napoli, you don't fight *il sistema*. You respect it, or flowers will be dropped over the stain you leave on the pavement."

"What the hell is *il sistema*?" I asked.

"For you? It is a wolf pack circling a crippled deer. You will be torn to pieces." He turned, not caring if we responded. "*Vattene a casa*. Go home, and don't die."

We watched him strut down the long blue corridor and disappear around a corner.

CHAPTER EIGHT

"SO WHAT IS *IL SISTEMA*?" BO ASKED, his voice cutting through the soft chatter of the waiting room.

Lamberto shoved his phone into his jacket and nervously scanned the gathered families. Heads whipped around as if a fire alarm had sounded, and the room fell into an eerie silence. Lamberto took Bo's elbow and steered him toward the exit. I trailed behind, offering a sheepish grin and apologetic nods, feeling every bit like the blundering tourist.

"That is not something we discuss openly here," whispered Lamberto in the empty corridor. "It is the Camorra, the Naples mafia. They call it *il sistema*—the system." A nurse hurried by, and he paused until she turned a corner. "In this part of Italy, the Camorra is a social, financial, and political institution. It is not just part of the culture; it *is* the culture."

"We have organized crime in the US as well," I interrupted dismissively.

"No, it is not the same," he said. "In *Napoli*, it is an intangible presence, a pervasive and undeniable force."

Bo and I looked at him as if he'd stopped talking in English. He read our faces, took his car keys out of his pocket, and purposely dropped them. The clatter resonated down the hollow corridor. "*Il sistema* and gravity are the same—an inescapable fact of life."

"You keep saying Naples—is the mafia divided by cities?" I asked.

"No, it's divided by geography." Lamberto picked up his keys. "The Sicilian mafia is called Cosa Nostra. You saw *The Godfather*?" Bo and I nodded. "Then, moving up the toe of the Italian boot, in *Calabria*, there's the 'Ndrangheta, which is the biggest. Then move north along the boot," he lifted his leg and slapped his shin. "This is *Campania*, where Naples is, where we are right now, and it is the home of Camorra—the most violent mafia."

"I'm feeling better already," mumbled Bo caustically.

"Why the most violent?" I asked.

"It is Italy's original mafia, older than the others by over a century. It was born in the prisons of Naples, which are older than Rome. Initially, the Cosa Nostra and 'Ndrangheta were formed to protect farmers from roving bandits; the Camorra *were* the bandits. It's a confederation of different clans competing for territory, and unlike the Cosa Nostra and 'Ndrangheta, they are not bound by honor codes." He paused, breathed, and looked down the long, bleak corridor. "What is not well known is that the Camorra is more powerful than the others. It is so embedded in Naples that their legal income exceeds their illegal income."

"How do they earn their legal income?" asked Bo.

"Restaurants, bars, construction, garbage—service business mostly." He looked around, tucked his chin to his neck, and said softly, "Sometimes hospital services like cleaning and security."

"And the illegal?" I asked.

"Drugs, extortion, counterfeiting, and money laundering." He counted them out on his fingers. "Every clan has a *capo*, the boss, and the soldiers are grouped into *paranza*, which translates to a small fishing trawler that collects the 'fish.'" He made air quotes. "The delinquents in the trawlers are called *piranhas*—violent kids—who push drugs and kill for sport and machismo."

"Kinda like American street gangs," said Bo.

"A little different," he replied. "Here, violence is personal, intimate. In America, gangs shoot at each other from their cars. In Napoli, they cut your throat while you sit in the backseat."

"Everything's a bit more refined in Italy," I said dryly.

A doctor, speaking rapidly in Italian to an accompanying nurse, passed by, stopped, turned, and said something, both hands flipping in a backhanded wave.

"We need to get out of the corridor," Lamberto translated. We all stepped back into the waiting room, where everyone looked at us. Lamberto pointed at the coffee machine and offered to buy. Bo and I shook our heads as he wandered over to get a cup of the black brew.

"God, that stuff is poison," I lamented.

"We're in a hospital, Marty. They'll pump your stomach," Bo replied with a flat grin.

I smirked.

"Sounds like everyone in Naples is mafia," said Bo to the attorney when he returned. I casually looked at the other family groups. No one was listening anymore.

"No, but it spreads through the city like blood through fabric, and everyone pays for it, some more than others, mainly the shopkeepers and businesses who pay *pizzo*."

"Pay what?"

"That's the squeeze, the protection money. It sucks billions out of the economy."

I had an epiphany. "I know what's going on," I whispered. "Our foundry chimney sweep, Rosa, is a Camorra man, and he's scared that our acquisition will stop the *pizzo* payments."

Lamberto looked confused. I realized we hadn't told him about our conversation with Alessio Rosa, and Bo repeated what he'd said.

"He threatened you?"

"He said the foundry is dangerous—that it holds our death—and he asked who should die, the pretty lady, Dante, Marty, or me." Bo pointed both thumbs at his chest.

Lamberto took a sip of his coffee, and I grimaced for him.

"Does the mafia have anything to do with the foundry?" I asked.

"No. The Chiurazzi is whitelisted and always has been."

"What does that mean?"

"The *Carabinieri*—the cops—have a department called the DIA, the Anti-Mafia Investigation Directorate. It publishes a whitelist that registers all the companies the Camorra clans have *not* infiltrated. The DIA updates the list constantly, and the Chiurazzi has been on it since its beginning. The Vatican would never have granted it a license unless it was on the DIA Whitelist."

"Maybe the DIA is wrong," said Bo. "Have they ever been wrong?"

"Maybe, but not about this. I know the Chiurazzi family, and they're clean. Everyone in Napoli knows the foundry."

Natalya entered the waiting room, conversing in broken Italian with a nurse, which surprised me. I didn't know she spoke Italian— even if only a little. After signing something on a clipboard, she returned it to the nurse and joined us.

"I have signed more papers than a mother giving up her child for adoption," she said through a sigh. "I even pay for special food."

I filled her in on what had happened.

She looked nonplussed. "Why does Alessio want to scare us? Is he bidding on the foundry?"

"It is an open bid auction," said Lamberto, blushing slightly. "But it doesn't matter who bids on the Chiurazzi. The Vatican has already determined that your company is the winner."

His answer was purposely vague, and I glanced at Bo to see if he'd picked up on it.

"I don't feel like a winner," I said cynically.

"Why does the Vatican decide?" asked Bo.

"Because the Chiurazzi owes it money, the Vatican license cannot be transferred to any new owner. If the Church pulls the license, it will never be renewed."

Natalya's phone rang. Who could be calling her here in Italy? Leo's phones were preprogrammed with only our group.

"Is that one of Leo's phones?" I asked.

She shook her head and answered the call with "*Da milyy*," then stepped back into the corridor.

"Can you fire Alessio?" asked Bo.

"This is Italy," said Lamberto. "I don't know if I have the authority, and even if I did, he'll sue you. He'll win, and you'll be forced to pay him several years of salary as severance."

About twenty minutes later, Natalya strode back into the waiting room. Doctor Rossi and Nurse Lucia flanked her like an entourage, momentarily looking as if they worked for her. A sarcastic chuckle rose inside me.

The doctor explained that Dante's surgery had gone smoothly. The metal rod had been successfully removed, and the wound debrided. His vitals were stable, and Dante would suffer only a minor scar, as if he'd been shot with a small caliber bullet. He was recovering in the post-operative unit, where we could not go, and his anticipated discharge would be in two days, barring any unforeseen circumstances.

//

Lamberto drove us back to Napoli Centrale after a detour to Natalya's hotel for her suitcase and then to Marina Chiaia for a waiting boat to Capri. Bo repeated my earlier question in the car: "What are you doing in Capri?"

Natalya's reply pulsed with the same unyielding finality she'd used on me earlier: "Visiting a friend."

But in my head, the conversation continued. *"Do I know this friend?"* I replayed, anticipating her taunting response: *"Not as well as I do."*

As night fell, we walked down a narrow floating dock at the small marina, helping Natalya with her bags as a sleek mahogany launch named *Mermaid Whisper* bobbed patiently, waiting for its intended passenger. A towering silhouette tipped his hat in greeting. "*Signorina,*" he said in a low rumble while extending a gloved hand to pull her luggage aboard.

Natalya turned to Lamberto and asked, "So, for sure—no one else is trying to buy our foundry?"

Even in the night's settling darkness, I could see her eyes trying to catch mine.

Lamberto hesitated and looked at his shoes, their black leather invisible against the pier planks. "I cannot tell you officially, but unofficially, no," he said.

It was a small lie, but he'd cast it into a still pond—and the ripples would expand wider than anyone expected.

CHAPTER NINE

BO AND I CAUGHT THE LAST BULLET TRAIN from Naples to Rome. The *Frecciarossa* executive class compartment was again empty except for us.

"It's feeling more and more like a dumpster fire," I said, looking out the dark window, seeing the distant lights of Cassino through my reflection. "I can't shake it."

"Forever the rain at my picnic," he replied.

"Is this funny to you?"

"Lighten up, Marty. Dante will be fine."

Bo thought I was worried about Dante, but I wasn't. I understood why he might think that. Since his brother's murder two years ago, Dante had become my responsibility. I kept him close—he was one of the few who knew the truth of what had happened. The death of Nico Scava changed Dante, and he bore a deep guilt for his role in it. Gone were his excesses—the ganja binges, the old biker friends, the aimless sloth—replaced by long, obsessive painting benders producing some of the best counterfeit art in the world. Dante didn't just emerge from the shadow of his murdered sibling. He grew like sugarcane after the rain.

I worried for a while about Dante's fragile conscience. While he was locked into the secret like we all were, he'd been a passive rather than active participant, so his commitment to secrecy was more tenuous than ours. I was concerned when he started courting Nico's wife, Charley—his grieving sister-in-law.

Charley's feelings about her husband's disappearance had gradually shifted from rage and disbelief to a perpetual state of limbo. It was different for her than for us. We knew what had happened to Nico, while for her, he'd just vanished—poof—gone, a waning memory connected only to her photographs of their past. Her loss became a consuming sadness that Dante sought to soothe. I was sure that Dante would never confess his knowledge of the murder to Charley. He'd been the catalyst that set it in motion, and he could never reveal the truth if he wanted to keep her affection. Over time, as Charley realized her husband would never return, she gradually, with more fatigue than fire, allowed Dante to move in and occupy his brother's bed.

"It's not Dante I'm worried about," I said, looking at Bo. "It's this whole deal."

He took a swig from his Pellegrino. "I love it. We'll be VIPs to the Vatican, Marty—the Vatican! That's serious progress, given where we were a couple of years ago. Just imagine the doors it'll open."

"I'm not sure I want those doors opened," I said. "It feels wrong. The Vatican wouldn't know Paladin if they tripped over it. They haven't had a chance to vet us, and Leo couldn't tell a Picasso from a finger painting. Yet suddenly 'they' lay the portfolio of the most valuable library in the world and a stockpile of masterpiece castings at our feet." I turned back to stare out the window at the gliding darkness.

"So what?" Bo said and sighed. "The money comes from Dmitry, which means he found some loose change in his couch." His eyes drifted shut.

"I don't care about Dmitry's upholstery, Bo. I'm trying to determine if we're abetting money laundering."

Bo's eyes shot open, cold and severe. His smile evaporated. The banter was over.

"Goddamnit! Marty, we've had this conversation so many times I've memorized it—I can set it to music."

He was referring to our constant speculation about what Dmitry Chernyshevsky, one of the wealthiest men on earth, was doing with a couple of small-timers like us—investing rounding-error money in our modest conglomerate. We had reasoned that there were only three possibilities: 1) we were nominal mules in a massive money laundering operation; 2) Dmitry was willing to throw hobby money at his favorite booty call, Natalya; or 3) he was a sharp investor using Paladin's steady growth to diversify his holdings. With jaded hubris, we rationalized it as a combination of 2 and 3, which, if true, made our collaboration with him unsavory but lawful.

We could live with that.

To clarify, money laundering is pushing dirty money through a funnel of other companies, called in the trade "empty boxes," so that the money coming out the other end of the funnel is unrecognizable from the money that went in. But the entire enterprise depends on the word "dirty." There is a distinction between "illegal" and "illicit." While drug cartel money, for example, is legitimately dirty, oligarch money, for lack of a better term, is not so much dirty as it is—"dingy."

Dmitry owned many companies, the biggest being Rakhmetov Korporatsiya, an oil transportation and trading company that President Vladimir Putin sold to him for scraps after he'd bribed Boris Yeltsin to pick Putin as his successor. He was a robber baron in a kleptocracy. In Russia, wealth wasn't illegal—it just came with strong strings attached.

He sold oil produced in a sovereign state on the international market. His trains, trucks, and tankers were legal transport. His sales were lawful and legitimate. His dealings may have been unscrupulous inside the venerable borders of the US, but they were benign, even customary, inside the corrupt walls of Mother Russia.

Bo liked to say there was no difference between a Russian plutocrat and a Saudi sheikh. They both lived lavish, decadent lives, and their wealth came from corrupt cronyism. In Saudi Arabia, it's the royal family; in Russia, it's Putin's oligarchs (Russia's royal family without the pedigree). However, the Western financial world coveted Saudi riyals while shunning Russian rubles, although both were earned similarly. In the welter of global trade, nationality trumps geopolitics.

If a sheikh had funded Paladin Holdings, we would have had a grand IPO, be a publicly traded company, and our equity would be liquid. With an oligarch, however, we had to settle for private ownership, with less transparency but more flexibility. One reason we could swallow the entire Vatican-Chiurazzi venture was that we could count our shareholders on the fingers of one hand.

"We don't launder money for Dmitry, Natalya, or anyone else," Bo carped at me as if scolding an errant child.

"Well, we're giving it a damn good rinse then," I shot back.

He stared at me for a solid minute. "Yeah, OK, that's fair," he said with a slight grin. "But we've got to stick together on this. You've got to stop second-guessing everything. Natalya wants to sell art. The Vatican has more art than God. Nobody's laundering anything. The lead for this deal didn't even come from Dmitry or Natalya. It came from Dante, for Christ's sake."

We sat quietly for a while. Bo thought Dmitry was judged unfairly. He wasn't.

In Russia, wealth correlated with malice. The more menacing you were, the richer you became—and vice versa. Dmitry used to be the eighth richest man in Russia, but then the fourth fell out of a window, and Putin put the second in prison to make a point.

You can do the math.

Natalya once described Dmitry Chernyshevsky to me as *khitryy chelovek*—a cunning man with a vicious determination. True or not, the next few days would prove he was also one malignant son of a bitch.

"She's meeting up with Dmitry on Capri," I said.

"I figured that."

"You think it's odd that Dmitry doesn't want to meet with us? When we're this close?"

"Yes, very odd. Like he's purposely avoiding us."

"Maybe he wants plausible deniability."

"From what?"

"Money laundering," I smirked.

CHAPTER TEN

I TOPPLED INTO BED LIKE A FELLED TREE.

I hadn't even taken off my shoes. My clothes still carried a patina of foundry grit. All I wanted was temporary oblivion, but when I sank into the plump white duvet it belched up a cloud of down feathers that I didn't see so much as taste. I coughed and gasped while sitting up, thinking I was still at the foundry, breathing in soot.

It took a second to realize my duvet had been sliced open like a book and another second to see my sheets and mattress peeled wide. A surge of panic shot through my bloodstream, as if a hydrant had been uncapped.

I bolted out of bed. Instinct and adrenaline drove me to the closet, where my clothes hung in tatters. I opened the dresser drawers; things were still folded but carelessly, and as I lifted them out, they fell apart in my hands.

Someone had taken box cutters to every piece of fabric in the suite. The mattress, the sheets, the duvet, the couch, the armchair, the desk chair, and my clothes—suits, shirts, pants, sweaters, even underwear—had all been sliced into long material tassels, like fringes on a leather jacket. There was a menacing civility to it, invisible incisions that took their time to bleed.

In a frenzy, I raced two doors down from my room to Bo's. I pounded on the heavy wood door, but there was no answer. In my mind, I saw Bo lying in his bed, staring at the ceiling, his throat cut open and bleeding into the feathers of his ruptured pillow. I sped past the elevator and took the stairs three steps at a time, hitting the lobby floor with a final leap that threw me into the wall. I was running toward the front desk when I saw Bo and our Vatican envoy, Leo Giacobbe, strolling out of the Dome restaurant. Bo saw my face and the halo of goose down still orbiting my head and shoulders.

"Are you fucking chickens again, Marty?" he asked through a laugh. "We've talked about this—it's an unhealthy compulsion."

Out of breath, for a moment I couldn't talk. "My room's been sabotaged," I panted. "I was worried you were hit, too."

I explained quickly, and Bo and I took the elevator to the third floor. Visibly shaken, Leo ran to the reception desk to get an attendant.

Bo's room was vandalized in the same way. Everything was sliced into bits, and his clothes were an ensemble of ribbons.

Leo, breathing heavily, and the hotel manager, barely breathing, showed up as we pulled Bo's slashed clothes out of the closet. The manager, a tall, thin man with curly black hair, introduced himself as Vincenzo Vincenzi and asked to see my room once he'd examined Bo's. Vincenzo was curiously calm, but given my adrenaline, anyone not screaming struck me as annoyingly composed. He asked us if anything had been stolen. I didn't think so. Then he asked if Bo and I still had our passports, which we did, as we'd taken them to Naples with us.

Vincenzo inspected my room, shaking his head at my bed, which looked like a pillow fight gone wrong. He also fingered my clothes, which were just shreds of material. Then he called the *Carabinieri*.

I returned to Bo's room, where he and Leo talked quietly but intensely. Leo held a folded card, which he handed to me as I approached them. I had the same card in my room, sitting tent-like on my desk near the lamp, welcoming me personally to the Michelangelo and reminding me to take advantage of the complimentary breakfast in the lobby restaurant. Someone had written over the menu items in all caps with a black marker: *VAI A CASA O MUORI.*

"Leo found it," said Bo. "I never even noticed it had been moved. It says, 'Go home or die.'"

Alessio Rosa's ugly face loomed in my mind, and my heart palpitated a full beat.

"This is about the Chiurazzi," whispered Bo, and I looked behind me to see why he was whispering. He noted my concern and added, "Leo said we have to be careful about what we say to the cops."

"Did you tell him about Naples? What happened to Dante?"

"That's what I was doing in the bar when you ran up looking like Big Bird just mugged you."

"You can't claim this as anything other than a random hotel robbery," said Leo. "Don't talk about the accident at the Chiurazzi."

"What happened at the Chiurazzi wasn't an accident," I insisted.

"Do not talk about it," said Leo in a fierce murmur.

"Piss off, Leo," I barked. "You got us into this clusterfuck, and right now, I'm not sure I want to do anything you say. Was your room ransacked?"

"No," he said.

"You sure?" I spat, and moved my face close to his.

"Yes, I just checked."

"Why is that?" I asked acidly.

"Stop talking to me like I had something to do with this." He met my evil eye without hesitation and with equal aggression. He dropped the fawning veneer. "I'm trying to make sure you don't lose your passports. You attach this shitshow with a threat in Naples, and the police will immediately link it to organized crime. That means they'll investigate what you're doing in Italy, confiscate your passports, assume the worst, and shove a flashlight up your ass. You'll need to involve the US Embassy to untangle the mess, and the Vatican will expel you like a virus."

He marched out of the room.

I looked at Bo and thought about a cabin in the woods two years ago. "You afraid I'm going to piss myself?" I griped.

"No—we're wearing our only clothes, and I'm not loaning you my undies."

I knew what he was doing, and I appreciated it. I plopped onto his bed, landing clumsily and a geyser of pillow guts plumed upward. Bo and I both laughed. Then we strained to stop laughing, which made it worse, and our laughter intensified, so we were wiping tears from our eyes when the police entered the room.

The *Carabinieri* officer was a stocky woman wearing a black uniform with a Sam Browne belt and a Beretta 9mm in a cross-draw carry. Her lipstick looked freshly applied, which surprised me given the late hour. Accompanying her were two husky men from the *polizia* in dark blue jackets with their 9mms in a right-draw carry. They did not give their names nor shake our hands. All three looked exceptionally serious, though, to be honest, the lipstick helped ease some of my anxiety.

Vincenzo Vincenzi helped translate. "*L'ufficiale vorrebbe sapere…*"— "The officer would like to know…"—went on for about half an hour. While the woman cop asked questions and took notes, her two companions took pictures with pocket cameras. I noted that the *polizia* guys glanced smugly at each other when they saw the feather explosion in my room and the down dust still on my shoulders. One of them snapped my photo. He said, "Cheese," but I didn't smile.

Bo showed the woman officer the folded card, and I retrieved the one from my room with the same message. She put them in her note portfolio. She interviewed Leo (who reappeared after sulking in his room) and then the rest of the small crew on night duty. Her reassuring authority reminded me of my daughter's soccer coach. Leo eavesdropped as much as possible, telling us the questioning revolved around room access. The consensus was that the vandals had preprogrammed key cards because no hotel doors had been damaged.

None of us talked about the staged sabotage at the foundry or

Alessio Rosa's threats at the hospital. Bo and I were experts at strategic omissions; apparently, Leo was too. The hostilities were obviously linked, but Leo's instinct was correct. If we had told the *Ufficiale* about the threats, she would have made a phone call, a different officer would have been assigned, and our passports would have been confiscated while they determined if our business dealings were somehow affiliated with mafia interests, specifically *La Camorra*.

It was 2 a.m. when the *polizia* left, and I'd been up for almost forty-eight hours. Vincenzo had an attendant move Bo and me into different rooms. Watching him hang our frayed clothes on the porter's cart and wheel them to another room was sad and comical. I dropped exhausted onto my new bed, still seeking blissful oblivion. This time, as I belly-flopped, the duvet embraced me in a warm hug instead of spewing its contents everywhere.

I managed to get four hours of sleep before waking in a warm sweat, anxious and with no memory of dreams.

I stayed in bed, my mind inevitably drifting to her.

CHAPTER ELEVEN

Miami, one year ago.

"DO YOU THINK WE SHOULD GO TO BED TOGETHER?" Natalya asked, bringing the shot glass to her lips.

"Is that an option?" I asked, startled at her directness.

"If you want it to be," she replied.

I loved the sound of her thick contralto—warm, throaty, and suffused with a sensual Russian rhythm. Her deep brown eyes, usually cool and detached, were now flirtatious and inviting. Her dark blonde hair was getting shorter again. When we first met, it brushed her shoulders, but over the months, it had retreated inch by inch as if it were always in the way, now framing her face in a short boyish cut that only enhanced her natural curves.

"In that case, I'm all in," I replied.

"That is a very agreeable answer," she said after downing the vodka with a slight grimace and shudder. Briefly studying a thin slice of Polish sausage on the *zakuska* platter, she picked it up and slid it between her lips, which still showed a faint glaze of lipstick, indelibly elegant, like the rest of her face.

"I want to be a good partner," I said, tossing back my vodka and repeating her grimace but not the shudder.

"So, you are saying you will take one for the team," she jested with an inviting smile.

"Well, Bo insisted he be in charge of investor relations, but I'm happy to assist."

"Bo doesn't like me, I think." She gave a mock frown and foraged from the platter, settling on a sliced pickle.

"Bo likes you enough but keeps attractive women at a careful distance."

"He has happy marriage, yes?"

"Yes." I took another sip of vodka. I knew where the conversation was going and weighed how much to reveal. I'd caved to her blindsiding advance quickly—too quickly—but I had my reasons, valid or not.

I'd flown to Miami for our monthly face-to-face and she'd picked me up at the airport. Bo hated the meetings, which he thought were redundant and unnecessary, so I attended alone. Usually, I would take a cab to my hotel and then visit her gallery office in the morning, but on this trip she'd surprised me by picking me up at the airport and inviting me to her place at SoFi in South Beach.

She'd asked me if I liked to drink vodka, and I lied, saying I did. Delighted, she said she would teach me how to drink Russian style. We stopped at a Fresh Market and headed to the deli section, where she bought sausages, salted herring, and slices of cured pork fatback called *Salo*. Then she guided us through the vegetable section, picking radishes, green onions, potatoes, a jar of sauerkraut, and one of pickles. Finally, she added a rye baguette and a loaf of black bread.

"I will make *zakuska*, small bites—how do you say—to arouse the vodka."

"How about dinner?" I asked.

"If I do it right, you will forget about dinner," she said.

When we arrived at her waterfront townhouse, she told me to make myself comfortable while she prepared things. Pulling a bottle of Stolichnaya Elit from her Sub-Zero, she shooed me out of the kitchen, and I explored. She'd decorated her place with a Versace-style grandeur: Italian marble floors and Venetian plaster walls. Arched entrances and thick, ornate wooden doors separated the spaces. Antique furniture was mixed artistically with modern plush, and large tapestries graced every room. Window walls were every-where, and elaborate brocaded drapes framed the unobstructed view of the marina, where mega-yachts floated indulgently in the night water, the lights of Miami shimmering in the distance.

She waited until I swallowed my vodka and finally asked me the question I thought she would: "And, Martin, you have a happy marriage, too?"

She picked up a piece of black bread topped with sauerkraut.

"Happy is a relative term," I said, looking into her beautiful face and deciding to say more than I should. "Abbie and I had a great relationship, but then I tried my hand at entrepreneurship, and we went through some rough times financially. Paladin was the last straw, and the marriage, like the company, nearly went under. We separated for a while, and then you and Dmitry made your investment and saved the company and, to a degree, the marriage."

"You were not together when we met?" she asked, startled.

"Nothing official," I answered, thinking furiously about how much I should betray. "She thought a separation would save the marriage—make me quit Paladin and find a job with a steady income and a secure future. I lived at a Marriott Residence Inn for a while, and after your five million dollar infusion, I moved back home."

"And now you are happy?" I could tell the *you* was not meant to be plural. Her question took no interest in Abbie—she was exploring my fealty, my fidelity.

"Not really. The marriage didn't bend—it broke. We glued it back together, but there's a scar, a fault line, and any sudden jolt..." I trailed off.

"Ah." She nodded pensively, and I could see the shift in her eyes. "I do not want to be that jolt." She took another shot of the Stoli.

"You're not—she's fucking her boss," I said too quickly and regretted it immediately.

Natalya squinted, set her glass down, and said, "You should not have told me that."

I apologized, and we talked about unimportant things for a while. But my comment hovered over us like an albatross, and eventually, she veered back to it and asked, "How do you know this?"

"That Abbie is sleeping with her boss? I don't know for sure. She hasn't confessed or anything. She's good with secrets. But she took a job a year ago with a software firm headquartered in Geneva, Switzerland, and she travels there often with her boss, the company's CEO."

"It is a nice city to travel to," she said.

"Yes, it is, and I notice little things—things only I can see and obsess over."

She raised her eyebrows instead of asking, *Like what?*

I hesitated, knowing I was about to breach the privacy barrier that wraps and protects a marriage. Still, I was stricken by then, willing to crash through any boundary to get what I wanted.

"Like she comes home from a week in Geneva with her boss and has more sexual energy than when she left." I waved my hands nervously. "She's been gone for a week, so sex when she returns is…"—I searched for the right word—"…our rhythm. And when we get together, there's an enthusiasm that feels residual…like she's coming down from a mood."

I looked directly into Natalya's eyes. "And she's always a little more groomed—moisturized skin, shaved legs, everything smooth, all her parts primped and preened. After a week of hard work in Geneva, I expect her to be tired and scruffy. Instead, she comes home and makes love to me with a passion that feels guilty and a body that looks refurbished. I think it should be the other way around."

I hesitated, questioning if I should go further. "And then there's the underwear thing."

Again, Natalya raised her eyebrows inquisitively but said nothing.

"Abbie has this separate stash: pretty, lacy, sexy, for special occasions. She stopped wearing spicy lingerie for me years ago, but weirdly, she now packs it for her trips. Her 'special' underwear,"—I made air quotes—"has become her 'travel' underwear. After fifteen years of marriage, I notice stuff like that."

We sat silently for a minute, and I regretted my rhetorical spasm, feeling like a snitch.

"Are there many trips?" she asked.

"Not when she started, but now frequently. One week in Geneva, five weeks at home. It's a great gig, especially if you like to travel."

Another spell of silence. I was aware of her looking at me as I wallowed in self-pity, staring into my vodka glass. "She also works out all the time now. It started after her first few trips. Abbie's always kept herself in good shape, but still, she's a mom with teenage kids. She spends an hour at the gym every day now, rain or shine, transforming herself from good to great."

"When she travels, who looks after the children?"

"Andrew and Ali are in high school, so they don't need constant attention, and we have a cleaning lady who doubles as a nanny."

She glanced at the food platter, but I could see her mind working.

I continued. "And she never calls me when she travels. She calls the kids. They have their phones, and she'll check in with them daily. I once asked her why she doesn't call me, and she said because she doesn't worry about me." I swirled the ice in the Stoli. "I doubt she even *thinks* about me—why would she want to interrupt her romance by revisiting her reality?"

I emptied my glass and expelled the residual air in my lungs, wanting to rid myself of my confessional guilt.

Then Natalya said soberly, "You say Abbie is good with secrets."

"Yes, she is," I answered.

"And you?" She stood up and crooked her finger at me as she walked out of the lounge. "Are you also good with secrets, Martin?"

///////////////////////////////////

The sex was incredible.

I can't explain why.

It wasn't like we did anything new—it was just effortless. Surprisingly, Natalya was as comfortable with my body as I was. I learned over the years (don't ask me how) that some women possess an instinctual sense for sex—intuitively knowing what to do and when to do it with such confidence and skill it conveys a sublime proficiency that is a little jarring and blissful at the same time.

I couldn't get enough.

Afterward, we indulged in languorous conversation. Natalya placed her pillow at the foot of the bed, lying in the opposite direction, our heads facing each other. She then put her manicured feet on my chest and asked me to stroke them.

"Just gentle," she instructed. Which I did, and she closed her eyes, smiled, and sighed.

"How can you tolerate this? I could never stand it," I said.

"Hmm...no, it is beautiful feeling. I learned it from Mikhail—he would stroke me after lovemaking—my palms, my underarms, *moy zadnitsa*—my bum, and bottom of my feet, which I love the most."

"Mikhail, your second husband, after you came to the States."

"Yes, my stepson's father. He was a good man. For me, a perfect match, except his age."

"Tell me about him...tell me your life story," I said, my fingers brushing against the arch of her foot.

"Ha," she laughed. "You make me feel old. A life story should not be a peek at the middle. I will start at the beginning and tell you more another time."

"Then there'll be another time," I teased.

"Of course, Martin. I am not a one-night stand."

"I was hoping you'd say that."

////////////////////////////////////

Natalya, the older of twin sisters, entered the world pink and perfect, while her twin, Krystina, was laid transversely and had to be delivered by caesarean, bloody and screaming. The additional time moved her sister's birth past midnight to the following day, so Natalya was always celebrated, in one form or another—first.

The girls were identical, blessed with coils of tawny blonde hair, soft brown eyes, straight teeth, and olive skin. They grew up in a low-rise brick housing complex in Kapotnya, a dreadfully poor district about nineteen kilometers southeast of Moscow's center. The area was home to a large oil processing plant, condemning its residents to foul air, an inescapable fetor, and a ubiquitous greasy veneer on everything, even their sky. In such squalor, the girls were treated like two flowers in tar sand, enjoying all the benefits their striking beauty gifted them. They appeared as mirror images to the outside world, yet in their private lives, they became opposites of each other. Natalya was confident and friendly, while Krystina was dark and reclusive.

"When we were little girls meeting new people, we stood side by side in our pretty dresses. I looked up at the faces of the strangers, but Krystina looked down at their shoes. Mama would scold her and say, 'Dogs look at feet, not pretty girls.' Mama was not kind to Krystina."

With their mother's determination, the sisters achieved minor celebrity status—if not across all of Moscow, at least in Kapotnya. Life in the Soviet Union was so dreary back then that anything mildly unconventional attracted extravagant attention. Two lovely identical twins from an impoverished part of the city stood out, earning features in local newspapers through human-interest articles filled with childhood anecdotes and sprinkled with party propaganda.

When the sisters turned eighteen, the Hotel Ukraina, the only five-star luxury hotel in Moscow, hired them to tend the lobby bar. It was a job befitting their small fame and a gateway to their futures. The monstrous hotel, built by Stalin, was strategically located between Spaso House, home to the entire US diplomatic corps, and the Russian Federation buildings known as the Russian White House. Consequently, the hotel's cavernous grand bar swelled most afternoons with diplomats, dignitaries, apparatchiks, spooks, and snoops. In this chowder of the powerful, soon-to-be-powerful, or wannabe powerful, the twins thrived. Natalya's allure and Krystina's aloofness captivated the exclusive assembly of male patrons seeking suitable companions.

"My sister," Natalya yawned, "was a temptress. She learned her power over men and liked to play. For her, sex was money; it bought things for her. She was beautiful, so she was rich. You understand?"

"You are equally rich," I said.

She smiled approvingly. "Yes, but I used *my* money to look for husband, and I got two of them. Both were good to me, and both were wrong for me." She yawned again. "We have expression in Russia—*Besplatnyi syr tolko v myshelovke*—it means free cheese is only found in a mousetrap—you understand this, yes?"

She closed her eyes, drifting away.

"Yes," I said. "But over here, we say, 'You get what you pay for.'"

CHAPTER TWELVE

Rome, Saturday, January 17th

CLIMBING OUT OF BED, I felt a familiar griminess cling to me, a physical and emotional residue of the previous day's events. I'd slept in my clothes—a desperate armor against my newfound vulnerability—just as I had two years earlier when Natalya's nephew, Vasili, tried to kill me.

After showering and applying lots of deodorant, I brushed and spanked my wrinkled clothes with the complimentary hotel lint brush. Then, still rumpled and unkempt, I strolled downstairs, looking for what the natives laughingly referred to as *caffe*.

A small vase with a single red anthurium adorned the center of the table where Bo and Leo sat. The nearly empty restaurant smelled of freshly baked cornetti and espresso. Leo sipped his cappuccino while Bo stared into his with dread.

"Morning," I grumbled.

Bo didn't look up. "I think this stuff might interfere with the ability of cells to divide and grow," he said, gently poking a spoon into the black brew.

"You're describing chemotherapy," I said, sitting opposite him.

"Exactly," he said, frowning at me.

"Chemo can save your life," I pointed out.

"And make you nauseous," he returned.

We filed through the breakfast buffet, selecting warm brioche, fruit, and slices of ham and cheese. I poured myself half a cup of java and diluted it with another half-cup of cream while Bo studied me.

"I need the caffeine," I said, shrugging.

We engaged in casual conversation while we ate. I watched other guests arrive and fill the tables. No one sat near us, and after a young lady in a grey skirt and white blouse brought us more *caffe* and a full bottle of cream, we leaned closer and started to talk more seriously.

"Vincenzo went home, but the day manager told me the investigation into how your rooms were vandalized continues," said Leo.

"We have to get new clothes," I said, shifting my head to sniff my underarms.

"First, we have to meet His Eminence Cardinal Bertolini, so shopping must wait," said Leo. I wondered if he had taste buds as he downed more undiluted black mud.

"How'd the Church ever get into the licensing business?" asked Bo unexpectedly. He'd evidently been mulling it for a while.

Knowing our preference for brevity, Leo offered, "It's a long story, but I can condense it."

"Pretend you're getting paid by the hour," said Bo, "and we only have a dollar."

Leo smiled. "I don't get paid by the hour."

Bo looked at his watch and smiled back. "Tick-tock."

Leo scraped at a small dollop of jam on his plate with his finger, savored it, and then launched into Vatican history.

"Popes in the Middle Ages would dispatch their emissaries throughout the known world to acquire, or steal, all the documents that had survived the Dark Ages. Over the next five centuries, the Catholic Church became the global repository of Western history's most precious documents, manuscripts, and books. But, by tradition, the Church is highly secretive, so this massive archive remained closed in self-imposed sequestration, and its library became better known as a mausoleum."

"Lots of thrillers have been written about the Vatican's hidden archives," I said.

"It's practically a genre." Leo took a deep breath. "Fast forward about five hundred years to 1984, and everything changed when Father Leonard Boyle, an Irish priest, was appointed the library's prefect. Boyle believed that the most important reservoir of knowledge in the Christian world should function more as a library, not a cemetery. Millions of ancient writings were still cataloged by pencil and paper, and he wanted to computerize them. But there was little money available for modernization. The Vatican's treatment of its prized inventory was perfunctory at best, barely a footnote in its operating budget."

"The Vatican has an operating budget?" asked Bo.

"Of course it does. The only person not on salary in the Vatican is the pope." He sipped some of his coffee and continued. "For years, the library had scraped by on meager earnings from selling postcards and photos of images in its portfolio. So, Father Boyle—may he rest in peace—moved aggressively to fund his plans and, in his ambition, cut some dubious business deals. His showstopper came in 1988 when he exclusively licensed the global rights to all the images in the library to a California businesswoman named Elaine Peconi for $3 million."

Bo's eyebrows arched while I frowned—our typical and contrasting expressions for being impressed.

"She'd sold him on her idea to allow sacred images to adorn everything from silk scarves to coffee mugs—all blessed and certified by the stamp of pontifical endorsement, the Vatican Library Seal."

"A marketing godsend," said Bo.

"Manna from heaven," I added.

"Correct," Leo said. "Peconi convinced—you might even say bamboozled—Father Boyle into believing he was sitting atop a giant pile of intellectual property that could be licensed the way Disney licenses the image of its cartoon characters to be put on T-shirts and children's pajamas. The only difference was that the masterpieces in the Vatican Library had never been seen before. But the naive Father Boyle did not know that Peconi had recently declared bankruptcy, and her financial backer was a disgraced owner of a failed S&L."

"Hmmm—I'll bet the gods weren't pleased," I quipped, and both Bo and Leo furrowed their brows at my irreverence.

"Well, certainly not the Roman Curia," said Leo. "Everything in the library—in the Vatican, for that matter—belongs to the pope by divine right. In Father Boyle's case, a simple priest with perhaps too much authority had signed over the rights of the apostolic treasure to a determined dilettante as if it were his own."

The same young waitress in a grey apron and white blouse came by to pick up our dishes and invited us to return for seconds. We thanked her. From her smile, I could see she would blossom into a true heartbreaker someday.

"The Vatican has forever suffered with the same problem," continued Leo after she stepped away. "The pursuit of both religion and reward. The Church is much better at the former than the latter. It took a few years for the Ecclesiastical Authority to figure out what was happening. Once it did, the Church removed Father Boyle, installed a new prefect, and demanded the licenses back."

"We heard about the litigation yesterday from the attorney, Lamberto," I said.

"Father Boyle had gone rogue, you see—but what he did is quite typical in the Church. Men of God instinctively trust individuals over large corporations. The good Reverend signed binding contracts without seeing so much as a resume."

"And Gennaro Chiurazzi bought one of the licenses and then couldn't keep up with the required fees," added Bo.

"Correct," said Leo. "Mrs. Peconi was very aggressive with Gennaro, demanding payment, so he did what all Italian men do when provoked by a belligerent American woman: he went around her and asked Father Boyle for divine forgiveness." Leo smiled.

"Father Boyle got Peconi off Gennaro's back by letting him collateralize his obligation with the foundry mold collection. That's how the IOR is owed money."

"By the IOR, you mean the Vatican Bank," clarified Bo.

"Yes, the IOR—Institute for the Works of Religion—is the Vatican Bank. We also call it the VAT. Angelo Caloia is the bank's president, and you are scheduled to meet him in an hour."

At that moment, a short, bald man in a black suit—like the one worn by the night manager—approached our table and introduced himself as Giuseppe, the hotel's day manager. He apologized for the room invasions, and though his English wasn't as fluent as Vincenzo's, he made up for it with animated theatrics, expressing his concern with an expressive face and arms that flew about carelessly. Giuseppe assured us that such an incident had never happened at the Michelangelo and would not happen again. He upgraded both Bo's and my rooms to the two presidential suites, handing Bo the key to the Michelangelo Suite and giving me the Raphael Suite. He also told us that we wouldn't have to pay for anything for the rest of our stay.

"*L'hotel è tutto vostro*," he said, bowing.

"The hotel is all yours," translated Leo.

We thanked him, and he picked up our tab from the table, ripped it in half, made the *perfetto* gesture (which I call a chef's kiss), and walked away.

"Wow!" said Leo. "Those suites are two thousand euros a night, twice that in summer."

"Seems fair," said Bo. "I have to buy all-new underwear."

"Ditto," I added. I suddenly felt even dirtier as Leo's tailored suit, white shirt, and tie registered with me for the first time.

"No better place than Rome for that," said Leo. "What happened is almost enviable."

"Not really," I said.

"Will you check in with Dante later?" asked Leo.

"Yes, of course," I said. "I'm telling you again, that forklift driver slammed purposely into the shelf. He meant to kill us."

"That's overly paranoid," said Bo. "I don't think Alessio is trying to kill us; he's trying to scare us off so he can do a management buyout."

Leo fidgeted nervously with his cup and saucer. I asked him, "What do you think?"

"I don't know," he said hesitantly. "It feels like a low-level shake-down. Camorra clans no longer handle street work; they farm it out to baby gangs, juveniles working their way up to clan status. From what Bo told me, Alessio sounds like a guy who's seen one too many gangster films. But what happened to your rooms? That's something else entirely. I'd bet a baby gang hit them." He shrugged slightly, though the tension in his shoulders and the way his eyes shifted hinted he knew more than he let on.

He checked his watch. "We've got to go. We're meeting His Eminence in an hour, and I need to grab the small gift I brought for him. I'll meet you outside the lobby in five minutes."

Bo and I sat quietly, watching Leo leave. The restaurant had emptied again, and my eyes drifted toward two men in black clothes positioned against the far inside wall. I'd seen the same men at the same table yesterday.

Bo focused on them, too. "You see those guys over there? They never speak to each other."

"Maybe they're married," I replied sullenly.

"I think they're Mafioso."

"Or maybe they're like us—friends in Rome on business."

He stood up, put on his wrinkled sports jacket, and looked at them again. "Or a baby gang—past its prime."

CHAPTER THIRTEEN

"LET'S WALK," SAID LEO as we stepped out of the Michelangelo into the crisp morning air. *"Palazzo del Sant'Uffizio*—The Palace of the Holy Office—is ten minutes from here."

The sun lit up the street, making it feel warmer. We walked down *Via di S. Pietro* toward St. Peter's Dome, turned on *Via Allessandro* and then onto *dei Cavalleggeri*, a narrow one-way street lined with Vespas and Fiats like a parking garage.

A heavy woman wrestled with an equally heavy postcard kiosk, preparing to open her small restaurant. Across the cramped and shaded street, a stout man hauled a crate of fruit from the boot of his double-parked Fiat to fill up a portable fruit stand wedged against the building and blocking most of the sidewalk. We maneuvered around them, wishing them good morning and enjoying the Fellini scene.

I've heard people say that Rome is a museum-turned-city, while others claim it's a city-turned-museum. Either way, I wanted to immerse myself in its culture and charm, linger in its vibrant streets and absorb its unique persona. I was a bit chafed at Leo, hurrying along in his fancy suit, carrying a brown paper bag with *Fincato* printed on it. He paid little attention to his surroundings, concentrating instead on something ahead of him, invisible and out of reach.

"What's in the bag?" I asked.

"Cigars," he said. "Cardinal Bertolini likes a good Davidoff."

"The *gift*," said Bo, looking at me and cocking his eyebrows in amusement, referencing the reason Leo had returned to his hotel room after breakfast.

"A *taste*," replied Leo, as if he were redefining the word *gift*.

He could see that Bo and I didn't understand. "The Vatican works like no other organization on earth," he explained. "It's a holy place, but it operates under a dense mesh of obligations and favors."

"Bribes," I submitted.

"Not bribes," he answered, slightly out of breath. "*Favors* is more accurate."

A tall man wearing a flat tweed cap pulled low over his eyes and a matching scarf tied in a Parisian knot walked toward us, and Leo stopped talking until he passed. "Favors come in all shapes and sizes. They can be as subtle as a kind act or as overt as a gift bag."

"Of expensive cigars," I gibed.

"Or an envelope of money," said Bo.

Leo ignored us and continued, "Favors lubricate the machinery."

"Sounds a little klepto to me," said Bo. I could tell he was purposely pushing Leo's buttons.

"You're being obnoxious," puffed Leo. "The Church's purpose is spiritual, but its operation is human. Hundreds of chaste men compete for power, which often elicits favors. I can't do much for a cardinal, so I provide a *taste*—in respect."

"A *taste* for *grace*," I said.

"Now you get it."

We turned onto *Via Cavalleggeri*, a bustling avenue where scooters weaved between cars like water bugs juiced on adrenaline. Despite the hour, the street flowed with people to dodge and sidestep. Spotting American tourists was easy. My countrymen, clad in baseball caps, cargo pants, and beer-logo sweatshirts, sported an unconscious uniform that blared "Ugly American" as conspicuously as a Vespa horn. In contrast, Italians wore scarves, felt hats, and leather jackets draped with effortless style.

"Don't talk about last night's vandalism and Dante's accident," said Leo. "They're complications I don't want the cardinals to worry about. Let me explain it my way—follow my lead." He breathed heavily, jogging every other step to keep pace with us. Bo always walked like he was racing toward a checkered flag, and over the years, I'd learned to speed walk.

We strode along the ancient thirty-foot wall of Vatican City for five minutes and turned into Piazza del Sant' Uffizio, with the Palace of the Holy Office on our left. Almost five hundred years old, the giant structure occupied the entire piazza. Its scale was staggering. The street-level walls were travertine stone, while the upper floors were faced with rough red brick. Its windows were framed with shutters like metal curtains, and the lower windows were encased in iron gratings, giving it a prison look. A massive arched door, like the entrance to a cave, dominated the center of the building. My eyes were pulled to a narrow balcony and an enormous window framed by tufa stone carved with the Vatican coat of arms.

"Michelangelo designed that part of the building," said Leo. He checked his watch. "We've got a few minutes; let's look at the square." Turning, he headed toward the plaza.

Bo and I followed, staring at Bernini's colossal colonnade and the band of sculptures atop the basilica gazing down at us. It was early, but already a hundred tourists were milling about.

"Welcome to Vatican City," said Leo. "Population nine hundred and twenty-one."

"With its own army," added Bo.

"Yes, the smallest in the world—about one hundred and thirty-five men."

"I still think their uniform makes them look like a court jester without the funny hat," I whispered as we walked further into the row of gigantic Doric columns.

"Don't tell them that," said Bo. "They'll put you in a hospital and not think twice."

"It's against the law to make fun of the Swiss Guard uniform. You'll be ejected from the city and never allowed to return," said Leo.

I threw up my hands in surrender as we stepped out into the papal plaza. I'd already felt small in the colonnade, but now I felt Lilliputian. The square was a lake of grey stone, about the size of six football fields—half of it shrouded in chilly morning shade, and the other half bathed in the warm morning sun.

"Impressive, isn't it?" said Leo.

"I feel like an ant crossing a freeway," said Bo.

In the distance, tourists mustered on *Via della Conciliazione*, the broad avenue connecting St. Peter's Square with Castel Sant'Angelo. A smattering of priests, nuns, and pedestrians walked about, their destinations unknown. Everything seemed to move slowly, as if in space where scale slows time.

St. Peter's Basilica loomed behind us in all its Renaissance glory. The largest church in the world, as majestic and imposing as any royal palace, its massive baroque façade was so exuberantly ornate and lavish that Bernini himself could have sculpted it out of a giant travertine block. Thirteen sculptures of Christ and his apostles crowned the cathedral like sentinels guarding the iconic dome, a colossal celestial orb hovering over the giant edifice like an ashlar halo.

There's a discrepant scale to the Vatican that is hard to grasp—a balance between size and space. I repeatedly felt small, dwarfed by everything—buildings, interiors, sculptures, tapestries, and furniture. There's a bulk to it, an existential immensity that's difficult to describe except to say it's how I saw the world as a child before I grew into it.

Leo checked his watch, and we trekked back to the Palace of the Holy Office.

"The lines are starting to form," said Bo.

"Not for us," said Leo. He walked to the gated Petriano entrance and stood behind a young priest under a sign that read *Solo Personale*

Autorizzato. Wearing his clerical robe, the priest showed his ID and walked through. The Vatican guard, dressed in his billowy baroque uniform with a black beret, took Leo's ID and looked at Bo and me like we were luggage.

"They're with me," said Leo, showing him a folded letter and our passports.

"*Avanti, Buongiorno,*" he said.

Once inside the building, our voices echoed off the honed stone floors, caroming between the coffered thirty-foot ceilings and the faded tapestries—woven narratives—floating on the granite walls, interspersed with religious frescoes.

"This place used to house the Congregation for the Doctrine of the Faith," said Leo, his voice lingering as if it was reluctant to leave. "You would know it better as the Inquisition."

Bo and I stopped walking, Leo proceeding a few steps before realizing he'd left us behind.

"As in *The* Inquisition," I responded too loudly.

"Yes, the entire basement used to be a prison. The Church held Galileo here."

"Holy shit!" exclaimed Bo, his voice reverberating down hallways and vanishing around corners.

"You might want to find a different way to express yourself," said Leo.

Bo blushed a little, and I grinned.

"We're going to the third floor to the cell where the father of astronomy was held," Leo continued. "It's now the office of Economic Affairs—Cardinal Bertolini's office."

Bo and I looked at each other in disbelief. "The office of Economic Affairs was a former prison cell?" asked Bo.

"Of course not," Leo smiled. He was playing with us to get even for the poking Bo did earlier. "Galileo was imprisoned, but not in the basement where the real cells were located. He was held in a five-room suite on the third floor with a valet and a servant who brought him his daily meals. When the building was renovated at the turn of the century, his suite was converted into a single large office. It's now Bertolini's office."

"Imagine occupying the same space every day as Galileo," I said.

"And I thought we had a great office in Lake Oswego," muttered Bo.

We started to climb a large marble staircase.

"How is it you know so much?" I asked.

"My wife and I were always devout Catholics. After she passed away, I moved to Orvieto, a place we discovered on our honeymoon and visited often during our marriage. We always dreamed of retiring there, but God had other plans, and I made the journey alone. I began traveling to Rome, volunteering for various roles within Vatican City. I forged friendships with members of the Curia—the pope's administrators—and was honored with the titles of Papal Usher and Vatican Docent. I've come to understand how things operate here."

Bo and I made our usual impressed faces.

"Then docent on," said Bo.

The third floor was equally formidable. We walked down a cavernous hall lined with heavy oak doors spaced far apart, small brass plates announcing the offices locked behind them. Life-size paintings of popes adorned the walls, their imposing portraits amplifying the already suffocating sanctity of the place. I imagined myself as Galileo, trapped between two Vatican guards in their flamboyant outfits, shuffling down the hall to my so-called cell after another interrogation by the inquisitor cardinals.

Near the end of the hallway, Leo stopped, opened a dark wood door, no different than all the doors we'd passed, and waved us in like a porter. We entered a small monochromatic room with a bare metal desk in the center, a matching metal locker against one wall, and a stark metal crucifix hanging on the opposite. A handsome young Black priest greeted us from behind the desk. Leo showed his ID and discreetly dropped the bag of cigars on the desk, explaining it was for His Eminence. Without opening it, the priest pushed it dismissively aside, came around the desk, opened a side door, and said with what sounded like a Nigerian accent, "Gentlemen, their Eminences will see you now."

Leaving the front office's austere minimalism, we stepped into a spacious room so lavish and opulent that the contrast was jaw-dropping. Bo and I hung back hesitantly as Leo marched toward a diminutive, delicate man in a black cassock with red buttons and a gold pectoral cross that swung slightly when he moved. A small black skullcap—*zucchetto*—covered his thinning black hair; thick glasses obscured his eyes and much of his face. He smiled by pursing his lips, which were surprisingly warm and friendly.

"*Benvenuto, Mr. Giacobbe, è bello rivederla,*" he greeted in a soft, almost haunting voice while reaching out his hand, which Leo took, bowing deeply as he touched it to his forehead.

Should I do that? What if I screw it up—wipe my nose against his hand?

For a second, I panicked and looked at Bo, who seemed completely at ease, like he was about to meet a new neighbor.

"Your Eminence," said Leo as he quickly moved to the other cardinal, dressed also in a black cassock with red buttons and a small gold cross around his neck. His expansive forehead extended to his red *zucchetto*, fringed by thick silver hair. He, too, wore glasses, but they were smaller and thinner, so I could see his weary brown eyes. As Leo took his hand and touched it to his forehead, the cardinal offered a thin smile constricted by deeply indented jowls.

With the same speed Leo passed from one cardinal to another, he moved to a man standing beside the most imposing leather sofa I'd ever seen. He wore a perfectly fitted grey suit, white shirt, and blue silk tie. A wide, pleasant smile completely contradicted his sad, sunken eyes. Leo only shook hands with him.

I can do that.

"*Signors,*" said the first cardinal, opening his arms to us, standing before a massive giltwood table with gold cherub legs. *"Prego, entrate."*

Bo and I stepped forward. The cardinal gesturing us in was Bartolomeo Bertolini, the head of economic affairs for the Holy See. It was his office, his meeting, and his deal. The other cardinal was Claude Rautan, the Vatican Librarian who oversaw the secret archives and the library. The third man was Angelo Caloia, President of the Institute for the Works of Religion (IOR), also known as the Vatican Bank.

Cardinal Bertolini approached me and reached out his hand, vaporizing my nervousness. I didn't have to bow, curtsy, or accidentally wipe my nose on it. I just had to accept it and say, "Very honored to meet you, Your Eminence." His hand felt like sun-warmed lambskin.

After introductions Bo winked at me, like he wanted to say *I told you so.*

Cardinal Bertolini waved his arm, inviting us to sit anywhere in his vast, stately office, which was filled with meticulously arranged baroque and traditional furniture. The blue-grey plaster walls, reminiscent of antique marble, were ornamented with paintings and tapestries. Velvet burgundy curtains draped the ten-foot windows, and in a far corner stood a boardroom table long enough to seat twenty, with a bronze bust of Michelangelo's *Madonna* as its centerpiece.

As I scanned the art on the walls, my eyes snagged on a familiar face—a memory—like flipping through a magazine and catching a photo of someone you once knew but thought dead. I was paralyzed momentarily. My heart lurched, my knees locked, and I stopped breathing as if someone had pressed a Beretta to my forehead. Bo stood behind me, but I knew he'd seen it, too.

On the wall before us, next to a pale painting of an elderly, white-bearded Galileo, hung Raphael's Renaissance masterpiece *Portrait of a Young Man*, encased in an ornate gold frame.

Bo and I had a history with the painting. It had changed our lives.

It was the reason Nico Scava was murdered, the reason Paladin existed, and the reason Natalya was in my life.

The world believed it lost or destroyed, with a $100 million reward fueling its legend. Few knew the truth: the original now hung in Dmitry's private vault, alongside the forgery Dante had painstakingly crafted to replace it.

The delicate, androgynous face of Raphael seemed to peer back at me, a haunting echo of the past I'd spent two years trying to bury. The sight of it was impossible. It shouldn't have been here. It couldn't have been here. Bo and I had ensured there was only one place it could ever be.

Yet here it was—this horrifying reminder of everything we'd endured, of the blood spilled over its discovery.

I felt the recoil from Bo, a palpable shift in energy.

Then, in a flash of clarity, a disturbing revelation hit me. What I had mistaken for a capricious whim from my bewitching partner, Natalya—buying an Italian foundry—was, in fact, a much more complicated and deliberate scheme, driven covertly by Dmitry, my other partner: the billionaire.

That would be the lethal part.

CHAPTER FOURTEEN

"IT IS BEAUTIFUL—NO?" Cardinal Bertolini said sotto voce, standing beside me, his gaze fixed on Raphael's portrait. He smelled faintly of incense.

"No…I…I mean…yes," I stuttered, trying to sound reverent though I didn't feel it—I feared it.

"Where did you get it?" Bo asked stoically.

"A gift," the cardinal replied.

I nodded slightly, murmuring more to myself than to him, "A taste."

Bertolini studied the side of my face. "*Si*—taste and see that the Lord is good," he responded, his tone demure.

But we were on different tracks; he'd invoked his deity while I thought of mine. Dmitry Chernyshevsky might have been partying on Capri with Natalya, but his machinations loomed large, leaving me to wonder how much we hadn't been told.

"Well, gentlemen," Leo said, breaking the disquieting pall in the room, "I think we have things to discuss."

I jerked out of my trance, exhaling as if to pop my ears, and exclaimed, "You have a beautiful office, Your Eminence." Sinking into the tufted sofa, I added, "I understand Galileo was held here during his trial."

Bertolini shrugged slightly and settled into a twin sofa across from me, a long mahogany coffee table separating us. He said something in Italian. Cardinal Rautan approached slowly, wincing as he shuffled closer and lowered himself beside Bertolini as if his muscles were angry with him.

"His Eminence says, perhaps yes, perhaps no. If he shares this space with the spirit of Galileo, he is honored; if not, he is blessed by its possibility."

Bo sat beside me, facing the Cardinals, while Leo and Angelo Caloia settled into two flanking chenille armchairs. Everyone aimed for casual friendliness while a faint trace of parchment and leather hung in the air, fitting the stiff solemnity of the meeting.

Cardinal Rautan spoke exemplary English, telling us he'd spent many years in the US as the Vatican Ambassador. In contrast, Cardinal Bertolini understood English better than he spoke it. During our conversation, Bertolini looked pensive and stayed quiet, listening, conceivably reflecting on something else—I wasn't sure. I glanced at him often because his gentle and winsome smile reminded me of my mother.

Cardinal Rautan spoke about the library and the archives, sounding very much like he was reading from a brochure. After a twenty-minute exposition, he shifted gears and invited us to talk about ourselves.

Bo dusted off some of his wisest and funniest stories. He was on comfortable ground. We'd spent years cultivating relationships with investors over carefully crafted tales of our histories and families. But things had changed for me, so while Bo dispensed endearing anecdotes about his wife and daughters, I was out of practice, and it wasn't easy anymore.

Cardinal Bertolini studied my face, and I felt it burn as I talked about Abbie. I tripped, stammered, and stared at my shoes. I was boasting about my wife (and children) to not one but two leading cardinals of the Roman Curia only hours after sulking like a lovesick teenager because my plans for a carnal tryst in Rome with my Russian girlfriend were disrupted.

At one point, Leo explained that the airline had lost our luggage, excusing our disheveled appearance. The president of the bank, Caloia, jumped in and told us he would make a call immediately and get us an appointment at Battistoni on *Via Condotti*. I'd never heard of Battistoni, but I knew *Via Condotti* was the famous shopping avenue near the Spanish Steps. Bo and I declined the offer, but Caloia insisted, pulling out his phone and walking to a corner of the office so far away only shouting would get his attention.

While Angelo Caloia pulled strings at his favorite tailor, Cardinal Bertolini leaned forward and said softy, "*Un bel vestito per il concerto.*"

Bo and I didn't understand, but Leo's eyes widened.

"Gentlemen," said Cardinal Rautan, turning his head to all of us. "His Eminence says you will need a nice suit to be his guests at the Concert of Reconciliation this evening at Audience Hall, right next door. *Il Papa* will be attending. The concert celebrates Christian unity and the twenty-fifth anniversary of *Il Papa's* papacy. To be invited is a great honor. This year, we have combined the Epiphany concert with the Reconciliation Concert to accommodate the Holy Father's schedule. The music will be *bellissimo*."

"*Grazie*, Your Eminence," said Leo, bowing in his chair.

Bo and I followed Leo's example. I was too timid to halt the conversation. We would soon go shopping for clothes to wear at a concert hosted by Pope John Paul II and attended by dignitaries from around the world. I had assumed we'd buy sweatshirts and jeans, grab dinner at a restaurant overlooking the Colosseum, and get wasted on twelve-year-old Barolo La Morra.

Things weren't going as planned.

We never talked about money. It simply didn't come up. The cardinals proffered piety, not price. To them, our compact was a matter of heart, not hand. Bo and I discussed our company, Paladin Holdings, and its charity operation. Cardinal Rautan asked the questions while Cardinal Bertolini listened. Angelo Caloia fidgeted, looking like he wanted to be somewhere else—doing something else. Doubtless, he had no more interest in our company's altruistic activities than Bo or me.

Paladin's charity program had always been our red-headed stepchild, functioning to contribute free art, mostly sculptures, to charity auctions. Catholic fundraising campaigns were the primary beneficiaries. Dmitry wanted Paladin to cultivate a strong CSR (Corporate Social Responsibility) score, while Natalya aimed to attend multiple black-tie events to recruit new clients for her gallery.

Bo and I paid little attention to it. We hired a compassionate and competent woman to run it and then abandoned ship, trusting her to weather any storms. The operation held the remnants of our dying business and the crypt of our previous crimes.

In retrospect, I see the irony—a venture we'd treated as a leftover, like broccoli on a child's plate, had become a portal to the shitstorm heading our way, proving once again that the road to hell is paved with good intentions.

Later in the meeting, I crossed my legs, and the tip of my shoe struck the edge of the coffee table between our couches. A hefty tome resting in the middle shifted and settled with a thud. I grabbed it quickly, apologizing for my clumsiness, and glimpsed at its title: *Philosophiae Naturalis Principia Mathematica Autore Is. Newton.* I was stunned for a second, and Cardinal Bertolini noticed my disbelief.

"*Guardate, per favore,*" he said, waving his hand gently.

"Please look," translated Cardinal Rautan.

I picked up a leather-bound sheath that protected a finely grained volume inside. Pulling it free, Bo and I sat, enthralled, gingerly leafing through brittle pages filled with spidery text.

"It's not the 1687 original of *Principia* by Isaac Newton," said Rautan. "That one is in our library. This edition from 1726 was donated by a private collector some years ago. After God's holy book, it is the most important book in Christian culture."

Bo smiled wryly at Cardinal Bertolini and said, "And now it's *your* coffee table book."

Bertolini's puckered grin stretched into a thin, inscrutable smile.

"His Eminence has always been fascinated with science. Possibly, it is the ghost of Galileo, after all," said Rautan, speaking for Bertolini.

The minor disruption brought our meeting to an early close. Both cardinals stood and began moving toward the door. Their full-length robes cloaked their legs, making them seem to float above the carpeting.

"Your Eminence, may I ask you something about the Raphael portrait?" I asked Bertolini.

"*Prego*," he said, turning back to me.

"Is it real? Did Raphael paint it?"

His furrowed lips curled even more. "No. The *originale*, she is lost…to war. But…she is best *copia*…ever made."

"It is, Your Eminence," I said, recalling how I wept over the original in an airport hangar, standing over the body of Vasili, the man who had killed my partner, Nico. "Have you had it long?"

"No…was a gift from your *collego*," he said in a puzzled tone, as though he believed I already knew.

Leo huddled with Caloia, getting details for Battistoni's. Caloia suggested we go right away in case the tailor needed to make adjustments. He also assured us that our names would be on a list with the Vatican Guard at the entrance of Audience Hall for that evening.

As we were about to leave, Cardinal Rautan looked at Leo and said, "*Signor* Giacobbe, I am pleased. *Signors* Bishop and Schott will make good shepherds of the Chiurazzi. I will no longer worry that the foundry will fall into the hands of lost souls."

I took Cardinal Rautan's outstretched hand and asked, "Lost souls?"

"Certainly not you, Martin. You and Bo are different from the

others. There is a light in you. I believe it comes from the fire within."
Dimples parenthesized his grin.

I wasn't sure what he meant. It sounded like a meaningless plat-
itude thrown out at the end of a meeting—a kind of ecclesiastical
farewell. I glanced at Leo, who looked at Caloia, and I surmised it
wasn't just Dmitry and Natalya keeping secrets.

Standing close to me, Cardinal Bertolini added in a subdued but
knowing voice, "Let the fire in you burn like peat...not like paper."

A silence so thick I could have rested against it kept everyone
motionless. After several seconds, Bertolini broke the stillness with
a sharp intake of breath. He took my hand, his intelligent, sagacious
eyes searching my face, breaching my guilty conscience. I was sure
my forehead had the names of Abbie and Natalya tattooed on it.
Could he feel the rapid pulse in my hand? Did he know I lied about
my happy marriage?

Finally, he leaned toward me and whispered something in my
ear, his voice a thin rasp.

After our exit, as Leo, Bo, and I walked down the long hall, Bo
pulled me back a few steps and asked, "What did he say?"

"I'm not sure, but I think it was, 'Life is a labyrinth—the soul
is your compass.'"

After a few more steps, I added, "Basically, I'm screwed."

CHAPTER FIFTEEN

BATTISTONI'S WAS MAGNIFICENT.

Its interior wore the scent of wool, wax, wood, and wonder. Glossy mahogany shelves filled with cashmere, silk, and vicuna sweaters lined the walls. Suits hung in polished wood displays arranged by brands: Armani, Brioni, Canali, Kiton. Stately poised mannequins were so well dressed I wanted to be friends with them.

A sign on the counter read *Lusso Discreto*—Discreet Luxury— but I begged to differ. Luxury is bold—demanding attention like a Ferrari parked outside a McDonald's. For me, it was the reward for achievement. Bo had always felt the same. He'd grown up on a small ranch in eastern Oregon while I grew up in the remnant ruins of Berlin and immigrated when I was still a boy. For both of us, luxury had once been a greyscale—a limited palette of possibilities constrained by the boundaries of class and circumstance. But, with success, that greyscale had faded, replaced by a kaleidoscope of colors, and we embraced it.

Tailors Piero and Giacomo expected us and prepped the place before we arrived. I kept getting their names wrong until I realized Piero had a tape measure around his neck, and Giacomo had a wrist pincushion. They fussed over Bo and me as if we were their grandchildren dressing for our first school day. The only thing they didn't do was comb our hair.

Leo sat on a velvet sofa and watched contentedly.

Bo looked better than I did in everything. He'd never lost his athletic build, even years after he stopped playing football. He barely fit into the cockpit when he started racing Formula GTP cars. He was naturally muscular, while I was (and still am) thin but without definition, or as my kids liked to say, "skinny fat."

Piero and Giacomo fawned over us all the way out the door. Our suits and a curated assortment of other clothes would be adjusted and delivered to the Michelangelo by 5 p.m. The visit cost us a couple of hours and serious money. Still, we'd attend the concert in style. With a chorus of "*Grazie arrivederci,*" we reluctantly exited the shop.

It was early afternoon, and *Via dei Condotti's* foot traffic had swollen to holiday mall levels. Across the street from Battistoni's was a narrow arched alley leading to a neighboring street. I caught a glimpse of someone leaning against the stone wall. His face was in shadow, but his figure was hauntingly familiar—the robust frame trim yet thick. His right shoulder drooped slightly as if his right arm held something heavy—*like a 9mm Beretta.*

Bo and Leo were already twenty paces ahead, and I squinted, craning my neck toward the hulking silhouette. As he turned to walk in the opposite direction, his face briefly caught the sunlight, pulled from the shadows for a moment.

I nearly pissed myself.

It was Brody Lynch.

It was the *Irishman.*

My spine stiffened, and my stomach turned to ice.

Brody—fucking—Lynch!

We'd crossed paths three times—each one bloody. The first time was in a dank fishing cabin where Nico was killed. The second time was in a dank cellar where the Baron was killed. The third time was in a dank airplane hangar where Vasili was killed.

I carried a dark past with that bastard. He scared the bejesus out of me—the living embodiment of my nightmares. I chased Bo and Leo down the street, grabbing Bo by his jacket.

"Lynch!" I managed to force out. "Brody Lynch!"

Bo reacted as if I'd slapped him, and Leo stepped back. People swerved around us like we were an impromptu street performance.

"What! Where?" asked Bo, looking over my shoulders and seeing nothing but a heaving wave of shoppers.

"In that arched alleyway," I said, pointing at the empty space.

Bo maneuvered back through the crowd and peered into the alley. Brody wasn't there.

"You're seeing phantoms, Marty," he said close to my ear. "We're in Rome…*R-O-M-E*! Get a hold of yourself."

"I have no idea who you are talking about, but I see look-alikes all the time," added Leo. "I think the older I get, the more people tend to resemble each other."

For a moment, I stared down at my new shoes. I grasped how crazy I sounded. I took deep breaths and began to doubt what I had just seen. Had I imagined it? Was I delusional? I stood still in the street, my whole body shaking, cold sweat on my brow. Then I stuffed my hands into my pockets and wandered toward Caffè Greco, Bo and Leo trailing behind, their voices muffled by the din of ghosts fighting in my head.

A line had formed outside the restaurant. Fortunately, when Angelo Caloia called Battistoni from Bertolini's grand office, he'd also reserved his table for us. I knew little about Angelo (who'd barely spoken during our meeting) other than he was president of the Vatican Bank, but I liked him more with every hour.

A stern-faced, tuxedoed *cameriere* guided us through the oldest café in Rome, which had opened sixteen years before John Hancock signed the Declaration of Independence. The landmark restaurant was a cacophony of art and kitsch—a treasure trove of paintings mixed pell-mell with porcelain plates and figurines.

We were routed to the rear salon, next to a drawing room lined with old bookcases and a worn parquet floor that reminded me of Sunday school. The salon was a red room filled with velvet banquettes and marble-topped tables. Ours was in an alcove with a large sculpture of a satyr crouching next to it. The air smelled of coffee and vanilla, with an undertone of damp stone.

I ordered a vodka martini, Bo ordered his usual scotch, and Leo ordered an Aperol spritz.

"When did you start drinking vodka?" asked Bo.

"A while back," I said, hiding my face behind the menu.

His lips pursed as he eyed me skeptically. To my relief, Bo then shifted his focus. "Leo," he said, "Lamberto mentioned something—what did he call it? *Pizzo*. Do you know how that works?"

"*Pizzo* is paid to the various clans. It is a security tax, so your business doesn't burn down," said Leo. "It comes in many forms, paid however each business can afford it. Sometimes it's a percentage of revenue. Sometimes it's a no-show salary. Sometimes it's buying from a specific supplier. In Naples, *pizzo* is as rife as moss. Camorra gangs are very parasitic."

"Why don't business owners tell the scumbags to pound sand?" I asked.

"That's naive, Marty. In Naples, the Camorra is a part of the cultural ethos. Think of it as…" he hesitated, looking for the right word, "…an *understanding*. If every business in the neighborhood buys from one vendor, then you buy from the same vendor. No one threatens you. Thick necks with pinky rings don't show up one day and lock your door. That's great for movies, but it never happens in real life. If you don't buy from the designated supplier, a brick goes through your front window. If you still don't comply, there's a second brick, and by the third brick, your insurance stops covering the repairs. Then you conform. It's that simple."

The *cameriere* brought our drinks, and I contemplated Leo's words. Over here, everything—from the secular to the sacred—functioned on a system of tacit cues. Even a sanctified monolith like the Church operated within this framework of *understanding*, where acquiescence was as natural as breathing. I appreciated the parallels.

A minute later, the phone in my pocket buzzed. The screen read *Dante*. I hit the green answer button.

"Dante?"

All I heard was disjointed static. "You said these phones worked better than our own," I commented to Leo, but before he could reply, a voice emerged.

"They tried to kill me! Right in the hospital! Can you believe that shit?!" Dante's words burst out like they were escaping a burning building.

Bo could see my face and knew something was wrong. "What's happening?" he said.

I held up my forefinger, blocking his interruption, and held the phone closer. "What did you say?"

"Here, in the damn hospital, mafia muscle—I'm guessing it was mafia, *goombahs* for sure—came into my room and scared the shit out of me!"

I felt besieged. An hour ago, I saw the Raphael. A minute ago, I thought I saw Brody Lynch. Now, Dante was yelping hysterically in my ear. Things were happening too fast, like staccato bursts of machine gun fire.

I left the table for more privacy. "How the hell did they get into your room?"

"How should I know, Marty!" he barked. "Maybe they used their cloak of invisibility."

"Did you know any of them?"

"Yeah, Marty, they're old buddies. We used to hang out together back when I snuffed people for shits and giggles…no. Never saw them before in my life."

"I thought one of them might have been from the foundry, like Rosa," I answered defensively.

"No," he said. "I told the nurse to call the police, but she looked at me like I was drunk."

Navigating the restaurant's meandering layout, I sidled between tables, listening intently to Dante's frenetic voice. Finding a quiet spot in Caffè Greco at lunchtime was like hunting for solitude in a mosh pit.

"Start at the beginning," I instructed, trying to calm his rapid rhetoric.

"The hospital is great. The nurses treat me like I'm a celebrity. I'm on oxycodone for pain and was sleeping. Suddenly I couldn't breathe, and opened my eyes. Some asshole the size of Sasquatch was pinching my nose shut while another guy on the other side of the bed had his hand over my mouth. I tried to sit up, but the pain was too much, and I screamed into his smelly palm. I tried to bite him, but when I did he hit me in the solar plexus before taking his hand away. I spasmed and still couldn't breathe. I thought I'd suffocate right here in the hospital. Then the guy holding my nose let go, held a finger to his lips, and shushed me."

Dante stopped to catch his breath. "He shushed me, Marty. I couldn't find air, and this dirtbag pretended he was throwing a surprise birthday party!"

"What did he say?" I asked, trying to get him to focus.

"A bunch of crap in Italian, but then he stopped and started again in English." Dante switched to a mock Italian accent. "'Go back to America. Naples does not welcome you. Tell your friends to leave while they can. The Chiurazzi is no longer for sale. *Capisce*?' I shook my head like a stupid bobblehead 'cause I still couldn't breathe. He said, 'Good. We have mutual respect. If you break that respect, you will never breathe again. Do you understand my English?' I kept nodding my head. Then they left. I have a private room, so no one saw them."

I cracked a humorless smile, remembering how hard Natalya had worked to get him that room; no good deed goes unpunished. "You said you told the nurse?"

"I hit my call button and told everybody: the doctor, the nurse, the attendant, the janitor. The security guy said he didn't see anyone out of the ordinary. Everyone thinks I had a nightmare."

"Yeah, I know how you feel," I said. I thought about what Lamberto had said about Camorra-controlled security in some hospitals.

Winding through the restaurant, phone fastened to my ear, I peripherally caught a flash of ruby. Looking up, I saw a woman wearing almost neon red lipstick. We made eye contact as I neared her table. Compact and intent, she was dressed in a black pleated peplum coat with silver buttons, her dark hair secured in a tight bun. Not a tourist—tourists didn't dress like that. She was dining alone, and her brown eyes followed me with a steady curiosity as I paced back and forth through the restaurant. I nodded to her in apology for disrupting her solitary lunch and moved on.

"Are you packed?" I asked Dante. "Where's your passport?"

"Lamberto Liuzzo said he'll bring my stuff to the hospital. Natalya called me this morning. She said she'd be here Monday to take me to her plane."

Nomadically, I wandered into a long, narrow room flooded with sunlight. I strolled past a table where the same two men we'd seen that morning at the Dome restaurant were seated. Once again, they observed me silently, not talking to each other.

They were following us.

"Do you need me to come to Naples?" I asked.

"No. Stay in Rome and cancel this damn deal. The Chiurazzi is bad news…it's UXO."

"What's UXO?"

"Unexploded ordnance."

Then the line went dead.

CHAPTER SIXTEEN

I RETURNED TO OUR TABLE.

Ignoring the vodka martini in front of my empty chair, I grabbed the scotch perched before Bo and downed it in one gulp. Bo stared at me as I interrupted a *cameriere* taking an order at another table, handed him the empty glass, and told him to bring two more immediately. Then I returned to our table and relayed what had happened while Leo sipped his Aperol spritz.

"How often do we need to be kicked in the balls before we get the message?" I hissed.

"I thought we were getting squeezed by Rosa, but this is beyond his ability." Bo turned to Leo, trying to connect the dots. "Who are these lost souls Cardinal Rautan mentioned?"

Leo sighed, resigned. "I wasn't supposed to tell you. Lamberto swore me to secrecy." He lowered his voice and scanned the room, though it wasn't necessary. The surrounding tables pulsed with noisy chatter and clatter swallowing our words.

"The Chiurazzi has another bidder—an unacceptable buyer," he said with a slight bob of his head and a sheepish grin.

"Unacceptable to whom?"

"Everyone," Leo replied. "The Church, the lawyers, the Italian government."

The *cameriere* delivered two scotches, and I pressed a twenty euro note into his palm for having interrupted him earlier.

"*Gracie mille*," he said with a nod, letting me know he'd bring more if needed.

"*Eccellente*," I said, and he hurried away.

"You lied to us," growled Bo, moving his face closer to Leo, who arched back.

"I was told not to tell you. I didn't think it was important because the other bidder can't win. It's not about money. The Chiurazzi will never be sold to them. It's not so much a lie as an omission."

Bo and I exchanged glances. We'd done the same thing ourselves many times when necessary.

"Make it good, Leo," I said. "Make it really good."

"It happened before I was hired," he started.

"Wait, what? You were hired?" I cut in.

"Of course I was hired. I work for Cardinal Bertolini, who asked me to assist Angelo Caloia and Cardinal Rautan. They were helping Lamberto Liuzzo sell the foundry, so I suppose I work for all of them."

"Aren't you the overachiever," said Bo, his voice dripping with vitriol.

"Back off, Bo," pushed Leo. "I did what I was told. I'm a facilitator, not an agitator."

"Your 'facilitation' nearly got Dante killed," I injected, bitterness fueled by disappointment. I'd grudgingly started to like him, but that was gone now.

He continued, "When old man Gennaro Chiurazzi died, Lamberto thought the foundry would be a quick sale and a nice commission for the Liuzzo firm." Leo swirled the straw in his drink and took another gurgling pull. "But then, the shit hit the proverbial fan," he said after swallowing.

Bo and I drank our scotches simultaneously. I held up a finger to stop Leo from saying any more, then flagged down the *cameriere* I'd tipped earlier. I showed him two fingers, signaling we needed two more, and he gave me a thumbs up. I knew we would need liquid fortitude to hear whatever the "shit" was that "hit the fan." Then, I pointed at Leo to continue.

"Within a day of putting the foundry on the market, Lamberto was visited by two attorneys representing the *Impresa Artistica Vesuviana Srl*, which translates to the Vesuvian Art Company Ltd. They said they represented the owner, who intended to submit a bid to buy the Chiurazzi. Lamberto had never heard of the company, so he checked into it. He has a contact in the DIA—that's the Anti-Mafia agency that maintains the Whitelist. It turned out the Vesuvian Art Company was owned by another company, which was owned by another company, which was owned by yet another company, registered to Cosimo and Gemma Di Lupo. Do you know who they are?" Leo shifted a quizzical gaze between us.

Neither of us answered, but my stomach tightened because I knew what was coming.

"Cosimo and Gemma Di Lupo are two of the children of Mauro Di Lupo, the *capo di capi*, boss of bosses, head of the most powerful Camorra family in Naples—the *Scampia clan*."

I stared into my empty scotch glass. "Shit."

"Lamberto never responded to the attorneys," Leo continued. "He couldn't say, 'No, sorry, we're not going to sell this iconic foundry to people who would fill the treasured molds with the bones of their enemies.'"

"Yes, that would have been awkward," I said, and we stopped talking momentarily as the *cameriere* brought us more scotch.

"At first, Lamberto was very stressed," Leo continued. "No other buyers were stepping up. He even called the prime minister, Silvio Berlusconi, who is a billionaire. Lamberto implored him to buy the foundry because he's a big art lover. But Berlusconi said no.

"This left the Di Lupos as the only bidders. Rejecting them was very dangerous. Lamberto was scared for his family. He made the sign of the cross before starting his car. His father, Gabriele, finally called his friend Angelo Caloia to ask if the Vatican Bank would buy the foundry. The Church was already owed money, so the purchase could be a simple debt-equity swap. That way, the Di Lupos couldn't hold Lamberto responsible. The Church is the only organization in Naples more powerful than the *Scampia clan*—so, problem solved."

"Problem solved is a common refrain from fools and children," rumbled Bo.

"Well, apparently Caloia had a different idea. He said he knew someone who would buy the foundry. Cardinal Bertolini asked me to help with the sale. I called Lamberto, and he told me to talk with Dante Scava."

"What? Why? I'm not tracking," said Bo, and neither was I.

Leo took another swallow of his spritz. "I knew Dante wasn't the buyer," he corrected. "I was told to *talk* with Dante and follow the breadcrumbs."

"That's insane," said Bo. "Why would Lamberto have you talk to Dante instead of us?"

"You'll have to ask him that. I did what I was told."

"You put a target on our backs, you idiot." I wanted to slap his face.

"I did no such thing," he declared. "I was hired to enable the purchase—to bring Paladin on board."

"What do you know about the Di Lupo clan?" I asked.

"More than I want to. The family's been in the papers for years."

We leaned forward, our heads drawn close like conspirators. To the tables around us, it must have seemed like we were gossiping about them.

The Di Lupo territory, according to Leo, was Scampia, a northern neighborhood of Naples. The gang engaged in drugs, extortion, prostitution, and counterfeiting while also operating legitimate businesses, including bars, restaurants, and shops. The old man, *Capo* Mauro Di Lupo, also known as *Riccione*—Rich One—started as a small-time dealer in black market cigarettes in the early sixties. Ambitious and driven, he kept moving up the criminal ladder, and before turning thirty killed his gang leader, stepping into the vacancy.

"Where's HR when you need it?" I quipped.

Leo ignored me.

"Di Lupo amassed power and wealth incrementally," he went on. "The organization was so secret no one working in it could say Di Lupo's name without risking having their tongue ripped out. Stealth allowed Mauro to forge his empire over many years without the *Carabinieri* or the DIA knowing he existed.

"He imported cocaine from Colombia, heroin from Afghanistan, and hashish from Morocco. The drugs fed into an extensive network throughout Italy, Germany, and France. Instead of fighting other clans for territory, he partnered with them to franchise the business. His most potent partnership was with the Casertani family, who controlled the flourishing counterfeit brands business—shipping fake Louis Vuitton, Versace, Gucci, and Prada into Russia." He paused to take a breath and another slurp of his drink.

"Mauro grew his fortune and his family," he continued. "There are eight Di Lupo children: seven sons and one daughter. There used to be nine. They're all adults now."

"Why would any guy into that much crap want to buy an art foundry?" asked Bo.

"His daughter Gemma wants to buy it. Cosimo, her older brother, is providing the money."

"Just how violent are these sociopaths?" asked Bo.

"The most—Cosimo Di Lupo thinks he's Al Pacino in *Scarface*." Leo paused, rotating the straw in his empty drink. "Cosimo is the new *capo*. His father, Mauro, gave up the crown when his youngest son, Antonio, was killed in a motor-scooter accident a year ago. I read it in the Naples papers. The kid was on the back of the bike and fell off when the driver took a sharp turn. They were goofing around—being kids. He wasn't wearing a helmet, and the car following the scooter drove over his head.

"They found the car's driver a week later in the *Sebeto* canal; his head was cut off with a handsaw. They never found the rider of the scooter, only his arms and legs, which had been torn off his body. The rumor is that Mauro was inconsolable, and in his grief, he turned over daily operations to his oldest son. Cosimo just turned thirty-five, and he's a full-blown psychopath renowned for his cruelty, which says a lot given his father's no Mother Teresa."

"I think Di Lupo means *wolf* in Italian," said Bo in a non sequitur.

"There've been rumors that the Di Lupos are in a turf feud with the Casertani clan. It's all rumor and street talk, but I read somewhere that as the new *capo*, Cosimo is making changes, and the other clans are unhappy. But none of it matters because they can't buy the Chiurazzi. Paladin will win the deal."

"As decided by Angelo Caloia—what are we missing here?" I said, exhaling my frustration.

"Caloia didn't decide," Bo replied, pushing his scotch away. "Dmitry did. We just fell in line." His eyes bore into mine. "The bank president works for Cardinal Bertolini, and Raphael's *Portrait of a Young Man* is hanging in his office as a gift. It could only have come from Dmitry—a gift for what?"

My eyebrows arched, warning Bo not to say more. I abandoned my scotch as well and got up from the table. "Bo and I know more about psycho mobsters than you might think, Leo."

I beckoned our *cameriere* and pressed another twenty euro note into his palm. "I'm not hungry anymore. You stay and eat Leo—Bo and I will meet you at the hotel. You can pay for the drinks."

He frowned and shrugged. "Your loss," he said. "The tiramisu is sublime."

Bo rose and followed me away from the table. "I think we've got a couple of Di Lupo cretins following us," I whispered, and he cocked his head at me.

"Wait a minute," Leo called out as if an errant thought had just struck him. He waved an open hand to stop us from leaving.

"Who the hell is Dmitry?"

CHAPTER SEVENTEEN

"WHAT DO YOU MEAN WE'RE BEING FOLLOWED?" ASKED BO, slipping into his worn sports coat.

"When I was on the phone with Dante and walking through the restaurant, I saw the same two guys we saw this morning."

"The guys who didn't talk to each other?"

"Yup."

"Where?"

"Table in the narrow corridor room."

"That's dumb," said Bo. "They can't see us from there."

"They don't have to see *us*. It's more important we don't see *them*. They didn't plan on me hiking around the restaurant."

Leo hailed us again. "Answer my question."

"What?" Bo snapped back.

"Who's Dmitry?"

"Natalya's boyfriend," he barked, leaving Leo puzzled.

Bo slalomed through tables, diners ducking and dodging out of his way, rage beginning to pool around his eyes. I trailed in the furrow he left.

The two men at the round table blended seamlessly with the café crowd. There was nothing remarkable about them, and perhaps that was the point. They looked like regular working stiffs enjoying a drink on their day off, only their outfits hinting at their *sistema* association.

The bigger one, overweight with a shaved head, five-day stubble,

and a scarred nose, sipped a Negroni with casual ease. His nonde-
script brown eyes scanned the restaurant with a bored expression.
He wore an open black leather jacket—or *giubbotto*, as Piero at
Battistoni's called it. A crucifix tattoo peeked out from beneath the
coat's cuff. A black T-shirt clung to his body, revealing his paunch
and the indent of his navel. Around his neck he sported a single
gold chain, giving him the look of a man who aspired to make porn
movies.

The other man, smaller and leaner, nursed a glass of whiskey with
a more meditative air. His greasy hair was slicked back, exposing
a scar from his temple to his jawline. His bulging eyes gave him
the appearance of a startled tadpole. He wore a wrinkled black suit
over an equally crumpled white shirt, open at the collar. Despite his
shabby appearance, his demeanor exuded a broodiness reminiscent
of Peter Lorre in *The Maltese Falcon*. He seemed the more sinister
of the two—like a man who could hurt children.

They looked rattled when Bo approached and asked, "Have you
tried the tiramisu? I hear it's delicious." They exchanged a glance,
then looked behind themselves as if to confirm Bo was really talking
to them.

Bo carried a natural authority in his voice and bearing—organic
and unpracticed. I used to think it was his size and athletic training,
but concluded he was just born with it. He played cornerback in
college and could stand before you with a posture and expression
that chilled you to the bone. He glared at the two uncomfortable
men as if he were about to grind them to dust.

They stared up at him, and the one that looked like a tadpole
recovered first and said, "*Grazie*."

"Did you enjoy your breakfast at the Michelangelo?" asked Bo,
leaning slightly into their space.

"*Si*," answered Tadpole while Porn Guy straightened his slouch
and got ready to stand.

I stood beside Bo in the tight room, only two feet from Porn

Guy, wondering why he shaved his head but not his face—it made him look unfinished somehow. I smelled his cheap cologne. He glanced at my fists.

"Don't get up," said Bo, showing his palm. "Tell me why you're following us."

"*Vai Via*," said Tadpole, flicking his hand at us.

"I don't know Italian," said Bo.

"*Vaffanculo*," Tadpole snarled. "*Chi cazzo credi di essere.*"

Bo leaned closer and spoke in a low, suppressed cadence. "You just told me to fuck off. Tell me why you're following us, and I will."

"*Prendilo nel culo.*"

"English? *Lei parla inglese*," I interjected.

Porn Guy stood up, his body so close to mine that I felt trapped inside a bottle of Brute. Bo grabbed the sleeve of his leather coat to pull him back, but he twisted into Bo and threw a half-closed fist at Bo's face. Bo arched back, and the guy's knuckles grazed Bo's forehead. I was startled at the compact efficiency of his swing and impulsively pushed him into his seated partner. Everything crashed into the wall: the two goons, their chairs, their table, their drinks, the explosion of sound stunning everyone around us. Diners crouched or jumped out of their chairs.

The resulting fracas was immediate and short. Porn Guy and Tadpole lurched to their feet. Bo and I stood our ground. I swiveled my head, looking for random silverware—a knife or fork—but saw only spoons. Everyone had ordered *panna cotta* with their coffee.

Two *cameriere* ran into the room, grabbed us by our shoulders, and pulled us back, yelling, "*Scusa, scusa.*"

Bo spun away from the *cameriere*, squinted at Tadpole, and growled, "*Vaffanculo*—asshole—*capisce*?"

Porn Guy stepped forward but stumbled over an upturned chair leg. Tadpole caught him, hoisted him back up, and said, "*Capisco.*"

An overweight man with a pock-marked face, black suit, and

polished black shoes ran into the room so fast he almost collided with me.

Why do so many Italians wear black? I thought.

"*Cosa sta succedendo qui?*" panted the new guy, whose lapel pin read *Direttore*. Then he instantly recognized we were Americans and repeated in English, "What's happening here?"

Tadpole fired off rapid, furious Italian at the restaurant manager. People started slipping out behind us, emptying the room. As I watched them leave, I saw the woman with the red lips survey the scene as she strolled through on her way to the exit. She'd put on oversized sunglasses, and I couldn't read her face.

Leo rolled up and stood behind me, pretending he didn't know us.

"Why did you attack these men?" asked the manager as he picked up the whiskey glass that had rolled near his feet.

"We didn't attack anyone," I answered calmly.

"*Ci hanno attaccato*," said Porn Guy, pointing at Bo.

"I will call the police now," said the manager.

"We're leaving," said Bo.

"I must call the police," said the manager, stepping between us and the exit.

"Ask *them* if they want the police to come and ask questions," said Bo, nodding at the two men.

He did, and Tadpole said, "*No. Lasciali andare.*"

"I thought so," said Bo as he produced two fifty euro notes from his pocket and gave them to the manager. "This will cover any damages."

We walked out, Leo trailing behind, still acting like we were strangers. Every person in the café watched and judged us as the loud Americans we were. I took an optimistic view—we'd disrupted their lunch at the celebrated restaurant but left them with a story to tell for months.

Back on *Via dei Condotti*, Leo said, "I had a feeling about those guys."

I shot him a dry glance. "And yet you never mentioned it."

Bo cut in. "I'll call Natalya and tell her we're done."

"I'll do it," I said, careful to keep any smugness out of my voice.

"Fine, but leave Lamberto to me," Bo replied.

Leo, suddenly paying attention, snapped awake. "Wait—what are you saying?"

"We're out," Bo answered flatly. "You said it yourself. The Di Lupos will bury their competition, and we prefer to stay above ground."

Leo leaned forward, insistent. "I told you the Church won't approve their bid."

I shrugged. "Someone should explain that to them, because I'm not getting the sense they know."

We stepped into the crowded Spanish Square at the end of *Via dei Condotti* and made our way to the turquoise fountain at its center. The Spanish Steps rose ahead, crawling with camera-toting tourists.

"Listen carefully, Leo," I said, scanning the crowd around a large *Bottega di Fiori* for any signs of our surveillance. "Bo and I've dealt with mobsters before—not Italian, but worse. It wasn't fun. We're not walking into that pile of excrement again."

"Not voluntarily," Bo muttered.

I turned to Leo, my expression stern. "We're pulling our offer. But understand this—the Di Lupos think they're Italy's toughest, most dangerous clan. And maybe they are. We're getting out of their sandbox—not because we're scared, but because we don't want things to spiral further out of control. The Di Lupos have no idea who they're up against."

Bo locked eyes with Leo.

"They're toddlers playing with a loaded gun."

CHAPTER EIGHTEEN

WHEN WE RETURNED TO THE MICHELANGELO HOTEL, Bo said he needed to call home and decompress. I knew that meant he wanted to nap. Bo's body clock is as predictable as a recurring decimal. An early riser, his body seeks rest with an obsessive compulsion by midafternoon.

Leo retreated to his room as well, shoulders drooped in defeat. I assumed he'd make some calls and see if he could salvage the deal, or at least avoid the blame. He agreed to contact Lamberto and tell him to meet us in the hotel lobby before the concert, and to bring his father, Gabriele.

My sumptuous new quarters were named the Raphael Suite, which was amusing. It seemed I couldn't escape that haunting Renaissance master.

The room, or rather rooms, unfolded as a spacious oasis—dense velvety furniture sprawled atop a plush vermilion carpet. A warm glow emanated from the fireplace, and the walls were decorated with frescoes. The air carried the fragrance of the freshly cut flowers arranged on a glass table separating the two couches.

Since we hadn't eaten at Caffè Greco, I raided the sizable welcome basket on the kitchenette counter: hazelnut cookies from *Mulino Bianco*, a chocolate croissant from *Rispo Franca*, and a mandarin from the fruit cornucopia. I made a cup of coffee with enough cream to turn it the color of beach sand. I sat at my massive leather-top desk and searched the internet for information about the

Di Lupos. It wasn't difficult. They were infamous and dangerous, like psychopathic celebrities. I found a current article in *The Guardian*.

HEIR TO MAFIA THRONE WINS HEARTS OF TEENAGERS

By Mark Snyder in Rome

To the surprise of authorities losing their battle against the Camorra (the Neapolitan branch of Cosa Nostra), hundreds of schoolgirls in the crime-infested city are drooling over photos of Cosimo Di Lupo, 35, and sending them to each other over the internet.

With his actor's good looks, all-black clothes, and long stringy hair swept back in a ponytail, Di Lupo imitates a Gothic fantasy character from the movie The Crow. When he was arrested last month, teen hearts fluttered.

He is a heartthrob for working-class girls, who are thrilled by his aggression and style. Cosimo took over a criminal empire from his father, Mauro Di Lupo. The senior Di Lupo built his operation in the shadows, avoiding attention and publicity. The family's enterprise is estimated to have revenue of three hundred million euros annually and employs over two hundred soldiers.

"Jesus!" I said aloud. I scanned the photos and scrolled through more details to the final paragraph:

Mauro ran the business like a multi-tiered organization, but when Cosimo took over he centralized control, alienating the many clans his father had recruited. A feud involving the Di Lupo clan and its former allies, the Casertani clan, has been brewing. The Casertanis are called the "secessionisti" because they want to secede from the coalition. The rebellion is the result of Cosimo's changes. When Raffaele Casertani did not accept the new dictates, he appealed to the senior Di Lupo, who ordered his son to cease. Sources told me Cosimo responded, "Papa, you don't count anymore."

//

Nervousness prickled my skin as I paced, staring at Natalya's name on my programmed phone. It felt foreign. I was never nervous talking to her; if anything, I was usually giddy. My hand shook slightly, and I snapped, "Stop it!" before pressing the call button. It rang and connected after a slight delay.

"Natalya?" I asked, but there was no reply. Then, after a few seconds, "Martin?" she responded.

"Am I catching you at a bad time? Are you busy?" I asked too quickly, wondering if it sounded like a double entendre.

"No, it's good time," she said.

We discussed Dante first. She expressed concern, declaring she'd dispatched her copilot, Frank, to sit with Dante so he wouldn't be alone again. She planned to check him out of the hospital in two days, put him on her plane, and fly him back to Portland. The plane would then return to pick us up.

"Roundtripping Dante from Naples to Portland must cost a small fortune."

"It's no problem. Dmitry takes care of the cost."

"We've had a crazy day so far," I said.

"How crazy, Martin?"

I went in chronological order: the vandalized rooms, the meeting with Bertolini, Rautan, and Caloia, the big concert invitation, Leo's confession about a Camorra clan bidding on the Chiurazzi, and finally our run-in with the charming Porn Guy and Tadpole. I said nothing about seeing the Raphael painting in Bertolini's office, saving that card to play later, and kept my Brody Lynch delusion to myself.

I saved the clincher for last. "Bo and I are out. We're retracting our offer."

The silence from her end was grim but, for me, fortifying.

Finally, in a low and firm voice, she said, "No. We will go forward."

"Natalya," I said and sighed. "You need to understand how this works. There are three board members for the company. You, me, and Bo—and Bo and I have just voted no. It's done."

"No it is not. If you want to run back to America, hide in Portland, then go. I will close the deal on my own." More grim yet fortifying silence.

Shit! This would get ugly—she was pulling the coward card.

"Martin, I will call Lamberto and ask why he never told us about this mafia family. After I put Dante on the plane on Monday, I will catch train to Rome. I will get there early in afternoon and meet you at Caffè Domiziano in Piazza Navona by 2 p.m. Meanwhile, do nothing for the next two days. Go sightseeing. We will talk about things then—not over the phone."

The fact that she knew the name and location of a random cafe in Rome rattled me. I was reminded again of how little I knew about her life outside our insular bubble.

"Why not meet in our hotel lobby?" I asked.

"Because I'm not staying at the Michelangelo. I am staying somewhere else. I will walk to the cafe."

"Why are you not staying at our hotel?"

"It is not good idea, Martin."

"I've been upgraded to the presidential suite," I said meekly.

"It is not good idea," she repeated.

I didn't hide my disappointment. "I thought we were going to enjoy Rome together."

"Martin, this is not trip for enjoyment—we are here for business."

"Your point?"

"We are not alone in Rome. Two is alone, three is crowd, and four is—what is the right word—party. Yes?"

"It's never stopped us before," I lamented. "We always found a way."

"You are being difficult *again*," she warned.

"Yes, I'm sorry for what I said back at the hospital," I conceded. Her innuendo-laden words, *Not as well as I do,* left an unrelenting itch in my already bruised psyche.

"It was my fault," she acknowledged. "I made it sound like it was big secret, but it was not supposed to be. I am spending a few days with Dmitry on Capri."

"Why didn't you tell me you were hooking up with Dmitry?"

"Do not use that word, Martin. I am no teenager. I didn't tell you because it is *grubyy*—you understand—rude."

"Rude to spend time with Dmitry?"

"No, Martin, not to spend time with Dmitry. I love to spend time with Dmitry. It is *rude* to tell one lover I am spending time with another lover. Yes?"

"Yes," I said.

"Will you enjoy the big concert tonight?" she asked, a diversionary spring to her voice.

"I'm not a big concert guy."

"I will think of you," she said gently, and I felt better with the implied affection.

"I would prefer to hang out with you in my luxury suite."

"Yes, I can imagine that."

"It's a very nice suite," I admitted. "It cost me the shirt off my back."

CHAPTER NINETEEN

Mackinac Island, Michigan, six months earlier

SHE LAUGHED.

I loved hearing Natalya laugh. Her tenor pitch was warm and musical, as Cher might laugh privately.

"You are a good storyteller," she said, setting down her vodka martini.

We sat at a two-person table in the Cupola Bar atop the majestic Grand Hotel on Mackinac Island. We had arrived in northern Michigan four days earlier to inspect a lumber mill business. None of us knew much about the lumber industry, but the company was profitable and met Paladin's acquisition criteria. The mill was just a half-hour drive from the Bay Harbor Resort, a ribbon of land folded into the northern shore of Lake Michigan, home to two new golf courses and only a short drive from the Belvedere course, one of the best in the country. Bo was eager to play them, and I suspected his passion for golf spurred our new acquisition target.

I didn't mind. I don't play golf, but I played Natalya as often as possible, and I'd convinced her to join us on the trip for that specific purpose. The good news was that she loved playing golf (and me), and Bo had no complaints about her tagging along. We spent the mornings at the sawmill, the afternoons on the greens (I drove the cart), and the nights using the doorway between our adjoining rooms as a magical gateway to our private liaisons.

Bo remained blissfully unaware.

It was late June, and the weather was perfect.

At the end of the week, Bo flew back to Portland. I lied to him and said I'd stay a few extra days to visit my favorite resort town in Michigan, Charlevoix the Beautiful. Natalya pretended to fly back to Florida but didn't. We had the weekend to ourselves and took the ferry to visit the iconic hotel on the island, which has no cars.

After biking around all day, we changed to evening wear to accommodate the Grand Hotel's dinner dress code, savored the five-course banquet, and walked the length of the hotel's giant porch. Then we climbed to the bar, where we watched the sunset over the Straits of Mackinac, drinking vodka martinis and telling stories.

"You are rich with stories," she said. "You have so many." She held out her hand and counted on her fingers. "The poor immigrant story, the strong mother story, the Vietnam airplane story."

"Air traffic controller story," I corrected.

"Yes, of course," she said before continuing her tally. "The story of becoming rich in Silicon Valley—you have many of those—the story of how you lost your money and then how you built the part-nership with Bo and made it back. But no stories about Abbie or Andrew or Ali."

"I'm not comfortable talking about them with you. It feels—disrespectful."

"To them? Or to me?"

"Both."

"I am not a threat to them, Martin. You think about this too much."

I detoured. "Now I have a new story—our story."

"I think you should never tell it," she remarked with a chuckle. "It is a story with teeth, and it will bite you if you share it."

//////////////////////////////////////

There's an old joke that goes, "The sex was so good even the neigh-bors lit a cigarette," and I thought about that as we laid at opposite ends of the canopied bed in what had become our customary après-sex orientation.

For Natalya, our relationship had always been a confection. She was done with falling in love. Widowed twice and now the ardent mistress of a Russian billionaire who would never marry her, she had happily made her bed. She called our relationship an *uchastiye*, which means "involvement." She rejected the word "affair" because it carried too much consequence.

I favored "entanglement."

We'd been "entangled" for months by then, and the lovemaking was loose, sultry, and sensual. I questioned frequently if I was falling in love with her—or perhaps falling in love with the parts of her that reminded me of Abbie. I wasn't sure. The damn sex kept getting in the way. I knew I had an intense infatuation because I couldn't stop thinking about her. My obsession with Natalya subsumed my worries about Abbie and pacified my injured pride.

Meanwhile, my marriage improved. Like the relentless guilt that comes from long-term neglect, remorse pushed me to be a better husband. Abbie and I had been running on autopilot for the past couple of years, coasting on the routines we'd built in our early days together. There had been plenty of heat between us when we first met, but we'd let it cool abruptly and destructively, neither of us bothering to stoke the fire.

I stopped sulking and started paying more attention. Our intimacy remained the same—Abbie's interest often sparked after her travels—and I began spending more time with the kids. I'd pop into their rooms for "Dad chats," though they mostly found it awkward. As teenagers, they saw my visits as intrusions. My daughter dubbed them "Dad's ninja visits," and my son, quietly annoyed, just wanted to return to his gaming.

Natalya's eyes were drifting shut, but I didn't want the night to end, so I asked her to tell me about how she and Dmitry met.

"Now you want a story from me. Yes?"

"Yes."

"Will you stroke my feet while I tell my story?"

"Of course."

"Do you remember Yeltsin?"

What an odd non sequitur, I thought. "Yes. Boris Yeltsin, the first Russian President after the Soviet Union collapsed in '91."

"Yes. I was married then. But I worked with my sister ten years before at the bar in Hotel Ukraina. I searched for husband. My sister Krystina searched for *papiki,* you know, sugar daddies. Dmitry came to Ukraina with his friends all the time. He was handsome, smart, and interested in Krystina *and* me. Sex with twins attracted him. He went to bed with both of us."

My eyebrows shot up, and I squeezed her big toe in shock.

She smiled suggestively. "Dmitry dated us at same time."

"And?" I pushed.

With a sly smile and lusty lilt, she said, "*That* is a story for another time." As her eyes danced with erotic intent, she sighed and added, "Yes, you will like it," leaving me aroused by the provocative promise.

"Then Krystina became pregnant with Vasili," she continued, "and Dmitry stopped seeing her. But for me, he was—how do you say—*moyo varen'ye*—my jam—you understand?"

A dreadful realization slammed into me, and I blurted, "Dmitry got your sister pregnant? Dmitry was Vasili's father?"

"No—maybe yes—no one knows. Krystina had sex with many men. She had regular lovers and part-time lovers. One of her regular men was an American diplomat. She told me he was the father. She put his name on birth certificate. That is why Vasili had dual citizenship."

Natalya hesitated and locked her eyes with mine. "But maybe my sister lied to protect me, and Dmitry *was* the father. She knew I loved him, and perhaps she did too, but never told me. I thought about this many times. Maybe that is why she committed suicide. She suffered many secrets that will never be known."

Our stare held firm, acknowledging the private bombshell that had just detonated between us. We shared a wordless exchange filled with alternative realities. With chilling certainty, I realized that Natalya had never voiced her speculation to another soul, not even Dmitry.

Veering into new territory, she said, "Dmitry was best friends with Viktor Kukleva."

"Your first husband," I added.

"Yes. Viktor and Dmitry were young KGB officers, and I date them together."

My eyebrows executed an encore, and she again gave a sly smile. "I think you mean dated simultaneously," I amended.

"Yes, and there is no other story to excite you later," she said. "I date Viktor to make Dmitry jealous. Maybe push him to marry me—but I know now that Dmitry is not the marry type. In Russia, we say *truslivyy*. He is interested in the sex, not the marriage, just the sex."

She paused, and I wondered if she was thinking about "the sex" or what to say next.

"Dmitry went into business, and Viktor went into crime. He became a *Vor*, in the *Vory V Zakone*."

"That's the name of the Russian mafia, right?"

"*Da*. It has many names. It is also called *Bratva,* but mostly *Vory.* Viktor was big, strong, very hairy man—like Russian peasant. Dmitry was opposite, trim—sporty."

"Athletic," I said.

"Yes, and more dangerous. Dmitry and Viktor were savages, but not in same way. Viktor broke your bones. Dmitry broke your will." She took a sip of vodka from the glass on the nightstand and shuddered a little when she swallowed.

"Many *Vory* gangs operated in Moscow back then, and Viktor

took control of one quickly. Dmitry's new company needed money to make acquisitions, just like Paladin. So, he partnered with Viktor."

"I remember reading about that," I said. "When the Soviet Union folded, there was no infrastructure for borrowing money in a new market economy, and the *Vory* gangs became the early investors for many of the new private businesses being created. The Russian version of angel investors."

Natalya tapped the side of her nose. "Yes, and they make good team. Viktor put up money and muscle, and Dmitry picked targets. Dmitry knew what companies to raid, and Viktor knew how to be—*ubeditel'ny*—persuasive. Viktor told me they had simple method to take over other companies. Dmitry wrote contracts that signed all company assets over to his own company, and if CEO said '*Nyet*,' Viktor covered CEO's head with a plastic bag to change his mind. The CEO could not hold his breath for long, so he—how you say—rethought quickly."

"Reconsidered," I offered. My fingers grazed her feet and ankles.

She continued, "In Russia, we have expression called *Sarafannoye radio*. It is how news spreads between village women."

"We call it the grapevine," I said.

"Yes, Dmitry and Viktor became—*fol'klor*. Soon, they not needed plastic bags. Company owners agreed to sign over their assets without discussion. Dmitry's business grew fast—much bigger than Paladin."

"Well, suffocation is a highly effective form of negotiation," I responded. "Dmitry brings plastic bags; we bring a handshake and a smile."

"*Da*, he is efficient, but we are more friendly," she chortled.

"Social skills are for losers," I gibed.

She laughed her beautiful laugh. "Dmitry bought everything. Tractor companies, pig farms, insurance companies, even—do not laugh—sawmills. Over hundred companies in just a few years."

"Wow!"

"Yes, and at same time, Viktor became most powerful *Pakhan* in Moscow."

"*Pakhan* means boss of bosses, right?"

"Yes. It is a high position in the *Vory.*"

"And when did you marry Viktor?"

"Viktor asked me many times. I always say, *nyet*. I wanted Dmitry. But I was tired after many years of—*amúrnaya voznyá*—it means cupid fight. Poor Viktor was exhausted, but Dmitry found energy in the—*vzad i vpered*—back and forth, so I finally say *da* to Viktor."

"Then Viktor was killed," I said.

"Yes—*ubit*—assassinated. My marriage was short, only six months. Viktor was most powerful *Pakhan* because of Dmitry. Dmitry's company was so big, and he was so rich, he was now protector for Viktor, not other way around. This made Viktor look weak to his *kapitans*, and there was a power struggle—*myatezh*—mutiny.

"One day, Viktor drove me to my favorite spa. The assassin wired a bomb to our car, but it did not go off. When Viktor came home, the killer attacked and stabbed him in the throat; he bleed out in driveway. I was getting a pedicure."

She wiggled her toes, and I looked at her face. There was no sadness, no regret. Her eyes were closed. "After my sister Krystina committed suicide, I looked after her son, Vasili. I used his dual citizenship to come to Florida, where I met Mikhail, my second husband. He ran his art gallery. He was my teacher. I learn English and art. I took over the gallery when Mikhail died, which is now world respected. I didn't speak with Dmitry for many years. Then, one day, he called me to help him buy a painting."

"And Dmitry became an oligarch and—*again*—your boyfriend," I added.

"Yes, you understand," she said and sighed, drifting off. "Sometimes life knocks on your door to let you know fate walked in a circle."

CHAPTER TWENTY

Rome, Saturday evening

VINCENZO VINCENZI AND A PORTER pulling a clothing cart entered my suite with my new clothes. They placed them on the wide bed in the second bedroom, bowed, accepted my tip, and left. I showered and shaved on autopilot, dressing without the usual joy of putting on expensive new clothes. Natalya's baffling obstinacy filled my mind. I didn't want to quarrel with her, but I wasn't about to back down. The inevitable arguments would affect our relationship in ways I was trying to avoid. I wondered why she insisted the Chiurazzi purchase had to happen.

Standing before the full-length mirror, I confronted my reflection as a stranger. The Brioni suit fit perfectly, and the red cashmere scarf splashed against the dark blue like an intrepid flag. I looked ready to walk a red carpet, but it felt artificial and hollow.

I rapped on Bo's door, eager to share my conversation with Natalya, bracing myself for his response. He and I often clashed; he preferred clear-cut solutions while I was comfortable charting ambiguities. Over time, our friendship had nudged him—sometimes grudgingly—to consider the grey areas. But I knew Bo's position on the Chiurazzi venture was firm.

"You look like my high school drama teacher on opening night," he said, leaving the door ajar and walking back into his suite. He wore a shirt and tie sans pants and socks.

"And you look like Porky Pig," I replied, stepping inside and inspecting his digs. "You eat anything yet?"

"Yeah, I had room service bring me a burger. I don't trust the welcome basket."

I recounted Natalya's comments about not canceling the acquisition, omitting her observations about juggling her lovers. Pulling on his pants, Bo said, "I don't care. We have equity control of the company. It's done—I'm done—we're done."

"There's more to this," I said. "Why all the pretenses? At this point we know Natalya and, by extension, Dmitry are hiding something." I counted on my fingers as I continued, "Leo lied, Lamberto lied, Caloia lied, Bertolini lied, maybe even Rautan." I flinched in frustration. "Excuse me, but—what the f is going on? I feel like we're drunkards walking through a minefield."

"Speak for yourself, buddy," said Bo, lacing his new Ferragamo shoes. "I'm fully sober." Checking himself out in the mirror and satisfied with what he saw, he jiggled his Windsor knot and said, "Bishop—Bo Bishop."

"Are you seriously channeling James Bond right now?"

"Marty, I know you've had a tight sphincter about this deal from day one," he responded. "Unlike you, I jumped in with both feet. It excited me. Not because it made sense but because it didn't. It was unusual and different. We weren't buying another pub, hotel, or sawmill. It was a weird once-in-a-lifetime deal that's got—I don't know—swagger." He spoke to himself in the mirror. "We'd be able to brag about owning the world's largest collection of Renaissance art. Drop names like Michelangelo and Bernini like they were friends. Get invited to events like tonight's Papal Reconciliation concert—or whatever it's called." He dug into a bag and extracted his new Prada scarf. "We'd have reasons to dress like this! Hobnob with people we don't actually like but get to brag about it anyway."

He smiled, and I smiled back in agreement.

"But your instincts were spot on, Marty. First, no one tells us that a maniacal mafia family also wants the Chiurazzi, and then after that little tidbit drops, it's treated like an afterthought. It's a master class in pissing on our shoes and insisting it's rain." He shrugged his shoulders. "I don't know why the Vatican is lying about the Di Lupos, and I don't know why Dmitry and Natalya are treating the foundry like it's a personal inheritance. The only thing I do know is our favorite papal usher is a bit of a shyster, and the silver lining to this shit cloud is that we're getting out before anybody got dead. Given our history with Dmitry and Natalya—that feels like progress."

He picked up his phone. "Now, go get a drink. I'll meet you downstairs. I want to call Katherine and the kids."

"Sorry, I thought you'd done that already."

"No. There's a nine-hour time difference, remember. You would know that if you ever called home. They're all having breakfast now, so I'll catch them together."

His comment was not lost on me. I smiled guiltily, reminding myself to call the kids later.

I went to the Dome bar, looking out for the Di Lupo mongrels, and found instead Lamberto, Leo, and a third man, who I assumed was the senior Liuzzo, all huddled around a small round table in an otherwise empty place. Everyone wore dark suits and ties, in keeping with Vatican formal attire. Lamberto looked sullen, almost angry, while Leo looked defensive and contrite.

Their tension was palpable.

"Gentlemen," I said, pulling up a chair to join them. The elder Liuzzo stood to shake my hand, and I observed the resemblance between father and son—I tend to notice things like that because I, too, am my father's spitting image.

"Gabriele Liuzzo," he introduced himself, and I pegged him to be in his mid-seventies. We stumbled through some irrelevant small talk, and finally Gabriele said, "Leo tells us that you changed your intentions of buying the Chiurazzi."

"Yes we have, Gabriele. It's not the Chiurazzi—it's our competition. Neither Mr. Caloia nor your son Lamberto bothered to mention it during our negotiations." I avoided Leo's gaze.

"Indeed. Regrettably, Leo told you about that," interjected Lamberto. "He violated client confidentiality."

I looked at Lamberto and knitted my brows. "Really! That's what you're going to hide behind? Client confidentiality?"

"Martin," Gabriele said, touching me lightly on my sleeve. "Our firm must follow Italian law regarding auction purchases. It's no different in the US."

"Gabriele, with respect, you're bullshitting me. After Alessio Rosa made his threats at the hospital, Natalya and I asked Lamberto if there were any other bids on the foundry, and he said no—to my face." I looked at Lamberto. "Maybe you couldn't tell me who, but you could have hinted strongly—you know—that my life might be in danger."

"I understand, but Caloia asked us not to mention it," he answered.

"You don't work for Caloia," I pointed out. "You work for the Chiurazzi family."

"I work for both. The Vatican Bank is owed almost a million euros in back fees."

"I don't care," I said. "Feel free to collect the money from our competition. Bo and I are out."

"You're making a mistake," said Gabriele.

Anticipating Bo's preference, I ordered two Glenlivets, and the four of us settled into a shared silence, waiting for Bo, the scotch, or geniality to arrive.

"You know," said Gabriele, breaking the strained silence. "I have known Angelo Caloia for most of my life. We both studied at the University of Pennsylvania. I married his sister."

I looked at Lamberto, surprised. "You're Caloia's nephew?"

"Yes, it's a big family."

"We're all *sovrannumerario*—how do you say it—supernumeraries of Opus Dei," said Gabriele proudly.

"What's a supernumerary?" I asked, adjusting to the odd detour.

"Are you familiar with Opus Dei?" asked Lamberto.

"Like the secret order described in the recent bestseller?" I asked, referring to the blockbuster published a year ago and still flying off bookstore shelves.

"No. It's not a secret order. It is a personal prelature of the Church, with a membership of ninety thousand. It is Latin for God's Work. The book exaggerates for its thriller content—but yes—that Opus Dei."

I nodded while the bartender came around and placed the scotches on our table. He waved off my tip.

"Opus Dei categorizes its members into numeraries and supernumeraries," Gabriele continued.

"What's the difference?" I asked, wondering how we landed on such a strange subject.

"Numeraries are celibate; supernumeraries are not."

I smiled and thought maybe the book wasn't as fictional as I was told. "Well, that explains the '*super*' prefix," I quipped, and everyone laughed.

Taking advantage of the temporary affability, I asked, "Who told you about Paladin?"

Gabriele looked hard at his son and held up his hand. "I'm not sure we can tell you," he said before Lamberto could answer.

"I think you can, Gabriele," I countered. "You just don't want to."

Gabriele sighed in resignation. "I was talking to Angelo about Church matters and shared details about the Di Lupo offer for the Chiurazzi. My son and I were anxious about the potential reaction from the Di Lupos when we rejected their offer. Lamberto was losing sleep over it. Unexpectedly, Angelo became very excited and said he had a buyer." Gabriele took a deep breath. "A few days later,

Angelo called me and said that Natalya Danilenko would contact us to discuss acquiring the foundry. He'd solved our problem."

"Natalya called me," Lamberto took over, "and asked me to take the Chiurazzi information to a *Signore* Dante Scava in Portland, Oregon. I explained that I couldn't solicit anything because of my conflict of interest, but I had someone who could."

He pointed to Leo.

"Could what?" asked Bo, walking up behind me.

We took a moment to reintroduce Gabriele, and I handed Bo his scotch and summarized our conversation.

"*Signora* Natalya," Lamberto continued, "wanted Leo to introduce himself to *Signore* Dante and explain he had the Chiurazzi for sale, which would get the ball rolling."

"Why Dante? Why not Marty or me?" asked Bo while I nodded aggressively. Bo sipped his Glenlivet, put down the glass, and added, "Natalya isn't pulling the strings—Dmitry is."

He hit a nerve. Lamberto and Gabriele's expressions turned blank while Leo's face left the conversation entirely. The skin between his brows furrowed, his lips pursed, and his eyes narrowed in confusion and concern. "Isn't that the boyfriend?" he asked indignantly.

"Yes," said Bo. "Dmitry Chernyshevsky."

"What's he got to do with any of this?" His pitch rose.

"He's a silent partner in Paladin," I said.

"Son-of-a-bitch!"

All of us stared at him. "I'm sorry—that was uncalled for," he mumbled. Rising, he left the table and walked toward the lobby.

"We cannot discuss Mr. Chernyshevsky," said Gabriele, startled by Leo's sudden outburst. "We are bound by client-attorney privilege."

"Or client-attorney conspiracy," said Bo.

Lamberto checked his watch, stood with his father, and indicated we should all leave for the concert.

In the lobby, Leo paced in a circle. As we got closer, he hissed to Lamberto, "You never said anything about a *Dmitry*—whoever."

"I was told his participation was to remain confidential," said Lamberto, and he and Gabriele walked out of the lobby to a waiting car and driver.

I asked the doorman to hail us a cab.

"Scumbag lawyers," snarled Leo. "Mafia hitmen are monastic compared to them. I just figured it out—I cracked the code. I know what they're hiding. The Chiurazzi is a Trojan Horse."

Bo and I gazed quizzically at him.

"Those bastards aren't selling the Chiurazzi—they're selling the account. The Chiurazzi is just the vehicle that delivers it."

"What're you talking about?" asked Bo.

"It's not about the *foundry*, Bo. It's about the *license*!"

"The library license?" I jumped in.

"Yes," said Leo. "It's more valuable than the foundry and everything in it."

"What are we missing?" asked Bo, frustrated and impatient.

"The license, guys; the *license*!" he exclaimed. "If you have a library license, you have a 'unique and special' business tie to the Vatican." He made air quotes around the words *unique* and *special*. "Do you understand?"

"No!" I spat as we went through the lobby door. "What's the big deal?"

"A unique and special business relationship with the Church gives you access to the most valuable financial instrument on the planet."

Bo and I looked at each other. We felt lost in some weird linguistic labyrinth.

"What in the name of God are you talking about?" asked Bo.

"The account," Leo spouted. "The account!—The license comes with a Vatican Bank account!"

CHAPTER TWENTY-ONE

SIDEBAR:

At this point, for those unfamiliar with the history of the Institute for the Works of Religion, the IOR, aka the Vatican Bank—and I assume that's most of you—let me explain why this matters.

The Vatican is the world's smallest country. It could be squeezed into Manhattan's Central Park almost seven times. Shrouded and obscure, its economy relies exclusively on donations, investments, and tourism. As an institution, the Roman Catholic Church has always been rich in land, art, and sacred treasures, but due to poor management, it often teetered on the brink of financial ruin.

In 1929, shortly before it gained independence, its assets were, as usual, in a perilous state. In a desperate attempt to restore its solvency, Pope Pius XI signed the Lateran Treaty with Benito Mussolini, establishing the Vatican City as a sovereign state and securing a large sum of money in reparations for the papal lands stolen over the years by the Italian government.

The funds, however, came with conditions. The Church was obliged to channel a substantial portion of the money into the Italian banking system and commercial enterprises to fortify the nation's economy. This activity plunged the Church headfirst into '*usury*,' a practice traditionally deemed a mortal sin.

In response, the pope established the APSA (Administration of the Patrimony of the Apostolic See) to oversee these financial activities. Driven by pragmatism and adaptability, the Church underwent a transformative evolution, and the APSA thrived and surpassed all expectations. In less than a dozen years, the Holy See multiplied its initial sum of money by an astounding thousandfold, propelling the institution from financial obscurity to a commanding presence on the global stage—an economic behemoth wielding unprecedented influence.

In 1942, amidst a world engulfed in war, Pope Pius XII faced the challenge of safeguarding the Church's burgeoning wealth in the face of European uncertainty. Not knowing who would win the war, the Axis or the Allies, the pope wanted flexibility in navigating the financial terrain with utmost discretion. He aimed to invest in enterprises aligned with either side and adapt his portfolio to the fluctuating tides of war. In other words, the pope wanted to move money quietly to whichever side was winning.

To facilitate this fiscal agility, the pope established the IOR—the Vatican Bank. Situated on sovereign and neutral ground, the bank, or VAT, enjoyed immunity from wartime restrictions, rendering it the world's preeminent offshore bank. The pope could maneuver funds in complete obscurity, inadvertently building himself the perfect money laundering machine.

By now, it should be clear why the Vatican Bank might interest a Russian billionaire eager to move large sums worldwide.

But then, why not just open an account? Why all the subterfuge?

The answer (unknown to me then) was that Dmitry, Natalya, Bo, and I could never get an account. We simply weren't eligible. Few were, and certainly not dubious oligarchs, art dealers, or former entrepreneurs. In simpler terms, if you didn't wear a crucifix, clerical robes, or a Vatican name tag, getting an account in the bank was as likely as a heretic's prayer being answered.

I'll explain.

The pope owns the bank. He is its only shareholder and assigns its directors. It's housed in the Borgia Tower, a grim grey pillar built in the fifteenth century and attached to one side of the pope's residence—fittingly, once the papal prison.

This former medieval dungeon has been converted into a bank like no other. Its prison walls are now covered in marble, tellers wear clerical garb, ATMs are in Latin, priests use a private entrance, and a life-size portrait of the pope hangs on the wall.

The bank's sovereignty gives it "extraterritoriality," exempting it from local authority and allowing it to operate under its own legal system. With an unwavering determination reminiscent of the confessional booth, the bank meticulously guards its records, clientele, and transactions from the prying eyes of external authorities and regulators. Designed and purposed for discretion, the bank remains opaque, refusing to follow established rules, and whenever the global monetary infrastructure insists that it conform and answer to regulators, the Vatican Bank responds with, "We don't answer to regulators—we answer to God."

Bank accounts are granted only to citizens of Vatican City, global clergy, Catholic institutions, and privileged non-Catholics with a "unique and special business relationship" with the Holy See. Nuns—as a cardinal once jested—were excluded from holding an account because they'd taken a vow of poverty.

Now you understand why Dmitry wanted to buy a sculpture foundry in Naples. Through its license, the Chiurazzi had a business relationship with the IOR, which came with an active bank account. This meant Dmitry Chernyshevsky, Natalya Danilenko, Bo Bishop, and Marty Schott would all become anonymous account holders once the acquisition went through.

CHAPTER TWENTY-TWO

Back to Saturday

"HOW MUCH OF PALADIN DOES THIS DMITRY GUY OWN?" asked Leo as soon as we were all squeezed into the back of the cab. He breathed quickly, but not because he was winded. He was agitated.

"Cher-ny-shev-sky," I pronounced. "None of your business. What's wrong with you?"

"Please tell me he's not a Russian mobster," he said.

"I repeat—what the hell is wrong with you?" I shot back.

"But he's rich, right?"

"He's not poor," said Bo. "In the top thirty of the Forbes 400."

Leo's face turned the color of moonlight, his eyes burning with irritation, a shifting sense of dread, and what looked like urgent contemplation, as if he were plotting his next move.

"That explains Paladin," he muttered, more to himself than to us. "It's private; ownership is confidential; the Italian government and the DIA have no authority; the Chiurazzi remains on the Whitelist; and the VAT stays as secret as a black ops budget. Your Dmitry Cher-ny-shev-sky," he mimicked, "just hit all sevens on a cosmic slot machine."

Our cab moved as if it were stalled in a bumper car pileup.

"This will take forever," I bitched. "Let's walk."

I got out and paid the driver, who looked relieved to be rid of us. As I turned to catch up with Bo and Leo, I spotted Brody Lynch across the street, staring at me with the implacable scrutiny of a silent accusation. My breath lodged in my throat.

Delusion?

Maybe the first time.

Twice?

Not a chance.

I almost doubled over. "Fuck!" I expelled.

I looked for Bo, who was already thirty paces away, striding at his typical tempo. My skin crawled as if the chill in the air had turned inward. I opened my mouth to shout when Brody raised his hand, formed it into a gun, pointed it at me, and then disappeared into a side door. I raced after Bo and Leo, caught Bo by his trailing scarf and pulled.

"What the…!" he exclaimed.

"Brody Lynch!" I gasped and pointed to the sidewalk teeming with what seemed like everyone in Rome *but* the Irishman.

"Marty!" said Bo. "You're becoming unhinged."

"Who is this Brody Lynch?" asked Leo. "Please, not another Paladin owner."

"None of your business," I hissed at Leo, shoving my face so close our noses nearly collided.

Bo grabbed my lapels. "Calm down! You're acting crazy, and we're in the middle of a million people walking to the Vatican." Then he pulled me very close. "The Vatican. Marty. The damn Vatican! Get your act together!"

I pulled away from him, straightened my spine, flattened the wrinkles he'd made, and marched forward with unflinching conviction as Leo stared at me, temporarily forgetting his own distress.

Via Cavalleggeri, a battlefield of motor scooters, blaring horns, and roaming sightseers earlier that morning, was now hushed, transformed into a pedestrian path. The throng of elegantly dressed concertgoers flowed like a silk swell, parting effortlessly between the two main Vatican entrances. We drifted like twigs in a current toward the Petriano gate, where our invitations awaited. Unlike a stadium surge, this tony tide of suits and gowns—occasionally interrupted by the flutter of a cardinal's red sash—moved with serene purpose, orchestrated by some mystical alchemy into a procession. A steady, susurrant patter wove around us: Italian, French, English, Arabic, and Yiddish rolled together like the low thrumming of a polyglot chorus under the gentle light from dimmed lamps mounted on the Vatican wall.

"Angelo Caloia treats the Church like it's a real estate holding company with a bank attached," said Leo, his enmity for the bank president as blatant as a boil. Bo let him vent so he might reveal something. I scoured the crowd for another sighting of the Irishman to validate what I'd seen.

"Here, dying and banking go hand in hand," Leo continued, indifferent to the crowd around us, his voice stuck at a conversational volume. "The bank is the perfect portal for introducing corrupt money into the global financial network."

"Why?" I asked.

"What institution on this planet would reject a wire transfer from the largest church on earth?"

I frowned and nodded in agreement.

We arrived at the gate, and Leo spoke briefly to one of the Swiss Guards, who pointed to a large nun standing nearby. An air of quiet proficiency radiated from the starched folds of her habit, sharp as a card edge. She checked off our names on a clipboard. With our invites in hand, we moved with the crowd, carried along by the collective pulse.

"How does it work, Leo?" Bo asked nonchalantly. "How does the Vatican Bank move money undetected?"

"It's not part of the global system. It exists in a kind of jurisdictional bubble. It's the least transparent bank in the world."

We found ourselves behind an Orthodox Jewish couple. The man wore a black skullcap perched over his curly sideburns, while his wife wore a long, modest skirt and a high-necked blouse. Her hair was neatly tucked under a floral-patterned scarf. I wondered if they were listening to us.

"Let's say you deposit money into your Chiurazzi account. You don't have to give your name—just deposit the cash. There are no limits. Then, one day, you direct the bank to transfer that money to a bank in Switzerland. Here's where the magic happens—the Vatican Bank has its own account within all its partner banks, operating like a secret vault. In the industry, it's called nesting. Your money travels through that network of accounts as Vatican money, with no transparency as to the source or destination. It's impossible to track."

We stepped into the breathtaking majesty of the Paul VI Audience Hall. Leo's words were swallowed by the overwhelming roar of sounds and voices, as if the Tower of Babel had tipped over, spilling its discordant noise in every direction. The scale of the hall was immense, with curved walls of exposed concrete rising in smooth, monolithic arcs, creating a sense of partial embrace. Overhead, the ceiling soared in undulating waves, illuminated by a profusion of light that gave the illusion of movement.

Rows of portable chairs extended across the arena in organized battalions, divided by open aisles. A staggering number of people flowed through them, mingling, chatting, and scrambling to find a spot in the battlefield of unassigned seats.

On stage, a brigade of tuxedos moved across a ruby-hued backdrop, bustling with activity. Glossy instruments gleamed in the soft light. Strings plucked, woodwinds moaned, and brass produced muted notes, creating a subtle melodic dissonance.

Further back, a giant chorus shifted like a colony of penguins, while against the back wall, bathed in a subterranean glow, stood a massive bronze leviathan: *La Resurrezione* by Pericle Fazzini. I'd read about this towering monument, a chaotic tangle of limbs and emotion, depicting Christ rising from a nuclear crater. Weighing in at eighty tons, it is the largest work of art in the Vatican after the

Sistine Chapel, so unwieldy that Fazzini molded it using polystyrene instead of clay or plaster. The fumes of the burning plastic ultimately formed blood clots in his lungs, leading to his untimely death a decade later.

To me, it looked demonic.

The three of us found a half-empty row, and I ushered Bo and Leo in ahead of me, following them down the queue. A gentleman stood as Bo reached his occupied seat, extending a handshake. Peering around Leo, I focused on the man with Bo, who bowed slightly, inviting him to sit. Even from a distance, I recognized the receding ruffled hair, the expansive forehead, the upward-sweeping eyebrows, and the beaming smile. The man sitting next to Bo (had I entered first instead of being polite, he would have been sitting next to me) was Luciano Pavarotti.

I cracked open the *Programma del Concerto per la Conciliazione*. It promised to be quite the spectacle: the London, Krakow, and Turkish Philharmonic Choirs, accompanied by the Pittsburgh Symphony Orchestra, performing Mahler's Second Symphony. I read the program twice; it was as incomprehensible to me as a wine list would be to my dog.

I scanned the front rows, occupied by cardinals in their black cassocks, red fascia, and red zucchettos, looking like a murder of crows perched on a wire. I spotted Cardinal Bertolini in the front row. I wondered if he was thinking about us.

"Bo is chatting with Pavarotti," whispered Leo, sitting between Bo and me. "I can't believe it."

"Yeah, I wish I'd slipped in first," I responded enviously.

"What's this Brody Lynch thing all about?" he asked.

I searched the audience of thousands for the Irishman. I was now sure that Brody was stalking us in Rome, but finding him in this sea of humanity would be like identifying a specific raindrop in a downpour.

"A few years back, Bo and I had an ugly encounter with a maniac.

He threatened our families. His sidekick was an Irishman named Brody Lynch."

"You think he's in Rome following you?"

"Him or his twin."

"Is the maniac with him?"

"I doubt it."

"Are you sure?"

"Yes."

"Why?"

"Because a rifle went off in his face."

"I'm sorry to hear that."

"Shit happens," I said, repeating his line about the Chiurazzi mold collection. I took a beat and asked, "Why'd you say earlier that dying and banking go hand in hand over here? And keep your voice down."

The last seats were filling up, and things were about to start.

"People involved with the VAT seem to drop like flies," he said quietly. "The last pope before this one was John Paul I, who died thirty-three days after being elevated. He wanted to reform the bank and clean it up, then—*pfft*—he died in his sleep in less time than it took for the smell of white smoke to leave his robes."

He turned to glance at Bo and Pavarotti to ensure they weren't listening, then continued, "There was the Banco Ambrosiano debacle. The bank funneled almost a billion dollars to shell companies in the Bahamas. The president of Ambrosiano, a guy named Roberto Calvi, was found hanging under the Blackfriars Bridge in London, with bricks and chunks of concrete stuffed in his crotch and pants pockets. Then there's the banker—nicknamed 'the Shark'—who washed heroin money for the mafia through the VAT. He was found poisoned in his prison cell. An attorney charged with investigating the bank for laundering activities was shot coming out of his house. And those are just the ones I remember."

"What about Angelo Caloia?" I asked.

"He was brought in to clean things up. Get the VAT placed on the DIA Whitelist."

Suddenly, silence swept over the hall. I glanced at Bo, who was staring straight ahead. I'd never seen an arena of seven thousand restless souls fall so completely still. It was an eerie quiet, thick with anticipation.

A Swiss Guard stood at attention in an alcove at the far-right corner of the stage. Then Pope John Paul II appeared, seated upright in a pontifical white chair that was wheeled to the center of the nook. Dressed in white, with a large gold pectoral cross on his chest, his head tilted slightly forward under the weight of Parkinson's. His face was gentle and full, touched with a faint, almost impish smile that hinted at a private amusement.

You could have heard a feather flutter.

As quickly as the arena fell quiet, it erupted in thunderous applause. The room surged to its feet; chairs scraped across the floor, and even the air felt reverent.

It was a moment forever burned into my memory.

I leaned toward Leo as we sat down, intrigued by a sudden realization. Under the crowd's rustle, I hissed, "Wait a minute…did you just say the Vatican Bank is *not* on the Whitelist?"

"Ironic, ain't it?" he tittered.

Bo shushed both of us.

CHAPTER TWENTY-THREE

WE SAT IN DEFERENTIAL STILLNESS THROUGH THE LONG CONCERT, clapping when appropriate and expressing our reactions solely through our eyes. Bo constantly checked his watch, as if trying to prod time into moving faster. Leo gazed vacantly, fixed on an invisible horizon, something worrisome playing out in his mind. My eyes drifted from the pope to the Fazzini sculpture, to Cardinal Bertolini, to the assembly—seeking another sighting of Brody Lynch. Pavarotti's eyes watered during the soprano solo, his lips moving gently as if he were singing along.

After the applause dissolved into the stone walls, silence enveloped the hall once more as the pope was swept away. The audience stirred, formal suits and gowns elegantly rumpled after two hours of sitting or napping, sequins catching the dimmed light.

The low hum of departure replaced the boisterous buzz of arrival. Voices formed a subdued murmur atop the sound of scraping chairs and clicking heels. The orchestra stood and mingled; everyone shook hands in triumphant relief. Along the perimeter, Swiss Guards used hand signals to direct the crowd toward the yellow glow of St. Peter's Square and into the cold, beckoning night.

I reached around Leo and Bo to shake Pavarotti's warm, fleshy hand, just so I could say I did. Then, we merged into the wave, moving with the current. Outside, the icy air clawed at my suit, setting my teeth chattering. I wrapped the red cashmere scarf tightly around my neck. As we poured into St. Peter's Square, the dense mass of attendees unraveled into its vastness before slowly reforming into a long phalanx that flowed down *Via della Conciliazione*. Like a sword, the broad avenue cleaved toward the brooding silhouette of Castel Sant'Angelo.

As we spilled into the historic avenue, the crowd thinned, seeping into its network of tributaries and side streets. I felt bad for the women in their delicate gowns, with too much skin exposed and only a small wrap or fur covering their shoulders. Many red lips were fading to blue.

"Where are we going?" I asked. "Our hotel is the other way."

"There's an after-party we must attend," said Leo, rubbing his hands together to stay warm. "The building is Palazzo dei Convertendi. You'll like it, Marty. I won't spoil the surprise."

"Does it matter if Dmitry uses the Chiurazzi account to move money around?" Bo asked, resurrecting our earlier conversation, his breath condensing in the cold. "It's just one account in one bank. He must have hundreds of accounts in dozens of banks around the world."

"You don't understand what an account at the VAT can do," Leo replied. "The bank once set up an account with the Milan branch of JPMorgan Chase. It was set up as a 'sweep facility,' meaning the account was zeroed out at the end of each day. Money bounced from Milan to Frankfurt, London, and New York—from one Vatican account to another inside JPMorgan. Deposits reached $3 million a day, every day, nonstop. By the end of one year, the account had moved over a billion dollars."

"Jesus Christ," I said aloud, earning a few glances from the moving crowd.

"One account, Bo," Leo continued. "One account, one bank, one year, one billion—totally anonymous."

"Jesus Christ," Bo echoed, mimicking me.

"We're here," Leo said.

In front of us stood a large beige building with a rusticated entrance and an imposing balcony. Much of the crowd had already scattered into nearby restaurants, shops, and other buildings, but the deeply recessed entrance to our destination was still packed, overflowing like a bursting abscess. Just a few feet ahead, a cardinal in a red sash and a bishop in a purple sash stood in line with the rest of the proletariat.

"You will like this, Marty," said Leo. "Back in the fifteen hundreds, this building was a bathhouse. Artists loved bathhouses because they could sketch nudes without getting punched in the face. The upper floors were apartments, and the artist Raphael Sanzio had one. He lived here while painting the frescoes in the Vatican. He also died here."

I shook my head in weariness. Raphael was everywhere, a historical gadfly that refused to stop buzzing. Inside the portico, we filed past a travertine plaque that read in Latin: *Here died Raphael Sanzio on 6 April 1520.*

Inside the parlor, the heat from a hundred people crammed into the space was overwhelming. The brick walls strained against the swelling human tide, bodies shoving and shimmying in every direction. I lost Bo and Leo after I spotted a bar against the far wall and began to burrow toward it, shoulders tucked, elbows out. A woman's shrill cackle punctuated the din as I undulated eel-like through a shoal of bodies, eyes locked on the liquor bottles marking my destination. As I got closer to the bar, a disembodied voice angrily informed me I was cutting past everyone in line, and I cried, "What line?" because there was only a sea of heads in no discernible order.

"Behind me," a female voice shouted, and I turned and stared into the face of the woman with the red lipstick who'd caught my eye at Caffè Greco. She was taller than I'd realized, our eyes level. Her hair was again coiled in a tight knot at the nape of her long neck, adorned with a double strand of pearls. A black gown clung to her, thin straps holding it in place, with just enough cleavage to pass Vatican decorum. A creamy embroidered scarf, likely a head covering for the concert, was wrapped around her shoulders.

"Hello," I said, startled.

She showed no surprise, meaning she'd either recognized me earlier or never recognized me at all.

"Are you stalking me?" I asked.

"Yes," she said, playfully dropping her voice.

Someone shoved me from behind, and I stumbled. She stepped back, or our faces would have bumped. Her features were so perfectly even they blurred into forgettable, the kind of face you could stare at a hundred times and never quite describe. Only her bold red lipstick stood out.

"Let's lock arms and plow to the bar!" she shouted. We did, and when momentum swept us to the front, I ordered two glasses of wine.

"White or red?" asked the frazzled bartender.

"I don't care; I'll probably spill most of it," I answered.

My new friend laughed and ordered red, and I signaled for the same. After the wine was poured into tiny plastic cups, she hollered, "I know this place—follow me!"

To my surprise, she took my free hand, held it tightly, and guided us along several walls to a staircase. Skillfully weaving through the melee, she ascended to the second floor, which was still crowded but less so. There, she tucked us into a corner where the overall noise was at a conversational level.

"My-name-is-Martin-Schott," I said, as if she might not understand me.

"My-name-is-Spina-Paulo," she said, as if I might not understand her.

We both laughed, and I followed up with, "You're American?"

"No, I'm Italian, but I've spoken English all my life. My mother grew up in England and taught me the language early on. I attended school there and received my *Laurea Magistrale* at the University of Sheffield in South Yorkshire."

I cocked my head.

"It's in England, east of Liverpool and south of Leeds. I lived there for five years. When I first came home, I spoke with a slight British accent, which was quite funny to my family, but over the years I lost it."

"Spina is an interesting name," I said.

"It's a nickname, not my proper name, but it's what my father calls me, and I prefer it. It means thorn."

"Did you like the concert?" I asked. Asking questions became my default reflex while I tried to figure out what was happening—were we flirting or just talking?

"No, I thought it was too long."

"Well, the concert was for the pope, not the audience," I said.

She laughed and sipped her wine. I glanced at her hands, which had multiple rings, camouflaging any potential wedding ring. "Did you go to the concert alone?"

"No," she said. "I came with my husband, who abandoned me immediately after the performance."

She's married, not flirting.

We talked for another fifteen minutes about nothing. She was disarmingly uncurious about me, as if she'd already formed her conclusions. I kept wondering why I was spending time with this woman. I wasn't attracted to her—not that I couldn't be—but her vibe felt decidedly non-sensual. During an awkward silence, I fix-ated on the red zucchetto of a cardinal standing a few feet away, surrounded by ordinary people in suits and gowns, all holding small cups of wine.

"Do you know him?" she asked, tracing my line of sight.

"No," I answered. "I'm just fascinated seeing a cardinal in this venue. It's like seeing the dean at a frat party. It's weirdly disturbing."

Bo barged through the crowd, with Leo trailing behind. He spotted me immediately and came over as Leo veered off in another direc-tion. I introduced Bo to Spina, and we quickly rehashed much of our earlier conversation. Bo paid little attention to either of us, scanning the crowd instead, likely searching for his new friend Pavarotti. He soon found a reason to excuse himself and left. I continued to watch Leo winding sinuously through the crowd until he finally made his way to us. He approached Spina with a burst of nervous energy, as if talking to a woman were somehow heretical. His obvious discomfort soon led him to wander off, leaving us alone again.

"It's hot in here and too loud," she said, finishing her wine and dropping the plastic cup. "Would you like to talk somewhere quieter?"

I briefly lost all ability to speak. Did our conversation just wade into deeper waters? Had *casual* turned into *carnal*?

For reasons I didn't fully understand, I nodded yes and flipped my hand in an Italian hand flick, indicating let's get out of here.

"I know a different way out," she said, taking my hand. We slinked along the walls of several rooms, passing a long string of nouveau religious paintings. "All painted by Leonida Brailowsky," she yelled. "A Russian architect who embraced Catholicism."

"I'm impressed!" I yelled back.

"With the paintings?"

"No, with your knowledge."

"I studied art at Sheffield."

Once outside, the frigid air slapped us, and she wrapped her scarf tightly around her. "We can go to the Michelangelo Hotel. It's close, and their bar is warm and nice," she quivered.

"I'm staying there—in the Raphael Suite." I wasn't sure if I was bragging or simply letting her know I had access to a bed. My mind was a tangle of strings, and I was pulling at them randomly.

"Perfect," she said, her cheerfulness unsettling.

Taxis lined *Via della Conciliazione* as if it were the airport, drivers eager for the night's action. Our ride was short and uncomfortably silent. I wondered what she was thinking as she sat motionless and composed. My mind raced, trying to make sense of it all.

Spina Paulo was attractive—though not beautiful in the way Abbie or Natalya were. She was married but oddly convivial, and I couldn't deny I was flattered and intrigued. Still, the speed with which things were unfolding was disorienting. I felt as though I were adrift on a raft, hurtling through a raging river, facing the teeth of the rapids and the threat of a perilous undertow.

CHAPTER TWENTY-FOUR

"WHAT DO YOU DRINK?" I ASKED, following her to a far corner of the Dome bar.

"I like Italian wine: Barolo or Brunello," she said.

Concertgoers occupied a few tables, their finery as tired as their faces, phantom timpani rolls still echoing in their ears. I walked to the bar and quietly asked for their most expensive Barolo, intending to test the hotel manager's assertion that the hotel would cover all my expenses. The bartender presented me with a bottle of Monforte d'Alba for a hundred and twenty euros, and I instructed him to put it on my room. Spina Paulo was impressed with my choice, and we drank the inaugural pour in silence, searching our minds for a topic to fall into.

"Tell me about your family," I said.

She smiled and replied matter-of-factly, "It's very rich."

That's not a common refrain, and it startled me. "Congratulations," I said, because I couldn't think of anything else.

"My father's friends call him Richie," she snickered. "When I was a little girl, we lived like eighteenth-century nobility—a huge house with huge furniture, everything baroque and swathed in gilt. My mother loved gold and massive floral décor. She may have grown up in England, but she's Italian to the core. We had so many servants they stood behind our chairs during meals to take our plates."

"What does your father do?" I asked, my interest piqued.

"He's a businessman. He came from Northern Italy, was as poor as a friar, and started as a *magliari*, which means he sold underwear and bedsheets to migrant factory workers door to door. When his boss died, he promoted himself because there was no one able to take his place."

"Nothing ventured, nothing gained," I said.

"He's retired now."

Our conversation drifted along, gliding through vapid tales that blurred together. After about twenty minutes, she unexpectedly said, "You've told me nothing about yourself; why is that?"

"I have a wonderful wife and two great kids. I live in Portland, Oregon, and I'm here on business. I'm leaving in two days. There's not much else to tell."

"Was your business successful?"

"Not really."

"Well, then you should at least enjoy your last few days in Rome," she said, her finger circling the rim of her glass.

I held her gaze and said, "I guess I'm not sure what is happening here."

"What do you think is happening?" she said coyly, taking another sip of the Barolo.

"I think we might be flirting," I said.

"Well, yes, of course. But why?"

"You stared at me in Caffè Greco," I said.

"Yes, I did," she admitted, a grin on her lips. "But you were strutting among the tables like an angry food inspector."

"Is that a thing here in Italy?"

"Ha!" she huffed. "And then you and your friend made such a scene."

"And then I meet you at the after-party," I said, grinning back.

"It is...suspiciously coincidental. Wouldn't you say?" Her voice deepened in a conspiratorial tone.

My mind suddenly settled on a whole new notion. "Where's your husband?" I asked.

"Where's your wife?" she countered.

My theory was beginning to gel. Was Spina Paulo a working girl? Did I accidentally reel in a high-end escort? But wouldn't she make herself a little more exotic? Did she think she needed to dim her wattage for a Vatican event?

What was happening?

"I have stayed at all the five-star hotels in Rome, including this one, but I have never seen the Raphael Suite. Would you show it to me?"

The words, "I'm not very good at this," tumbled out of my mouth, clumsy and unconvincing. I was already cheating on Abbie with Natalya, but this felt different—cold and opportunistic.

She emptied her glass and said quietly, "My father once told me if you want to wear horns, do it somewhere away from home, with someone French, Spanish, or even American. Stay out of the neighborhood…don't plant garlic in a rose garden. And if you get caught, stay calm; don't say more than necessary."

"That sounds like good advice," I said.

She stood and said, "I live in Naples, Martin—so I'm *not* in my neighborhood."

The unfinished bottle of Barolo felt cold in my hand as we walked to the elevator. I scoped the lobby like a mugger, reassuring myself that there were no witnesses. As we entered the elevator, I caught a slight scent of orange citrus from her hair. We didn't talk. It felt funereal rather than festive. What was I doing? I'm not a rake, not an operator. But I am drawn to enigmas, and at that moment, Spina Paulo was a loose thread inviting a tug.

With hindsight, it's clear to me now that the pull of consolation outweighed the simmering undercurrent of my guilt. Flirting with Spina wasn't aspirational; it was a compromise for not being with Natalya during a trip that had failed all expectations. Perhaps it was a way of getting back at her?

Once inside the suite, Spina wandered about, looking into every room. She homed in on the already ransacked welcome basket, digging through the paper spaghetti and pulling out a bottle of Chianti Classico.

"This is a beautiful suite, Martin. You must be an important guest."

I wasn't about to tell her it was free, so I said, "Thank you."

"If your business was unsuccessful, do you plan to return to Rome?"

I wondered if the question was her way of gauging repeat clientele.

"Can I open that bottle for you?" I asked.

"We still have Barolo, Martin. I'm in no hurry." She sat in the middle of one of the couches and removed her high heels. I remained standing.

"Sit, Martin. You look like a schoolboy," she said and smiled. "*Hai delle farfalle?*—Do you have butterflies?"

"Yes," I said with a fake frown. "Yes, I do."

"Tell me your phone number," she said, pulling her phone out of a small sequined purse.

I looked at her, puzzled.

"I'll call you, and you'll have my number. Then you can call me if you return to Rome—" she paused and smiled warmly, "or if you want to lodge a complaint."

I used the programmed phone Leo gave me. Strangely, having her phone number relaxed me. I sat on the opposite couch, and she asked me about sites in Rome I hadn't seen but wanted to.

A loud knock shook my door. I looked at Spina, and she looked at me and shrugged.

I went to the door and opened it. There stood Bo—his face covered in blood.

CHAPTER TWENTY-FIVE

DON'T CALL THE COPS, DON'T CALL ANYONE!

Those words rumbled through my brain as I saw Bo—blood smeared across his face, his nostrils clogged with cerise clots of congealed snot, and purple swells forming around his eyes.

"Holy shit!" I cried, yanking him into the room.

He pressed his elbow into his side and croaked, "Careful, Marty, my ribs…"

In that instant, Natalya's words from almost two years ago rebounded in my head: "*You are men who solved a big problem without going to the police, which is very attractive to Dmitry and me.*"

I instinctively knew Bo was thinking what I was thinking as I carried him slowly to the couch and eased him down. He spotted Spina before I could ask if he'd seen the car that hit him. Startled displeasure flashed across his face as he recognized her from the after-party, followed by a wince as he tried to straighten up.

"Can I help?" she asked him as a greeting.

"No," I answered for him. "Listen, Spina, I'm sorry, but you have to leave now."

"Should I call *polizia*?"

"No!" Bo and I chorused.

Her voice was flat and gratingly relaxed. I wondered how often a client had interrupted her work like this. She put on her shoes while

I stood close, urging her to hurry. When I lightly touched her back to guide her to the door, she sighed, "*Vabbe*—alright."

"I have your number. I'll call you," I lied.

"You won't, but I enjoyed meeting you, Martin. I hope Mr. Bishop will be OK."

She left.

I wondered how she knew Bo's last name as I closed the door. At the party, he'd introduced himself as Bo to her, not Bo Bishop.

Meanwhile, Bo managed to stumble to the bathroom and start running hot water in the tub. Every move was slow and deliberate. I helped him climb out of his new suit, marred with sundry street scars. The shoulders were torn at the seams, exposing the silk lining, and an oil slick soiled his left sleeve. His tie hung like a noose, and his shirt collar was squishy and crimson.

"Do you need a hospital?"

"No," he strained. "I need to sit in a hot bath."

Bracing against the double console sink he washed the blood from his face. "Mind if I use your tub? I might have a concussion—you need to keep me awake." He snorted a gob of red snot into his towel, sprouting a bloody rose.

"Did you get the license?"

"It wasn't a car, Marty," he slurred from behind a steaming towel that had turned pink. "It was Di Lupo's goons."

"You mean Porn Guy and Tadpole?" I felt adrenaline surge into my system.

"That's what you call 'em?" said Bo, steam rising, sheened with condensation on the marble tiles. "I just call 'em goons."

He threw the pink towel on the floor, grabbed another white one, dunked it under the hot water, and draped it over his head. It, too, began to turn pink. I couldn't tell if Bo's head had an open wound or if his hair was soaked in blood. He stripped to his underwear, gingerly stepped into the tub, and settled into the hot water so carefully it could have been liquid nitro.

A dull thud sounded at my door, and I looked at Bo.

"It's the night manager, Vincenzo," he said. "He helped me get to the freight elevator so no one would see me and said he'd bring a first aid kit and pain medicine to the room."

"*Scuza,*" said Vincenzo as I opened the door. "I first go to Mr. Bishop's room, but when he does not answer, I come here." Then, with the unsettling calm I'd come to expect, Vincenzo, a man seemingly unfazed by any crisis, walked past me to the bathroom and began unwinding a roll of gauze from the first aid kit.

"Not necessary," said Bo.

"You will bleed on my furniture, which will upset my cleaning people," he said, gently rolling the bandage around Bo's head. A blooming red stain revealed the blood oozing from a gash behind his right ear. "It's not deep," he said, then took a small tube of liquid skin from the kit and applied it with his finger. "This will seal it and stop the bleeding... it will become *crosta.*"

"When it scabs," I clarified.

"Yes," he replied, handing me a bottle of Spedifen. "Give him six. He's big, so more is better. Mr. Bishop asked me not to call the *polizia*. I won't, but I suspect you're not having a nice stay in Rome, *si?*"

"*Si,*" I acknowledged, guiding him to the door. "I appreciate your help, Vincenzo." I slipped two fifty euro notes into his hand.

"Let me know if I can be of more help." His words were subtle but intense, as if he wanted to communicate a message. I nodded like a conspirator, pretending I understood his code. I didn't, but I filed it away for future reference.

In the bathroom, Bo sank to his chin in the hot water.

"OK—now tell me what happened," I said.

"I was walking back to the hotel, hands in my pockets, and I got clobbered from behind with a wooden bat. I fell forward; my shoulders took most of the hit. I stayed upright, at least for a minute, and recognized the Di Lupo goon in the leather jacket. He kicked my knee, and I hit the pavement. Then the other guy, bug-eyes, started kicking me in the face and stomach—got a bunch of good ones in. Hit me square in the nose, and blood poured out like an open faucet."

"Son-ova…" I said, cupping my hands over my mouth.

"I got the bastard," Bo cut in proudly. "He came in for another kick, but after getting hit a lot playing football, I learned to keep my eyes open during the impact. I saw the little bastard coming, caught his foot, and twisted it. I'm pretty sure I broke his ankle. I heard it snap, and he howled. The other dirtbag came at me again with a club and got me in the head and ribs. I heard footsteps running toward us, so I rolled into the street—I couldn't figure out how many there were. A car swerved and slammed on the brakes. A woman and the driver jumped out. They must've thought I was just a drunk who stumbled into the street, but then they saw the other guys fighting and got the hell out of there. I staggered around for a second, trying to make sense of it all. It looked like one of them was beating the shit out of the others, but it was hard to see in the dark, and my eyes were screwed up from getting kicked, so I couldn't be sure what I was seeing."

He paused a minute, trying to remember. "Whatever—I figured I needed to get outta there, so I stayed out of the light and took alleys to get here. When I came into the lobby, Vincenzo saw me, grabbed me, and helped me get to the service elevator. A few guests noticed us, but Vincenzo signaled that everything was good."

"Yeah, about that. There's something not quite right about the night manager," I said.

"Vincenzo? What's not right?"

"He's too calm and collected. Remember how stolid he was last night with the vandalism? Now, he looks after you, even though you look like you've been in a fistfight with a train. He doesn't ask what happened, doesn't involve other employees, and doesn't call the cops. It's not normal."

"Would you prefer if he shrieked and ran around like his hair caught fire?"

I thought for a second. "Yes—actually—yes, I would."

"I think he's worried his hotel will get tainted from our stench. I think he wants us gone. The quicker, the better. He's discreet, not duplicitous."

"Speaking of duplicitous, where's Leo?" I asked.

"I'm not his keeper, Marty," he answered, annoyed. "I lost him early at the after-party. I mingled." He took a painful breath and continued, "What the hell was that woman doing in your room?"

"She's either a bored rich girl or a bad call girl," I said smoothly, trying to project the humor in it. "Either too much money or not enough."

"She didn't look like a hooker," he said. "More like a school teacher."

"Then probably a bored rich girl."

"Bored rich girls are dangerous, Marty. They're bored for a reason."

"Beggers can't be choosers," I said, staying with the vibe.

"What the hell, Marty," he said, wincing and sitting up. "Since when do you screw around on Abbie? I don't even know you anymore."

He didn't know the half of it, and I wanted to change the subject fast. "They say anything?"

"Who, the goons? Yeah, just before I got battered, I heard, 'Go home, asshole.'"

A swollen lump below Bo's right eye flared with anger, and I went to the fridge and heaped ice cubes into a towel. "Hold this to your cheekbone. It's boiling up."

"Bastard clubbed me like I was a baby seal."

He took a deep breath and slid underwater.

CHAPTER TWENTY-SIX

Sunday, January 18th

BO STAYED IN MY SUITE FOR THE NIGHT. We agreed to stick together. The Di Lupo men had attacked him when he was alone, and they'd proven they could get into our rooms.

I took the first watch.

Bo rattled out six Spedifen and washed them down with the last of the Barolo directly from the bottle. "That is an excellent wine," he said, staring at the label.

"You're gonna sleep like a tranquilized bear," I said.

Wrapping himself in the plush complimentary bathrobe, he carefully climbed into bed. I changed the wet bandage for a dry one and piled up all the pillows so he could sleep sitting up because his ribs were too tender to lie down. I left the door open so I could hear his breathing. His ability to fall asleep anywhere, anytime, was a benefit now. I listened to his stuttered snoring as I lay on the couch.

In the morning, I had room service deliver a cappuccino for me. Then I called Dante, knowing hospital protocol would have him awake early. It took a moment for the call to connect, and after the customary "How are you?" and the predictable "My life sucks," we settled into a more substantive conversation.

"Is Natalya's copilot Frank looking after you?" I asked.

"Like a personal bodyguard," he answered. "I talked to Natalya and told her to walk away from the Chiurazzi."

"Me too," I said. "I suppose you had the same luck convincing her."

· Stuck in the hospital, Dante had thought through the reasons behind the attack on him. His theory was on target for entirely different reasons than mine. Unaware of the bank account or the Di Lupo involvement but savvy about the art world, his analysis sprang from a different perspective. He suggested that the Chiurazzi could be used for money laundering—not through banking channels but the art market.

"I think Alessio Rosa wants the foundry to move mafia money. Art is treated differently than currency. Unlike selling stock or making money transfers, art sales—especially those through auction houses—are not subject to anti-laundering provisions."

"I don't understand."

"The laws that banks follow to fight financial crimes—you know—reporting large cash transactions or other suspicious activity. When art is sold, sellers don't have to identify the buyer or report the sales price. The entire market is a black box. Art is used to wash money all the time. Most sales happen through private dealers, who know to keep their mouths shut if they want to stay in business."

"Like Natalya," I said wryly.

"Like me," he scoffed.

But Dante's narrow perspective focused on a single pawn, leaving him oblivious to the checkmate unfolding across the board. He wasn't wrong; Chiurazzi art could be used for money laundering. He was just thinking too small. Leo's words from last night resonated: *"One account, one year, one billion."* Even all the Michelangelo, Bernini, and da Vinci originals combined couldn't pull that off. I decided not to tell him about the Di Lupos. The less he knew, the better. He needed to go home to Charley, his girlfriend, who would be waiting with open arms.

After Dante, I called Leo's room, his programmed phone, and his regular phone but they all went to voicemail.

Where was Leo? Was he also attacked? Is he safe?

My phone rang. I didn't recognize the number. Who would call me on this phone? I answered warily.

"Yes?"

"Marty, it's Spina Paulo."

I was dumbstruck. I looked at my watch. "Wow! Spina! I didn't expect you to call this soon," I sputtered.

Or ever.

"I've worried all night about your friend Bo. Is he alright?"

"I think so."

"What happened?"

I wasn't about to tell her the truth. I made up a story about a random hit-and-run and looked for a quick exit to the conversation. "Thank you for your concern."

"I hate the way things ended," she said.

I agreed.

"Then let's have breakfast," she said, her enthusiasm sparking.

I was surprised at her persistence. I glanced into Bo's room, briefly studying the rhythm of his snore, and thought, *What's going on here?*

"You know, Spina, last night was very nice, but…"

"If things had ended differently, we'd be having breakfast," she interrupted. "So, we can enjoy it now without the obligatory shame."

I smiled. "Well, that is true." But I wasn't persuaded.

"I'll entice you with a promise to tell you something about Leo Giacobbe you don't know."

My smile vanished. She had a knack for dropping lines that sucked the air out of my lungs. I briefly recalled Leo's nervousness and discomfort while talking to her at the after-party. Was he a former client? Is that why I couldn't reach him? When things flopped with me, did she make up for lost income by going to his room? What the hell?

"I thought you met him for the first time last night," I said.

"You're fishing for clues, Marty—breakfast?"

"Where?"

///

A smell of buttery yeast washed over me as I entered Rione del Fico. The outside air was still brisk, fogging the windows with morning mist. I chose a table far from the entrance but still within sight of it. A teenage waiter with disheveled hair set a steaming caffe latte before me. I pulled up the collar of my new jacket, almost hiding my face, and waited for Spina to arrive. I'd left Bo sleeping soundly; his body needed to heal, and until I found out what Spina had to tell me, there was no point in disturbing him.

I watched rivulets of dew trail down the glass of the entrance door. An elderly couple shuffled in, their worn coats and shoes marking them as locals. Another couple entered, their baseball caps identifying them as tourists. Then came a man in a navy blue peacoat. I recognized him immediately. He was here to kill me.

The Irishman…Brody Lynch!

My bladder cramped, and I tightened every muscle in my body as he strolled over and sat opposite me. We said nothing to each other for a stretch that felt like hours. I just stared at him. He hadn't changed, except he looked less oily. His dark hair was greaseless, and he'd shaved and lost his black leather jacket. He looked less mugger, more metropolitan—like he'd leaped an entire social class.

"You gonna piss yourself?" were his first words.

"Fuck you," were mine.

"I hoped I'd never see you again," he said.

"I hoped you were dead," I responded.

The teenage waiter, now in an apron, came to take his order, but he waved him off. "I won't be stayin'," he said.

"Good," I said.

"You've been actin' the maggot again."

I didn't answer, concentrating instead on keeping my hands in my lap where I could control their shaking.

"You've been runnin' your mouth about gettin' out of your business deal." He studied my face for a reaction I didn't give him. "You need to stop doin' that. It confuses things."

I clenched my bladder even tighter. "What's it to you?"

"It's nothin' to me, but if you keep doin' it, I'll 'ave to kill ye."

"If I had a nickel…" I shot back.

He gave me a derisive grin. "Understand—I don't wanna do that."

Reaching into his peacoat pocket, he pulled out a pack of cigarettes, its dented carton looking like a deflated lung, and dropped it on the table. "You know the difference between the price of a bullet and a cigarette?" He paused and stared hard at me. I stared back. Neither of us blinked. "About a dime. The bullet costs more. Don't make me shoot your sorry ass. I'd rather have a smoke—it saves me a dime."

"Good to know you're on a budget," I said. "You working for Natalya?"

"No."

"How'd you find us in Rome?"

"I know your meetin' schedule. I waited outside the big building and followed you to the fancy tailor—nice jacket."

"How do you know our schedule? And why do you care about our deal?"

"Still askin' stupid questions. You always did that. How'd you find me? Who do you work for? Why do you care?" He took a deep breath. "Two years, and you've learned nothin'. Start askin' smarter questions—like, how do I keep breathin'."

"I already know," I said. "Stay the hell away from you."

"Smart answer." He leaned forward. "And don't piss me off."

I stayed silent.

"Do what you're told, shithead. Buy the damn foundry—go

home—play with the kids—pet the dog—you still got the dog? Fook the wife—you still got the wife? She probably left and took the dog."

"I've got a mafia family threatening me *not* to buy the foundry. You threaten me *to* buy it. You kill me if I don't; they kill me if I do. Feels like a lose-lose situation." The sheer absurdity of the predicament provided a twisted comfort, and the knot of fear in my gut loosened a bit.

"Don't sweat the small stuff," he said.

I tilted my head. "The Di Lupos are no 'small stuff.'"

He picked up his cigarettes, stood up, and stuck both hands in his coat pockets.

"They are to me," he said. He strolled out without looking back.

I sat at my table for the next half hour, a fly trapped in amber. Gripped by a cold paralysis, my mind swirled while my body remained motionless. In that horrifying dissonance, I felt like a spectator in the unfolding disaster of my life.

Spina Paulo never showed.

I walked back to the hotel instead of taking a taxi. Head down, hands in pockets, I stopped looking for the Irishman. I knew he was precisely where he wanted to be, unpacked and living comfortably in my head.

CHAPTER TWENTY-SEVEN

RETURNING TO THE MICHELANGELO, I peeked into the Dome bar to see if the Di Lupo clowns were still present. They weren't, or if they were, I didn't see them.

In my suite, Bo was awake, stretching, flexing, and limbering his joints, which, judging from his groans, were reacting like rusted hinges. I followed him to his room and waited while he cleaned up. His digs were similar to mine, so I planted myself on one of his two couches.

"Do you want me to change the bandage?" I called out.

"No, it's scabbed up; I'll stick an adhesive pad on it," he called back.

"Guess who I had breakfast with?"

"Another hooker?"

"The Irishman."

The hush was thunderous. Even from a distant room, I heard Bo inhale. Then he released a string of profanity and stuck his head in the door frame.

"Well...details," he commanded.

I recounted Spina's call, how I left to discover what she had to tell me about Leo, and how Brody showed up instead.

"I should have pinched his cheek to be sure he wasn't a delusion," I said, not even trying to keep the smugness from my tone.

"Point made."

"He warned me—us—not to walk away from the Chiurazzi."

Bo's head disappeared again, and he said nothing for a while.

"None of this makes sense," he called out. "Who's he working for? Not the Di Lupos, obviously."

"I thought Natalya at first, but he said no."

"And you believe him because of his righteous moral code?"

"No, because Natalya wouldn't do that to me—to us. She wouldn't sic a rabid dog on us."

"Dmitry would," he said, tottering into the main room and sitting on the other couch. Although he'd combed his hair, brushed his teeth, cleaned his bandages, and put on a new bathrobe, he still looked like he'd gone twelve rounds with Mike Tyson. I filled a bag of ice from his fridge, and he held it to his face. I told him he looked like Quasimodo, and he thanked me, matching my sarcasm.

"We have another mystery," I announced. "I can't find Leo. He's fallen off the planet. He's not in his room, and he's not answering his phone."

"Those stupid phones he gave us are terrible," said Bo. "I don't use them. I tried to call home, and the latency was so bad I switched to my regular phone."

"I'm worried Leo was attacked like you were and is lying in a sewer somewhere."

"Yeah," he sighed, pressing the ice to his eyes. "And I'll assume he doesn't want us to call the cops."

///////////////////////////////////////

Shortly past noon, Vincenzo knocked on Bo's door with a lunch trolley filled with food and drinks: ham and mozzarella paninis, *minestra maritata*—Italian wedding soup—bread with olive oil, *panna cotta*, and Pellegrino. As always, he was alone, polite, and peculiarly professional.

"*Vorresti il pranzo?*" he asked, holding his hands together and making a subtle inclination.

"I thought you only worked the night shift?" I asked suspiciously.

"We are *mani corte* today, *signore*—how you say—no hands."

"Short-handed," I corrected.

"*Si*—so I stay and make sure your problems do not become hotel problems."

He pulled the cart into the room, went to Bo, and, with a nurse's scowl, inspected his head without touching it.

"Did you take pain medicine?"

"Yes, Mom," Bo answered with a smile.

Vincenzo smiled back and unloaded the trolley on the small wooden dining table by the kitchenette. Bo invited him to stay and eat with us, and he demurred, but Bo insisted. Even with one of Bo's eyes swollen shut and the other a red-veined marble, Vincenzo couldn't refuse him. I laughed inwardly, familiar with Bo's power of persuasion. Vincenzo rejected the food, poured himself a coffee, and sat with us at the table.

"Vincenzo, have you seen two men downstairs, probably in the bar or lobby?"

"*No signore*. But I know those you speak about—*il sistema*—I saw them yesterday."

"You can tell *sistema* men by just looking at them?" asked Bo.

"*Si signore*—*spicca*—they stand out like a priest in a whore house."

He explained that he'd grown up in Naples and experienced *il sistema* for much of his life, recognizing its members from their dress and conduct. He said the two men had shown up the first time for breakfast Friday morning but weren't hotel guests.

I studied his face as if I were hiring him to guard my children. "Have you been gone from Naples for a long time?" I asked.

"*Oh, si*," he said, holding his hands apart like he was exaggerating the size of a fish. "Life in Napoli is—*dolce-amara*—how to say—lemon and candy."

"Bittersweet," Bo interjected.

"*Si*. It is a proud city, but *mercer danneggiata*—damaged goods— like your clothes." He smiled meekly.

In broken but comprehensible English, he lamented the sad plight of his hometown. Naples, he explained, was the last great pagan city—a place of puppets, cards, and magic. Its tattered suburbs, among the poorest in Europe, throbbed with the mythologies of death and the afterlife. Superstition and *negromanzia*—necromancy—were a constant undercurrent of life. People wore the *cornicello* for fertility and virility, and the Church itself seemed more occultist. It was a city steeped in tradition, where the dark presence of the Camorra was pervasive and traditional.

I offered him more coffee, but Vincenzo declined. He nervously checked his watch as if worried the interview was going too long.

Bo asked him if he'd ever heard of the Di Lupo family.

"*Si Signore* Bishop—you do not want to know this family."

"I don't know them," said Bo. "But I think they know me."

"You think Di Lupo *vandalizzato* your rooms?" he asked.

"It's possible."

"What do you know about them?" I asked.

"*La diceria*," he said and then translated. "Rumors, gossip, what I read and hear. But only whispers—all bad."

He looked into his empty coffee cup, perhaps contemplating how much rumor he would share. Ultimately, he opted for caution, recounting the two stories everyone in Naples knew—legendary tales that may not have been entirely true but were shared like cherished recipes.

The first involved Mauro Di Lupo, *Capo di capi*, who was once furious with his top lieutenant. Word had reached him that the lieutenant had disrespected Mauro's oldest son, Cosimo, who was being groomed as his heir. While Mauro was out of town, Cosimo had acted on his behalf to gain leadership experience, but the lieutenant felt slighted by this sudden change in authority.

Upon Mauro's return, Cosimo complained of the lack of respect from his top man. Hearing of Mauro's anger, the lieutenant rushed to his house to apologize. Mauro accepted his apology and invited him in for a conciliatory drink. He poured himself a fine glass of wine and then took the other glass and pissed into it to the top. Mauro then drank his wine and handed his piss to the deputy, who, legend has it, drank the entire glass—emptied it without breathing. The man understood he could either drink the contents of his boss's kidneys or lose his own. The decision was an easy one.

"*Urgh*," I said, shuddered, and stopped spooning my soup.

"That is the first story," said Vincenzo. "The second story I know is true because I know the bar where it happened. It is no longer in business. *Capo* Mauro has many sons and one daughter. She is his angel, his *preferita*. When she was still *adolescente*, maybe sixteen, she not arrive home when expected. It was nighttime, and Mauro had strict rules for her safety. When she was late, her father got into a car with three of his men and drove around the neighborhood to look for her. They drove by a bar with many scooters parked out front—more than usual. Mauro stopped and sent a man inside to see if she was there. She was. Some young men had made a circle around her. Mauro's soldier pushed the young men aside and took the girl out of the bar."

Vincenzo shook his head somberly. "The men whistled and booed. They were playing a game with her. Outside, Mauro sat in the car and asked his daughter why she had not come home, and she told him the men in the bar blocked her way out, and she was not allowed to leave until she picked one to give—*pompino*—you know—blowjob in the bathroom."

He grinned directly at us to express he was not embarrassed.

"The old man asked if it was all the men in bar, and she said no. He took her back in, and she pointed at five men. They were a baby gang, very loud, very *cafoni*—rude, no manners. Mauro nodded to his men, left the bar, and walked his daughter home.

"His men pulled knives and axes out of trunk of car and go back into bar. They whispered to other customers to leave quickly. But not the baby gang. Mauro's men—how to say—*storpiate*—butchered them. They cut off their *cazzo e palle*—cock and balls—stuffed them into beer mugs and put them on the bar. Five men, five glasses." He held up his hands with spread fingers.

"*Urgh*," Bo said.

"In Napoli, there is now a saying, '*Bacia la spina e bevi le palle.*' It means kiss the thorn and drink your balls."

He sighed and stood, ready to exit. "Inside *sistema*, respect and fear are together." He interlaced his hands and wiggled his fingers. "The Di Lupos are respected only because they are feared."

He rechecked his watch and indicated he needed to go back to work. I walked him to the door, and he said, "*Signore* Schott, you and *Signore* Bishop, stay away from the Di Lupos. Keep your *cazzo e palle* safe." He pointed to my crotch.

I grinned and touched both hands to my zipper. "We'll keep that in mind, Vincenzo. Thank you."

"*Signore* Giacobbe should do the same—meeting with Di Lupos will not keep his *genitali al sicuro*."

I have a unique ability to keep my face serene even as my brain flares. My wife and children hate it because they can never read me in an argument. With tranquil composure, I asked, "When did Mr. Giacobbe meet with the Di Lupos?"

Bo knew not to startle him, so he eased himself from the table and cautiously approached us, his damaged face as placid as mine.

Vincenzo glanced at the ceiling, "I think two days before you arrive."

"How did you know it was Di Lupo?"

"It is good question," he said approvingly. "Gemma Di Lupo is not like her brother, Cosimo. She is private. She hides from paparazzi. Cosimo loves cameras, but she is like her father. She remains out of light…but I know her."

"You know Gemma Di Lupo?" asked Bo, his voice remaining nonchalant.

"No, not as you think. We are not friends. I know what she looks like because I went to same school when I lived in Naples. We are same age. I see her in Scampi when she goes shopping in stores and markets."

"You recognize her," Bo corrected.

"*Si*—she meet with *Signore* Giacobbe here in Dome bar—I was on duty." He bowed slightly, accepted my tip with a wink and complicit tsk, and left.

Bo's bruised and battered face reflected my rage.

"Leo's a yellow stain on a bathroom floor—something to step around," he muttered.

CHAPTER TWENTY-EIGHT

BO SWALLOWED ANOTHER HANDFUL OF PILLS, and I left him to sleep. Back in my suite, I called my family. Their questions bombarded me in rapid-fire succession: "Have you seen the pope? Can you describe the Vatican? What about the Colosseum? How's the food? When are we all going to Rome?" I spun a convincing web of lies and exaggerations, feeling no guilt as I did. To my surprise, Abbie was eager to start planning a family trip for our summer vacation.

That was not going to happen.

I spent the next few hours on my laptop, delving into the murky mysteries of the Vatican Bank, until a sharp ring from my regular phone shook me out of my concentration.

"I was just going to call you," I said to Natalya.

"How was the concert?" she asked.

It felt like a lifetime ago, and so much had happened that I needed to adjust to her lack of knowledge. I told her about Bo's ambush, deliberately leaving Spina Paulo out of the story. I saved Brody for last.

"Natalya," I asked over her silence. "Did you know Brody Lynch was in Rome?"

"No."

I believed her, but her terse answer hinted there was more to say.

"Did Dmitry know?"

"Probably."

"Does he work for you?"

"No."

"Does he work for Dmitry?"

"Yes."

"You never told me."

"Martin," she said and sighed softly. "How could I—why would I?"

"He threatened to kill me if we walked away from the Chiurazzi."

"I am sure Dmitry sent him. Brody is a bear with a toothache. He is meant to scare you, not hurt you. Fear has big eyes."

"I've heard that expression before."

"I will talk to Dmitry. Brody will leave you alone."

"Why doesn't Dmitry just pick up the damn phone and talk to us?"

She said nothing, knowing any response would sound placating.

"Why doesn't Dmitry meet us in Rome?" I pressed.

"He doesn't like crowded cities."

"I think it's because he doesn't like Bo and me."

"That is your speculation."

"We've been in business for two years, and I've never met him face-to-face."

"We have conference calls and went to a video site twice."

"Not the same thing," I said.

"He is your banker, Martin, not your buddy."

I passed over her comment and decided to play my ace. "How did Cardinal Bertolini get your Raphael—*Portrait of a Young Man*?"

She said nothing for several seconds. "Did you see it?" She sounded genuinely surprised.

"Hanging in his office, displayed in a big gold frame."

"The *real* Raphael?" she asked, pushing hard on *real*.

"No. Dante's forgery—which I thought you had."

"I gave it to Dmitry. He did not tell me he gave it away."

"To gift a forgery of the most valuable missing painting in the world to Cardinal Bertolini means Dmitry must have already known him—known he could be trusted."

"I can explain that." She perked up, eager to steer the conversation into positive territory. "Dmitry and I met the cardinal last summer at the Caritas Internationalis fundraising gala." She hummed, trying to remember. "It happened about a month after you and I had that wonderful week in Michigan. Do you remember?"

I grunted.

"It was called Gesture of Peace and held at the Palais de Chaillot. There were many—*shishka*—big shots—mostly rich Catholics and VIPs. Dmitry asked me to join him. We stayed at the Hôtel de Crillon and attended a fancy dinner party hosted by Francis Pinet-Dupont."

"Who?"

"Big money Catholic. He owns a very big company with many luxury brands. He also owns Christie's or maybe Sotheby's; I can't remember which one. He has a big winery in Bordeaux and owns a football club. Dmitry has a football club, too, so they know each other."

"OK, so what?" I asked irritably, barely masking my discomfort. In that brief moment, she'd opened a crack into her life, and the glimpse I caught shook me. With Dmitry, she moved in a world utterly foreign to me—a world that instantly made me feel smaller. I sensed she noticed the hit to my ego because she continued dispassionately, and I couldn't help but wonder if she saw me the way I suddenly saw myself—diminished.

"We sat at same table with Cardinal Bertolini and the bank president Angelo Caloia. Caritas Internationalis is Vatican's biggest charity, and many donors and politicians were there."

She lapsed a beat, uncomfortable with her disclosure.

"Dmitry already knew Angelo," she continued. "They did not introduce each other; they only shook hands. Then, during dinner, Angelo, Dmitry, and the cardinal stood together away from the table and talked for a long time. His food got cold. After dinner, Dmitry told me the cardinal was big fan of Raphael. I remember he wondered if—how you say—secret of the confession—protected him if he ever showed Bertolini the true Raphael."

"Why didn't you tell me this?" I asked, frustrated. "We negotiated with the Liuzzo lawyers for a week. You never said a word about meeting Bertolini or Caloia."

"I meet many people with Dmitry. I meet many people with *you*. I do not talk about who I meet at dinner or business."

"Really, Natalya! We were scheduled to meet Bertolini and Caloia yesterday, and you couldn't bring yourself to say, 'Oh—we once shared a lobster in Paris, along with a few other billionaires. We chewed the fat and had a lovely time.'"

"We didn't have lobster. We had Kobe beef. I didn't chew the fat—I don't like it, so I cut it to the side. Some people had fish. I remember Cardinal Bertolini had sea bass."

"Fuck me!" I exhaled in exasperation.

"I cannot do that right now. You will have to wait." She was playing with me, throwing me off track.

"Do you ever talk to Dmitry about me? About Bo? The company? You know—pillow talk."

"Dmitry and I don't talk over the pillow. Before now, he was not interested in Paladin. He never asked about it—or you. Then, the Chiurazzi deal happened. I did not tell him about it—he told me. Now, he asks questions about Paladin all the time."

"I thought Dante told you about the Chiurazzi?"

She sighed again. "Dmitry is doing something with the Church bank. It involves property, and he doesn't want me to discuss it. You understand this, yes?"

"Yes. But Dmitry needs to know Bo and I are out. Paladin will not buy the Chiurazzi. He can buy it, or you can buy it. But we want no part of it."

"No, Martin. Paladin must be the buyer." I could hear the stress in her voice. "I will do it myself."

"Nonsense, Natalya! Dmitry has more companies than I have shirts. Any one of his companies can buy the damn foundry!"

"Stop talking to me like I am your employee."

Her anger was palpable. I felt an elusive shift in the energy between us, the way waning steam carries heat from coffee, dissipating it inexorably into the air. I feared things might never be the same between us.

"I will explain it in a way you will understand, Natalya." I paused and took a deep breath. "Remember how we met? Remember your nephew, Vasili Bobrov? Remember how Bo and I were scared that the entire Miami *Bratva* would seek revenge on our families because I killed him?"

I paused, waiting for a response. There was none.

"I won't do that again. Not even for you. We are talking about the Camorra mafia. The family bidding on the Chiurazzi is the Di Lupo clan. They make the Miami *Bratva* look like a junior varsity team. Bo and I won't put our families in that danger. Am I clear?"

Silence.

"You keep saying Dmitry will make a phone call and clean everything up. But that doesn't make sense, Natalya. It just doesn't."

Continued silence.

"We're not in Russia, Natalya. We're in Rome. Dmitry has no juice in Rome."

She broke her silence. "Juice?"

"Influence, sway, power—we're not in Moscow. Dmitry can't just call off the dogs over here. He doesn't have the power—the juice."

She chuckled suggestively. "You really *don't* know him as well as I do."

CHAPTER TWENTY-NINE

IT IS SAID THAT MONEY FLOWS LIKE A RAMPANT RIVER, its teeming tributaries distributing its bounty.

Bullshit.

Money doesn't flow; it bounces, like hailstones, colliding chaotically, and destinies are determined by the decisions made between the ricochets.

Bo and I were now on the consequential side of those decisions, and I wondered just how insignificant we were in this grand scheme that seemed designed to manipulate us from the start.

We ate dinner in Bo's room, delivered again by our trusty night manager, Vincenzo, who apparently never went home. Bo's ribs, still tender, restricted his movement as he sat in his bathrobe. His face, a mosaic of welts and discolored bruises, reflected the pain etched into his posture. I replayed Natalya's conversation for him, and he listened intently, pushing his peppered pasta around the plate without a bite.

"Why do we care if Dmitry uses the bank to launder money?" I asked. "We're not part of it."

"Doesn't matter," he said. "Our names are attached to the account."

"But we're not using it."

"From the beginning, our names have never been tied to Dmitry's activities," Bo said. "He's an investor in Paladin, not an officer. He provides capital, which we pay back or trade for equity. What he does in his day job is as separate from us as a bank robber who owns stock in Apple. His connection to us has always been transactional. But this time, it's different. Paladin will own the bank account, and money will move under our management." He straightened his back and grimaced. "Once we open that door, we'll never be rid of Dmitry. He'll be like toe fungus."

A faint knock on his door made us exchange worried glances, both of us aware of the heightened threat.

"Vincenzo?" I asked.

Bo shook his head and stayed seated. "Who is it?"

No answer.

"Who is it?" Bo barked, holding his ribs.

"Me—Leo Giacobbe."

I pounced for the door, ripped it open, grabbed Leo by the wool of his fancy sweater, and hauled him into the room. "Where have you been?"

Leo pushed me away. Then, seeing Bo's condition, he clasped his hand over his mouth. "Holy shit!"

"You might want to find a different way to express yourself," said Bo, repeating Leo's words when we toured the Palazzo del Sant'Uffizio.

"Want to tell us where you've been? We've missed you," I said.

Leo ignored me and asked Bo what had happened. He explained that the Di Lupo goons we'd confronted in Caffè Greco evidently held a grudge.

"Leo," I snarled. "We know you're working with the Di Lupos. You've got some explaining to do."

He threw on a look of cartoonish bewilderment as if auditioning for a B movie.

"You were seen talking to Gemma Di Lupo in the lobby bar," said Bo.

He collapsed onto the couch in resigned defeat. "It's not my fault. I didn't want any of this to happen," he whined.

Bo went to his refrigerator and retrieved mini-bottles of Glenlivet. "I had them stock the fridge earlier—no charge." A thin, discolored grin creased his black-and-blue face, a fold in a weathered map. He poured the drinks, and then we sat, spacing ourselves far enough apart so neither of us could arbitrarily smack the other.

"I don't like scotch," said Leo.

Another reason to dislike him.

"You need to level with us," said Bo. "Stop with the lies and the attitude. People are getting hurt—look at my face."

"Officially, I'm a papal usher, so I interact with the higher echelons of the Curia," said Leo. "Unofficially, I function as Cardinal Bertolini's confidante and emissary to the outside world, managing delicate matters that require discretion."

"You're a fixer," I said.

"You already know this. Bertolini asked me to help Angelo Caloia, who told me to work with Lamberto Liuzzo." His face glowed in the warm light of the suite's fireplace. "I don't like any of them. Angelo Caloia, his brother-in-law Gabriele, and his nephew Lamberto are all bent. They're doing something with real estate, but I don't know the details. It's all conducted through the Liuzzo law firm."

"Is Cardinal Bertolini part of it?" Bo asked.

"I don't know how he's not," Leo said, shrugging slightly. "His Eminence controls all the Church-owned property. Caloia can't touch it without Bertolini knowing. I never discuss it with him. He's the most powerful cardinal in the Church. If I broach it with him, I'll be out on my ear like I just pissed the carpet."

Bewildered, I asked, "Why would a cardinal living in the lap of luxury be corrupt? He has everything he could ever want. He has no family. He's old. He'll die in a soft, warm bed. He's not spending money on hookers or drugs—hell, he even owns a copy of Newton's *Principia* and displays it like a common cookbook."

We all stared into the fireplace. Leo took a sip of his scotch. His mouth twitched, and he set the glass down quickly as if he wanted to distance himself from the taste. Bo and I grinned.

"None of them ever exposed the Di Lupo bid—Natalya and Dmitry never knew," I said.

"Would it have made a difference?" Bo asked.

I shrugged. "Leo, what's your connection to the Di Lupos?"

"The daughter, Gemma, came to me," said Leo.

"When?"

"A few weeks back. My guess is Alessio Rosa pointed me out. I think he's *sistema*."

He looked at me, and I replied, "Duh!"

"Lamberto gave Rosa a list of the due diligence team. I'm guessing Rosa passed the list to Gemma, who checked everyone out and decided to approach me. We met a couple of times, the last being here at the Michelangelo."

"You didn't think to tell anyone about it?" Bo asked.

"I was curious, and yeah, there was something in it for me." He moved further away from us. "Look, the Vatican isn't known for its compensation package. Unlike you, I don't have equity, and I do have debts. Maybe the Di Lupos knew about that." He sighed. "Gemma offered to solve my financial problems if I helped her. She told me she wanted the Chiurazzi—she loves art."

"So, what's your agreement?" I asked.

"She paid me $50K to keep her informed. If she gets the Chiurazzi, I get another $50K. I always knew I'd never see the second installment."

I was impressed. "A hundred grand—just for information?"

He stood up and took three steps back. "I also had to provide the preprogrammed phones—they're bugged."

For a second, the world froze like a snapshot. Then, with an agonizing guttural grunt, Bo sprang from the couch and hurled himself at Leo as if he were sacking a quarterback. Leo slammed against the wall, and a large, ornately framed reproduction of Michelangelo's

Adoration of the Magi fell with a loud thud, the glass cracking diagonally from corner to corner.

"I called my family on that phone, you bastard," Bo snarled, pinning him to the wall, his swollen eye an inch from Leo's.

"I'm sorry," Leo mewled.

I pulled Bo back, and Leo staggered, falling back onto the couch.

"I thought what happened at the foundry and then the room vandalism were just pressure tactics. I called Gemma and told her she was pushing too hard. She's used to getting her way. She's not as psycho as her brother, but she's not far off. Once I realized a Russian oligarch was involved, I figured this could go nuclear. I tried calling Gemma all night, but she never answered. I finally reached her this morning. I told her about your Dmitry guy, and she didn't care. She said Russians are only scary in Russia. In Italy, they're more annoying than dangerous.'"

"Where were you today?" I asked.

"I drove home to Orvieto. I hid out. Avoiding you! I checked on my daughter at Berkeley. I did this for her—to pay her tuition."

A thought struck me. "I talked to Natalya on the bugged phone yesterday. I told her we were walking away from the deal, but Natalya said no." Bo looked at me like he didn't understand my point. "It means they know their intimidation is working on us but not on Natalya."

"Di Lupo needs to understand Dmitry Chernyshevsky is very dangerous," said Bo. "Maybe we talk to her—explain things."

"Can you call Gemma and arrange a meeting?" I asked Leo.

"You call her," he shot back.

"I don't have her number, you idiot."

"You didn't get it last night?"

A tingle wove through my body, like a fraying wire sending shivers along my nerves. "What?"

"Last night," said Leo. "You drank with her."

I felt dizzy. "What the hell are you talking about?"

Bo turned to me with an expression of surprise. "You mean the hooker?"

"Are you talking about Spina Paulo?" I sputtered incredulously.

"Yes! Gemma—nickname Spina. Di Lupo—married name Paulo. Spina Paulo—Gemma Di Lupo."

CHAPTER THIRTY

Rome, Monday, January 19th

SOMETIME THAT MORNING, GEMMA DI LUPO—aka Spina Paulo—the only daughter of the most powerful mafia clan in Naples, kidnapped Natalya Danilenko, Paladin's chairperson, Dmitry's girlfriend, and my entanglement. They ripped a fingernail savagely from her right ring finger. God knows what else they did.

Natalya had planned to pick up Dante Scava from a hospital in Naples, where he was recovering after being skewered by a metal rod during our inspection of the Chiurazzi Foundry. Once she ensured his safe return to Portland on her private jet, she intended to catch the bullet train to Rome and meet Bo and me at Caffè Domiziano in Piazza Navona.

///

Bo and I slept in. I needed the rest; he needed the healing. The night before, we'd shoved Leo Giacobbe out of the suite after another round of grilling about the Di Lupos, then stayed up a few more hours dissecting our mess. Drained and frustrated, we finally called it a night, oblivious to how fast the ground was shifting beneath us.

After a late breakfast, I put on my favorite new shirt, hoping to impress Natalya. Walking the mile to Piazza Navona, Bo and I let the city's vibrant atmosphere wash over us—with the weariness of embittered tourists overstaying their welcome at a calamitous carnival.

I was eager to see Natalya. But, as you already know, I didn't.

I only got to see a small, sickening piece of her.

///////////////////////////////////

Ever notice how a house of cards collapses in a single breath, marked by a sudden whoosh of air? I thought about that while taking the cab back to our hotel, carrying Natalya's Birkin bag with her bloody fingernail inside. My world hadn't crumbled in stages—it vanished in a single, silent fold.

Bo and I didn't speak until we returned to the Michelangelo. We peered into the Dome bar, half-expecting to find Leo hiding there. I dialed his number, but it went straight to voicemail. Giuseppe, the day manager, offered us a tight-lipped smile from behind the front desk, his demeanor much diminished from the warm beam he'd given us two days earlier. I assumed he'd seen our bar bill, the damaged wall frame in Bo's room, and the bruised patchwork that was Bo's face.

Once in Bo's suite, he dialed his bugged phone the moment the door closed.

"Who are you calling?"

"Natalya," he said, putting it on speaker. It rang four times.

"*Pronto*," the voice was calm but hostile.

I looked at Bo and spoke before he could. "I want to talk with Natalya."

"She cannot go to phone now."

"Why not?" I demanded.

"She has swollen finger—*si*."

"Let her go," said Bo. "We're done with the Chiurazzi."

"*Quando vai a casa.*"

"English!" I hollered, then added under my breath, "You asshole."

"She leave when you are on plane to America," said the voice. It might have been Alessio Rosa, but I couldn't be sure. His English was better.

"We're not leaving without her," I said.

"But you must."

"Listen to me," snarled Bo. "You can have the Chiurazzi; choke on it. But the Vatican won't sell it to you. We've got nothing to do with that."

"You will convince *Il Vaticano* to sell the foundry to *Impresa Artistica Vesuviana*."

Bo spoke before I could, his voice remaining composed. "We can't do that. But, if we're out of the picture, maybe they'll change their mind."

"*Hai creato tu il problema.*"

"English—you asshole," I shouted.

Bo cupped the phone and hissed, "Are you trying to get her killed?" The phone went silent, and I thought we'd lost them. My heart raced.

"*Vaffanculo!*" growled the voice, then more silence. "You create this problem. Now, you fix it. Talk to the lawyers—*si*?"

"That won't work," said Bo.

"Then I send you her whole finger."

"You're crazy!" I shouted. "Goddamnit!"

Momentary silence again.

Then, "God is not on this call," said the voice calmly before the line went dead.

My hands shook as I misdialed, then redialed my untapped personal phone.

"They're not going to answer," said Bo.

"I'm not calling them. I'm calling Dmitry."

"You have his number?" Bo was taken aback.

"Natalya gave it to me once and said to use it only in an emergency."

"Shit," said Bo, pacing back and forth. "We're spiraling out of control."

"We were never in control," I said firmly and hit the speaker button.

Someone answered almost immediately. "*Privetstviye.*"

"Dmitry, this is Martin Schott."

There was a pause, and I heard movement. "*Odin moment.*" Then, "Martin?"

"Dmitry?"

"*Da*, my sorry…I have Valya join me." Valya, short for Valentin Kovalev, was Dmitry's interpreter. I'd learned from our calls that Dmitry understood English better than he spoke it, needing Valya more to speak than to listen. When Valya translated Dmitry's words, he even shifted pronouns, so we knew he meant Dmitry when he said I.

"Sorry to call you Dmitry," I managed, panting like I'd sprinted a mile.

Dmitry spoke Russian to Valya, who translated: "You never call, so I think this must be important."

"It is," I said, pausing as I glanced at Bo. His strained face told me his rib pain was back in full force. "Natalya is in danger. We're in Rome."

"I know you in Rome," Dmitry replied directly.

For a moment, the shift between accents disoriented me. Jumping between Italian and Russian felt vertiginous.

"Did she tell you about our problem here?" I asked.

Dmitry spoke, and Valya translated. "Yes, she said the Liuzzo law firm failed to tell us that a Camorra family had bid on the foundry." I heard Dmitry in the background. "I am already looking into it," said Valya.

"It's out of control now," I exclaimed. "The Camorra have Natalya."

"*Chto*—what!?" Dmitry asked, bypassing Valya.

"She's been taken hostage," I said.

A long silence followed. I heard muffled Russian, as if Valya held his hand loosely over the mouthpiece.

Eventually, "Was it the Di Lupo family?" asked Valya.

"Yes," said Bo.

"Bo?" came Dmitry's voice.

"Yes, Dmitry, it's me. A couple of Di Lupo's men came at me the other night—kicked the shit out of me. Ruined both my face and new suit."

Again, a long pause and muffled Russian.

"How did they contact you?" asked Valya.

"They dropped her purse on our restaurant table. It contained a photo of her, her ring, and her fingernail," I said.

Someone expelled air through their nose, maybe Dmitry, maybe Valya.

"*Yebát'*!" snapped Dmitry. I knew enough Russian to understand the expletive.

"They said the finger is…"

"Not over the phone," said Valya, cutting me off.

"We called her phone, and they answered. They told us they'll release her only after we leave the country, but first, we must convince the Vatican to sell the Chiurazzi to them."

"That won't happen," said Valya without hesitation.

Bo and I stared at each other in dismay.

"We don't want the Chiurazzi, Dmitry," I said. "It's not worth this trouble."

Muffled Russian, then Valya said, "Listen—you might not want the foundry, but I do, and Paladin must buy it. There is more to this than you know. The men involved have not been honest with us. I will take care of that. I will also fix the Di Lupo issue."

"Dmitry, maybe you can fix it," I said, "but what if Natalya gets killed in the process?"

While Dmitry talked in the background, Valya answered, "I am not far away—I will be in Rome in a few hours. You and Bo do nothing—talk to no one. The Camorra has spies everywhere. You are under watch. I own a hotel close to you. I will send you instructions. Can you get there without spies following you?"

"Yes," said Bo.

Then Dmitry's voice lowered, and Valya's voice did the same. "Martin, you are scared for Natalya right now. I understand. I feel like you. Love is evil—*Lyubov' zla*—yes?"

I hung my head and sighed. "Yes."

"Do nothing until I call you." He hung up.

Bo couldn't squint like he usually did, but he still tried. "Love is evil?" he asked, confused.

"It's a Russian expression."

"Meaning?"

"Love makes you irrational. Natalya says it all the time."

I avoided his eyes and caught my reflection in the glass of the broken picture frame leaning against the wall. I wondered if the fractured light carved the hollows beneath my cheekbones or if it was the corrosion from a lifetime of wrong choices.

Bo's gaze tunneled into me like a flashlight probing a dark well.

Finally, I inhaled, my voice cracking a little.

"I've been in love with her for a year now."

CHAPTER THIRTY-ONE

Miami, four months earlier

"I LOVE YOU," stumbled out of my mouth hesitantly, as if each word were a separate confession.

She blinked, a slow smile spreading across her face but not quite reaching her eyes. We sat on her bed naked, with a Scrabble board between us and two glasses of wine on a tray beside the game, along with our pile of concealed letter tiles.

We'd spent the day preparing her notes for the upcoming quarterly call with Dmitry. I had volunteered to fly to Miami to help build the presentation, and Bo agreed before I even finished the sentence. Getting time alone with Natalya was never a problem when the third member of our management troika worked tirelessly to avoid contact.

It wasn't that he didn't like Natalya; rather, she was too much like him. She sparked a subtle rivalry that ignited his natural alpha tendencies. With me, it was different. Bo saw me as a colleague but viewed her as a competitor.

"I do love you," I repeated, this time more forcibly.

"No, you don't," she said gently. "You think you love me, but I will not allow it."

"I didn't know I needed permission," I said, matching her tone.

She smiled broadly and took a sip of her wine. "Martin, *milyy*. You think you love me because I am *Russkaya*. I have nice accent and good looks, and I—how you say—support your fantasies."

"Satisfy," I interrupted. "You satisfy my fantasies."

"I think, maybe, it means the same."

Our eyes lit up with mutual amusement.

Natalya enjoyed playing Scrabble to improve her English. She'd openly cheat, swapping out tiles she didn't like, and I'd always let her get away with it. After rearranging her letters, she'd still frown at their incompatibility. I loved watching her face as she studied the board. I loved watching it do anything, really: think, talk, laugh. I'd never seen it cry, and hoped I never would.

"*Milyy*, I have married two men. First man, Viktor, was hard; second man, Mikhail, was soft. You understand?"

I shook my head.

"I think some women like hard men," Natalya said, making two fists and grunting a little. "Other women like soft men." She unclenched her fists. "I found out in my life I like both."

She studied my face. "Martin, you are soft. Dmitry is hard. For me, it is a good combination."

"I think I'm insulted."

She laughed. "I am not talking about muscles. I am talking about *kharakter*—what is in the eyes, not the flesh." She took a sip of wine. "I lived with hard and soft, but never at the same time. Now I have both, and it is balanced, and I like it very much."

"Does Dmitry know about us?" I asked, suspecting the answer.

"Yes. I don't keep secrets from Dmitry. To him, secrets and lies are more dangerous than guns and knives. He has no problems with how I live my life. I am not his only woman, but I *am* his closest—his most trusted. He had one bad marriage, but never again. He shares much with me, but because he wants to, not because he must. Dmitry loves me like a comrade. You should love me the same."

I finished my wine in a single swig. "Comrades are war-mates, not bed-mates."

She laughed. "You are being defensive, *milyy*. I will tell you something private to make you feel better. Dmitry is a fist." She raised her hand, curled her fingers into a ball, and shook it before me. "You, Martin; you are an open hand." She unfolded her fingers. "Dmitry doesn't sit with me in bed to talk and drink wine. Dmitry doesn't play Scrabble. Dmitry doesn't stroke my feet." She smiled. "You are different, but it is not a contest. You understand?"

I decided to change the subject. "Do you miss Russia?"

"No."

"What's the biggest difference between Russia and the US?"

"Toilet."

I laughed. "Toilet?"

"Yes, there are not enough in Russia. Finding toilet is impossible if you are outside shopping or eating. No one lets you use one. I visited Dmitry in *Moskva* and went shopping, and I had to take a taxi back to hotel to pee."

"You stay in a hotel when you visit Dmitry?" I was prying.

She smiled knowingly. "Yes, *milyy*. I stay at charming hotel because Dmitry owns it, and he built top floor into apartment."

"Do you go to Moscow often?"

"No, I do not like it. I go to Cyprus. It is beautiful."

She slipped off the bed and went to fetch more wine. I laid the game board aside, keeping the tiles in place. She filled our glasses.

"Dmitry has big property there. A private beach. Very good for sunbathing."

"That explains why you're always tanned."

"Sometimes Vova comes there to visit with Dmitry."

"Who is Vova?"

"Vladimir Putin. Dmitry calls him Vova from the time of friendship in KGB."

We settled in the middle of the bed, facing each other, our legs in the lotus position. "I tell you a secret you cannot repeat."

I made the gesture of locking my lips and throwing away the key.

"Dmitry helped Putin become president. They all knew each other from time in Leningrad and KGB: Vladimir, Dmitry, and Viktor.

When KGB broke apart, Putin went home to Leningrad, now called *Sankt Peterburg*."

"St. Petersburg," I interrupted.

"Yes. *Sankt Peterburg*. He went into politics by taking advisor job to mayor of city. Dmitry made it happen. He whispered in mayor's ear. In Russia, whispering in ear is done with money, not soft words."

"You whisper in my ears all the time," I teased. "I've never received a dime."

"Because it's not money you want." She ran her hand gently from my knee to my ankle, and my blood rushed.

"Dmitry helped Vova by whispering in many ears, and then Vova helped Dmitry. After he became president, Putin gave Dmitry oil contracts from *Rosneft*, Russia's biggest oil company. That is how Dmitry became oligarch and popular with *Siloviki*."

"What's that?"

"It is name for powerful people who make Russian politics work."

"Like our political elite," I said.

"No. America's elite are different from Russian elite. In America *elite* means brain—smart people. In Russia, *Siloviki* is not brain but muscle, which is more important than brain. Dmitry has muscle."

"You mean Dmitry has money," I said.

"No, that is in America. If you have money here, you have muscle. In Russia, you need *blat*. It means—access—you know—network. Dmitry has access to Vova, so he has a lot of muscle."

"Does Dmitry have access to the Russian mafia?"

"Yes. He is friends with the *Vory V Zakone*, just like he is friends with Vova. They all work together."

I felt a shiver run down my bare spine. At that moment, I was acutely aware that the person before me—naked, beautiful, composed, and assured—could address the world's most potent dictator and holder of the largest nuclear arsenal on earth simply as "Vova."

"So, Dmitry is Putin's bagman," I said snidely.

"No, Dmitry does not carry Vova's purse, but he is part of his choir."

I smiled. Her ability to refine an American colloquialism was delightful.

"I don't think I'll tell Bo what I'm learning about Dmitry. It's too unsettling."

"I think you won't tell Bo many things," she said with raised eyebrows and a beckoning smile.

"Do you want to finish the game?" I asked, nodding toward the Scrabble board.

"I don't think so," she pouted playfully. "Perhaps you have a better idea."

And I did.

CHAPTER THIRTY-TWO

Rome, Monday

I PULLED MYSELF FROM THE WARMTH OF THAT MEMORY to confront Bo's face, which reflected a brewing emotional storm. Regret clung to me like clammy sweat. In the tense silence that followed my revelation about Natalya, I feared I had shattered our friendship. An unspoken plea for understanding hung between us, and I braced myself, ready for the impending assault. In Bo's world, infidelity was the greatest sin—perhaps even worse than murder.

"What the fuck is wrong with you!" he yelled. Bo didn't yell at me often, so it caught me off balance even though I was prepared.

"It's not your business," I said quietly.

"Damn you, it's not my business!" he shouted. "I'm your best friend, and you don't tell me you're screwing around—with our goddamn partner! Our goddamn chairperson!"

"Calm down," I said.

Over the past two years, I'd watched Bo struggle with guilt. He'd witnessed me kill Natalya's nephew; he was complicit in my crime. Although Bo didn't pull the trigger, he shared the burden of culpability, and I occasionally sensed his resentment. We didn't discuss it much, but I felt his bitterness linger.

While his quiet, angry days had grown further apart, I still worried about relapses. He now steadied his breath and lowered his voice, his face a distorted mask; one eye swollen nearly shut, the other a bloodshot moon, and his lips taut as a bowstring.

"And Dmitry knows about it?" He threw his arms into the air.
"Yes."

"Bloody hell, Marty!" He huffed as if the game had ended and he'd played every down. Then, abruptly, he fell silent.

After a minute of heavy breathing, he said, "Dmitry said, 'Love is evil.' He actually said that." He began to pace between the couches. "Who talks like that? I feel like I'm in a depraved rom-com. Love is evil—love is blind—love is a many-splendored thing! What's next? All you need is love?" He punctuated his rant with the iconic descending drumbeats of the classic song—"Ba-ba-da-dee-DUM."

I let him pace and vent. He was on a roll, shock driving him to attack me with venomous sarcasm. But I could sense that the intensity of his anger, like the reverberations of a crash cymbal, would wane with each rhetorical gust. But then Bo's red eye narrowed. He'd suddenly had a new thought.

"What was going on last night? What was that all about? Were you going to cheat on Natalya while already cheating on Abbie?" He slapped his hand to his forehead, wincing from the sudden movement. "Were you doubling down? Who are you—and what have you done with my friend?"

He slumped onto the couch, drained of outrage.

To align with his anger and ease the tension, I muttered, "I'll probably burn in hell for this."

He sighed, releasing the last remnants of his anger. "It's not hell if you enjoy the burn, Marty."

We sat in silence for a moment. The verbal barrage was over. Then he asked, "Natalya? Really?"

"It just happened," I answered, sitting on the opposite couch.

"You know, Marty, the grass isn't always greener on the other side. Sometimes, it's fake."

"Nothing fake about this, Bo."

"I carry all your secrets, buddy. I don't want to carry this one. This one's too heavy."

"Cheating on Abbie is heavier than shooting Vasili?" I asked, puzzled.

"The killing was justified—the cheating is not. You were protecting Abbie. Now you're just hurting her."

"You want to keep lathering me up with guilt?" Now it was my turn to vent.

"Damn right! If it gets you to end it. Listen, Marty. The hardest thing sometimes is figuring out what bridge to cross and what bridge to burn." He paused. "Natalya is the bridge to burn." He rubbed his left hand over his ribs.

"What is this Dmitry thing? He knows. You know he knows. Natalya's in the middle. Is this some perverse threesome?"

"Nothing gets past you, does it," I said.

"Don't make me laugh. My ribs are killing me, and if you make me laugh, I'll be pissed."

"More than you already are?"

"Yes, you asshole."

An hour later, I received a text from Dmitry. It said: Hotel Raphael—dinner—8:00 p.m.

/////////////////////////////////

As we crossed the black brick of *Largo Febo*, a narrow side street branching off Piazza Navona, the percussion of our shoes echoed against the hard surface. Our obliging night manager, Vincenzo, had let us out through the alley entrance to the Michelangelo, and we quickly split up, each choosing winding back roads and narrow alleys to shake off any potential followers. I hustled past countless tightly parked cars and scooters, often ducking between them to wait and see if anyone was following me. No one was. Eventually, I reconnected with Bo in the bustling piazza, where we blended into the crowd before slipping into the side street that led to our destination.

The sight of the Hotel Raphael sent a chill down my spine. Known for its cascading vines of lush English ivy, bursting through the city's stoic stone like a spring bloom, the hotel was now draped in skeletal tendrils that hung like a tangle of witch's hair. A winter bleakness seeped from its ancient facade. I shivered as we entered.

The small lobby showcased vintage grandeur—worn Persian rugs sprawled beneath grey leather furniture accented with dark polished oak. The long, narrow reception desk, blockaded by several departing guests, was flanked by brass angel heads severed at the neck—macabre custodians of a previous era. Elegance was tucked into every corner.

I spotted Dmitry's translator, Valya, against a far wall, sitting in a plush antique chair with a sign over it that read *Louis XIV Bergère: DO NOT SIT.* I recognized his handsome Russian face from a previous video conference and gently elbowed Bo, who was absorbed by the commotion at the front desk.

As Valya came across the lobby to shake our hands, he expelled air from puckered lips. "They got you good," he said, looking at Bo.

"What's going on?" asked Bo, ignoring the comment and pointing at the pool of tourists surrounding the reception desk in animated chatter with the desk clerks.

"They are the last of the departing guests. We've emptied the hotel for safety."

"How do you empty a hotel?" I asked.

"We told everyone that inspectors found a small infestation from the ivy, and the entire building must be sprayed before infesting the neighboring buildings. It's January, so the hotel is not very full. We made it easy on the guests by moving them to another five-star hotel for the remainder of their stay at our expense."

"Wow," said Bo. "And they didn't even have to lose their underwear."

Valya squinted, not understanding, and Bo said, "Never mind."

We followed Valya to the elevator, and I thought about our

upcoming conversation with Dmitry. We had to get Natalya back, but we also needed to distance ourselves from the Chiurazzi. How much fight was left in us? A professional, polite "No," or a hand around the throat, kick-to-the-teeth "No"?

We took the Raphael's oak-lined elevator to the fifth floor. When the doors slid open, a large man in a dark-tailored suit—looking like a professional wrestler attending a wedding—blocked our exit. As soon as he recognized Valya, he moved aside, allowing us to pass.

"We're going to be sitting outside on the terrace," said Valya. "It's closed this time of year, but Dmitry assured me we would all be comfortable. He prefers sitting outside."

"All?" asked Bo.

"Yes. Dmitry has brought a friend, and more are coming. He will explain." Then he chuckled. "Or he will talk, and I will explain."

To get to the restaurant, we passed through a tunnel-like corridor and ascended a narrow staircase leading up to what seemed to be the building's attic. At its entrance, guarded by another imposing wrestler, we stepped out onto a multi-tiered roof. In a far corner, silhouetted by the dome of Santa Maria della Pace and St. Peter's Basilica glowing on the dark horizon, sat two men at a round table encircled by tall heater lamps.

Neither of them looked up or waved. Although Bo and I were one level above and thirty yards away, I felt the intensity of their conversation. I glanced at Bo, who was as relaxed as always. Even though he looked like a beat-up old boxer, he still radiated a confidence that warmed me for the coming confrontation.

"If he says 'Love is evil' again, I'm going to puke," whispered Bo from the side of his mouth.

"Me too," I whispered back.

CHAPTER THIRTY-THREE

IT FASCINATES ME HOW MENTAL IMAGES CAN SHIFT. When I finally stood before Dmitry Chernyshevsky, bathed in the soft red glow of heating lamps and patio lights, it felt like I was seeing him for the first time despite our previous video conversations. I had always imagined him taller; instead, he was nearly two inches shorter than me. His large, expressive eyes flickered beneath heavy lids, making it hard to tell if they were grey or green, but they hinted at a thoughtful observation. His face was soft and round, framed by a short, groomed beard the color of my golden retriever. His thick lips pursed together when he smiled as if to hide his perfectly set teeth. His hair was cut so short it required no attention. He projected a pleasant vibe that seemed unintentional, and I thought about what Natalya had said about him. He didn't look hard to me at all—he looked plush.

His companion stood in stark contrast. As I shook his tattooed hand, I was reminded of a familiar phrase—"built like a brick shit house." His body was a massive square of beef and muscle, with the pulpy face of a pugilist. Ink peeked over the top of his buttoned shirt.

His name was Sergei Sidorov. When he smiled, I could tell half his teeth were fake from the color difference. His close-shorn hair reminded me of my first day in boot camp when I was dubbed a "pinger" because my scalp had been buzzed to a near-metallic sheen. He smelled of cigarettes—not fine tobacco, but that acrid reek from cheap Turkish sticks.

There were blankets on our seats, but we ignored them. The heat lamps created a wall against the crisp night air.

"How is the damage?" asked Dmitry, looking at Bo with no discernible pity.

"Worse than it looks," said Bo, and Sergei laughed.

"You will stay here now," said Dmitry, sitting with Valya on his right and Sergei on his left. It wasn't a request, but it also wasn't an order. It was simply a statement of fact.

"We have luxury suites at the Michelangelo," responded Bo. "Everything is comped."

"There is no security there. Your throats will look like your clothes." Dmitry arched his right eyebrow, which felt like a signal that the discussion had ended. He began tapping his right forefinger on the table, the way I bounce my knee when I'm nervous or impatient.

"Is this your hotel, Dmitry?" I asked.

He responded in Russian, and Valya said, "Yes. It is a small museum with beautiful paintings, sculptures, and Picasso ceramics. Audrey Hepburn stayed here when she filmed *Roman Holiday*. But it needs repair. I will sell it soon."

"Have you contacted the Di Lupos?" I pressed.

"No, Marty." Dmitry continued in Russian, and Valya said, "It is not common anymore to kidnap people. It was popular in the seventies and eighties but is now an obsolete technique. It was probably done because things are moving too fast for the Di Lupos, and they ran out of options."

"They can let her go," said Bo. "They can have the Chiurazzi."

"*Nyet!*" snapped Dmitry. "You must stop talking like that."

His English was quite good when he wanted it to be, and his gaze, like a cat assessing a trapped bird, could disarm or devour in equal measure.

"Let's talk about what is necessary," said Sergei, speaking for the first time. "One, give me all your phones. I will give you new ones.

Two, don't return to the hotel. The rooms are probably bugged. My men will go and check you out. Three, no more taxis, no more walking, no more sightseeing. You will stay at this hotel behind guards."

Bo and I exchanged glances. His eyes flashed, and my instinct was to duck and take cover.

Bo smiled at Sergei like he was sizing up a nose tackle before the snap. With a firm cadence, he said, "I don't know you, Sergei. I'm sure you mean well, but don't tell us what to do, where to go, or where to stay. OK?"

I grinned idiotically, appreciating having Bo as my ally—like owning a Doberman who growls on cue.

Sergei smiled, too, looking uncomfortable. Dissent was foreign to him.

At that moment, a black-jacketed *cameriere* appeared carrying two bottles. He poured eighteen-year-old Macallan for Bo and me while Dmitry and Sergei received what looked like an expensive Barolo.

"I know you are Scotch men," said Dmitry, his finger still drumming.

"I would have preferred the Barolo," I mumbled.

"Leave the wine," said Dmitry, and Valya poured Bartolo Mascarello into my wine goblet. The *cameriere* announced that the chef would be serving in the next few minutes and then slipped away as quietly as he'd come.

"Bo, you need to understand something important now," said Valya. "I already know what Dmitry will tell me to say. He will say, I invited Sergei to Rome to help me get Natalya back. Without question, Sergei dropped everything and flew here in less than four hours. So, you will be polite and respectful to him. You should also know Sergei Sidorov is *Pakhan* of the *Solntsevo Bratva*, Moscow's biggest *Vory* brotherhood. He commands over a thousand men. You are still sitting in your chair and not lying in a puddle of blood because you are my guest, and Sergei is being polite—as you should be. Yes?"

Neither Bo nor I said anything in response. For the next few minutes, we sat in silence. My stomach growled, but not from hunger. Dmitry's restless finger tap had a disquieting staccato pulse, like he was mentally counting his money one dollar at a time.

The food arrived. Suffice it to say Dmitry ate like a billionaire: carpaccio of red tuna and crab on black lettuce for *antipasto*; truffle and ricotta-filled pasta for the *primo*; langoustine risotto with mushrooms for the *secondo*; blood orange granita for *intermezzo*; and lavender crème brûlée covered with blackberry compote for dessert.

"I do not eat meat in January," said Dmitry.

I couldn't enjoy any of it. My mind and my stomach frequently argued; typically, my stomach won, but at that moment, it was in severe torment, not just over Natalya but also over our precarious future, which looked increasingly grave.

Dmitry spoke mostly through Valya, focusing on his meal instead of juggling between languages. He asked us to detail our visit with Cardinal Bertolini, Cardinal Rautan, and bank president Angelo Caloia. Then, he wanted me to describe my derailed dalliance with Spina Paulo. Unlike Bo, Dmitry showed no curiosity about why I'd invited a strange woman to my room. In his world, there were always women waiting in his room.

Sergei asked us about the Di Lupo thugs. He grinned when I called them Porn Guy and Tadpole. I thought, *He would enjoy killing them*, and was not disgusted by the notion. I asked him about his excellent English; he said he'd been self-taught. I raised my glass to salute him.

The *cameriere* kept bringing bottles of Barolo, and I drank as if it were an obligation. After finishing my fourth glass, Bo quietly nudged my goblet out of reach, prompting me to switch to water. Over the years of our friendship, we'd learned to signal each other when the alcohol began to cloud our judgment. We were both heavy drinkers. I often wondered if I wasn't flirting with alcoholism, but I preferred to think of it as an open relationship.

"We know it's not the Chiurazzi you want; it's the bank account. But is it important enough to risk Natalya?" I asked, filled with the Dutch courage equivalent to a bottle of Barolo.

Still working on his brûlée, Dmitry spoke quietly while Valya translated. "This is not about Natalya; it is about Russia. I love my country. I am a patriot. It has made me and my friends rich. There are thirty-one of us in Moscow now—the most billionaires in any city. But we all understand Mother Russia is not a friendly place to keep money. It has a talent for misplacing its citizens' wealth." He stopped to drink wine, and Valya did the same.

I thought, *Can the ventriloquist make the dummy talk while drinking?*

"Do you know how many people have climbed Mount Everest?" Valya continued disjointedly.

Bo and I shook our heads.

"About two thousand. Do you know how many of them died? About two hundred. Most died on the way down, not on the way up. There is great danger after you reach the top. I call it *Paradoks Vershiny*—the Summit Paradox. You need a plan for it."

Dmitry then continued directly, saying, "Marty, Bo—the bank account is my insurance against the summit paradox. You understand?"

"But we don't belong in the middle of this, Dmitry," said Bo. "Our lives could be destroyed if we were caught laundering money."

Sergei Sidorov stood and said he needed to use the toilet. I figured he just wanted to smoke one of his Turkish cigarettes. Dmitry's meticulously groomed face distorted slightly as he leaned forward, drumming his fingers faster. I worried it was the tremor before the quake.

"You think I'm a laundryman?" he asked bluntly. "You think it wise to insult me?"

Valya leaned back, silent. His master was speaking.

I sobered up instantly, feeling a fist tighten in my stomach.

"I move my money. I don't wash it. My money is as clean…" Dmitry hesitated, scanning the table, "…as this tablecloth. You understand?"

Bo and I didn't respond. I glanced discreetly at the tablecloth, its smattering of ruby stains mapping the journey of empty wine bottles.

"You mistake yourselves for important," Dmitry continued as Valya scraped the remains of his crème brûlée. "You have nice little company. I have hundred little companies. I forget their names. My lawyers and employees tell me what they are. You understand?"

Bo and I stayed silent.

"Paladin—*malen'kaya zvezda v bol'shom sozvezdii.*"

Valya jumped in and translated, "Is a small star in a large constellation."

Dmitry stopped drumming, extended his forefinger, and pointed it at us like a weapon. He continued in Russian.

"Paladin is a tiny blink in a black sky," said Valya. "If I turn it off, no one will notice. Your company lives because I want Natalya to be happy. She has a toy to play with. But then—suddenly—without planning or intention, your company became important in a much bigger enterprise. It advanced from a blink to…"

"A nova," interrupted Bo.

"*Da!*" said Dmitry, slapping the table's top.

"When opportunity and company collide," I said.

"Did you trade away Dante's Raphael painting for it?" asked Bo.

Dmitry didn't skip a beat. He responded fiercely, "It is not Dante's Raphael. It is mine. I bought a *monastyr'* near Milan and will rebuild it into hotel. I sent Bertolini the painting, *znak priznatel'nosti.*"

"Token of appreciation, a thank you gift," translated Valya. "Here, it is called a *favor.* At home, it is called *smazka*—lubrication."

"In America, it's called a bribe," I said.

Valya paused as if Dmitry had said something he didn't want to translate. Then he looked at me hard and said, "Be careful, Martin. Just because we share some things does not make us friends."

"This deal could get Natalya killed," I said.

"You think I can't protect Natalya?" Dmitry snorted.

"She's not here for dinner," I pointed out, aware of the thinning ice I was on.

"We are all born to die," said Dmitry with the stoicism of a worn Russian proverb.

"And I am here to make sure it will *not* be Natalya," added Sergei, a pungent smell of smoke wafting past us. Dmitry spoke to him in Russian while Sergei looked at us like we were schoolchildren assigned to a time-out.

"Here is what will happen now," continued Valya, speaking for Dmitry. "I will leave. I have other work to do. You will do what Sergei tells you to do. He will deal with the Di Lupos. More men will arrive."

"Speaking of more men, why did you send Brody Lynch to threaten us?" I asked. I could see Valya suppressing his surprise.

"How did he threaten you?" asked Dmitry.

"He said he would kill me if we walked away from the Chiurazzi."

Dmitry showed his brilliant teeth and gave a loud snort. "Hah! Brody is good man." Then he converted to Russian, and Valya jumped in, saying, "Brody works for me in London. When Natalya came to Capri, she told me what happened to Dante. I sent Brody to protect you. He knows what you look like, so he can find you and keep an eye on you."

"He threatened to kill me."

Dmitry shrugged. "Brody is *primitivnyy*."

"Primitive," Valya interjected.

"Yeah, I got that." I exhaled and asked listlessly, "Can't we just talk to the Di Lupos?"

"And say what?" asked Sergei.

"Tell them to release Natalya before all hell breaks loose."

"You think hell has not broken loose? It is still locked up?" challenged Dmitry.

I stared at him, speechless.

Sergei jumped in, the scent of his cigarette hovering between us. "In Russia, we say *plokhoy nachalo imeyet plokhoy konets*—a bad beginning has a bad end."

Dmitry pressed on without his interpreter. "The Di Lupo people started this, and I will end it. I don't talk. I don't negotiate." He paused and leaned forward a little. "I don't offer salvation to the damned."

Why do Russians say stuff like that?

His persistent finger drumming clashed with the dull ache in my stomach. Our dinner was the longest I'd spent with Dmitry, and it was evident he was easier to take in small helpings. He was a contradiction—a plutocrat with the soul of a street thug, moving through the world with the quiet confidence of a king. He wasn't unpleasant, but his short fuse left me feeling neck-deep in eggshells. It was impossible to relax under those conditions. Bo was quieter than usual, which I took as a sign that he felt the same way.

Finally, Dmitry checked his platinum Patek Philip and said his helicopter at *Ciampino* airport was ready to take him back to Capri. He came around and shook our hands, told us again to follow Sergei's instructions, and assured us he would stay in touch until Natalya was safely returned. Then he and Valya left, leaving Sergei and the two dapper wrestlers with us.

To my great relief, the words "love is evil" never crossed his lips.

CHAPTER THIRTY-FOUR

SERGEI STARED AT HIS WATCH. "Tonight, you will call the Di Lupo woman and ask to meet her for breakfast at 10 a.m."

"What?" I asked.

"I will take care of all details."

A cool smirk curled his lips as he said something in Russian that sounded familiar. He translated, and my blood ran cold, remembering what Vasili had once said to me: "Big thieves hang little thieves."

"Do not take no for an answer," he continued.

"You don't want me to suggest a specific location?"

"No, that will bring suspicion. I don't care where you meet as long as it is a public place with open doors."

"Isn't it too late to call her?"

"Are you afraid you will wake her up? Hurt her feelings?"

Point made.

I didn't call right then. Instead, I followed Bo to his room and stared at my phone.

"I hate doing this."

"You got a better idea?" asked Bo.

I dialed Spina's number and put it on speaker.

"*Pronto.*"

"Hello, Spina, this is Marty Schott."

"How are you, Marty? It's late."

"I missed you at breakfast," I said.

"Yes. I saw you were busy talking to someone and decided not to interrupt."

She'd seen me with Brody.

"I want to try again. I'm interested in what you had to tell me about Leo."

"I'm not sure you will care anymore," she answered.

"Well, I want to see you again anyway," I insisted, nervous she might not agree to see me.

"You want to show me your suite again?" She was being artificially coy.

"No, I want to talk."

"About what, Marty?"

"About Natalya."

"Yes, that makes sense."

"Do you prefer that I call you Spina or Gemma?"

"My friends call me Spina."

"I think we can resolve our issues over coffee—Gemma."

She paused over the snub. "I think so too, Marty, but you should leave your friend at home."

"Bo?"

"No, the man sitting with you this morning. He looked like a bodyguard."

"I don't have a bodyguard, Gemma."

We agreed to meet at 10 a.m. at Trecaffè Due Macelli, on *Via Dei Due Macelli.*

"You won't get lost," she said. "Start at the Spanish Steps; walk south for five minutes; it will be on your left; you can't miss it. Remember to come alone."

"I'll go with you," said Bo after I hung up.

"You look like you played the Superbowl without a helmet," I said with an exasperated exhale.

"Flattery will get you everywhere," he said, grinning.

"She said no friends."

I left him to rest and found Sergei sitting with one of the wrestlers in the lobby. After giving him the address of the meeting restaurant, I retired to my new room, which would have been impressive at any other time but felt like a downgrade after the suite at the Michelangelo.

Near midnight, one of the wrestlers knocked on my door, carrying my luggage filled with my new clothes. He had gone to the Michelangelo and checked me out. I wondered what Vincenzo thought.

///

In the morning, after zero sleep, I found Bo in Relais Picasso, the snug lobby restaurant of the Hotel Raphael. It had a dozen tables and a gleaming steel counter buffet that threatened to restore a pound or two to my shrinking frame.

The place, populated with enormous burly men, looked like a weightlifter's locker room but smelled of pastries and espresso instead of sweat and talcum. I found Bo sitting alone, looking considerably better than the night before. The swelling around his eye had abated, allowing him to blink again, but it still showed as purple as plums.

"Is this seat taken?" I quipped, sitting down.

"Only 'til my date shows," responded Bo.

"What the hell is happening here?" I asked, scanning all the sheared and inked skulls that marked Sergei's soldiers.

"They came in overnight. I think Sergei plans to fill the hotel."

Two men at an adjacent table studied us, nodded sullenly, and returned to eating. Their tattoos painted a graffiti mural of their lives.

"'Hell is empty,'" Bo quoted Shakespeare, "'and all the devils are here.'"

"They're not devils," I said, lowering my voice to barely a whisper. "Natalya told me once they're called *gopniks*—men who hang on street corners and wear cheap tracksuits." My head rotated. "Jesus! They're arriving like kids to summer camp."

"You and I had different childhood experiences," Bo deadpanned.

"The Di Lupos are in deep shit," I said. "The *Solntsevo Vory* is more powerful than any local Camorra family. This bunch operates globally, while the Di Lupos operate locally. Gemma thinks she's part of a dangerous clan, but this crew will gut them like Friday's fish."

"What do you want to do, Marty?" asked Bo.

"I want to knock sense into Gemma, so she releases Natalya, and everyone goes to their respective corner."

"Oh, grasshopper," Bo sighed. "It's too late for that. They tore a fingernail off of Dmitry Chernyshevsky's girlfriend. I'm guessing that's the equivalent of a kick in the balls for him. I'll bet he told Sergei to go scorched earth. Leave nothing standing—man, woman, child, pet."

"You don't start a war over a torn nail," I said, a little too loud.

"It's not the nail, Marty. It's not even Natalya. It's Dmitry. No one does this to *him*." He took a deep breath. "We have to get out."

"We already agreed on that."

"No, I mean out. Out of it all. Paladin if necessary."

And that was the first time I heard Bo look for an exit.

Two years earlier, in a moment of prescience, still buzzed from celebrating our new alliance with Dmitry and Natalya, he had said, "We better not fail."

He'd been right, of course.

Our decision to team up with Natalya and Dmitry had been hazardous but born of desperation. We thought we could manage the risks—the potential blowback—like powdermen on a drill site.

We'd learned instead that when it comes to washing money, it's not the grime that gets you—it's the shine.

CHAPTER THIRTY-FIVE

Rome, Tuesday, January 20th

LEAVING OUR BREAKFAST TABLE, Bo and I followed the flow of *gopniks* into the lobby. A group of them surrounded Sergei, and when he saw us, he pushed through to come over.

"Bo, you will stay here. Do not leave the hotel." He spoke like a coach addressing his team before the big game. Unlike dinner the night before, Bo stayed silent.

"Marty, you will come with me. If you do as I tell you, you will not be hurt. Understand?"

I nodded.

"You will arrive a few minutes late," he continued. "They will know you're coming because they have someone following you. You will not see the person, but we will. The walk is maybe five—six minutes. You will walk on right side. The coffee shop is on left side. When you get close, the Di Lupo woman will see you. You will wave to her, and she will relax. Then you will slow your steps. Walk slowly, like—a strangler."

"Straggler," I corrected.

"Yes, good. When you see my men act, walk quickly into any shop. It is a street where people spend money and has many stores. You understand?"

I nodded obediently. "What will you do?"

"I will invite the woman to come with me. The Raphael is a five-star hotel. She will like it here."

I looked at Bo. His raccoon eyes were blank. I couldn't tell if he was relieved he wasn't joining me or the opposite.

"I guess I'm not the only one who got no sleep. How'd you pull all this together in just seven hours—at night?" I shook my head, trying to process it.

For a moment, Sergei looked insulted. "I'm a professional," he responded. "Now, I have a taxi waiting to take you to the Spanish Steps. The driver is mine. After I pick up the woman, you can step back on the street, and my driver will pick you up. It might take a few minutes. If you must walk, then walk back the way you came. Yes?"

"Yes."

Sergei's shirt collar was open, and I could see his tattoos dancing along his neck as he spoke.

"If something goes wrong, do not speak to anyone. You are a tourist. You are shopping. You know nothing. You understand this, yes?"

"This is crazy," I muttered.

"Marty," he said sternly. "They have Natalya. Be angry about that. Stop looking like *shavka*—little dog—look like *bol'shaya sobaka*—big dog. It is better."

He walked over to his men and continued giving instructions in Russian.

"OK, big dog, let's get you on your way," said Bo.

Walking toward the exit, my eyes bulged, pupils dilating like a camera lens. Strolling into the Hotel Raphael was Brody Lynch. I heard the air leave Bo's lungs.

"Aye, Bo," he said, ignoring me. "Long time."

"Not long enough," said Bo.

"Christ! Your eye looks like the bottom of a pint-o-Guinness."

"You should see the other guy." Bo's lips curled briefly.

"I did. You broke his ankle. I gave 'em both a good seein' to—put a flea in their ear," he said with a slight wink.

"What?" Bo's head snapped back.

"I gave them two eejits a right spankin'."

"You were the third guy?" Bo gasped.

"You can thank me later," he grinned.

"Martin—*Yebát'*!?" Sergei shouted from across the lobby, raising his arm to display the large chrome watch strapped over his intricate sleeve tattoo. "*Vremya!*"

///////////////////////////////////

The cab dropped me off at the Piazza di Spagna ten minutes before I met with Gemma. I walked south along *Via Dei Due Macelli*. The morning sun was warm again, as it had been every day since our arrival. Traffic was light, and I strolled leisurely, biding my time to arrive a little late. I wondered if it ever rained in Rome. I wondered if Brody Lynch would kill me. I wondered how much Natalya was suffering.

Walking away from the expansive piazza, the street gradually narrowed to a single lane, flanked by parked cars tightly aligned on either side. The shade from the constricting buildings shrouded the black bricks, giving the road a dull luster.

I scanned my reflection in the store windows, hoping to spot someone following me, but no one stood out among the early morning shoppers. As I approached my destination, my heart began to pound. Its beat had been surprisingly steady most of the morning—numbed, I'm sure, by the many shocks it had already endured.

I recognized Gemma sitting at one of four small tables outside the restaurant, her signature red lips animated in conversation with Porn Guy, who was seated beside her and heavily bruised. I waved at them casually and shortened my stride. I was about forty yards and half a minute away from unalterable bedlam.

In the distance, a large man dressed in black walked toward me on the opposite side of the street. I knew things had begun. As he moved along the row of parked cars, he neared a white BMW close to the small fenced-in patio where Gemma and Porn Guy were seated. Swiftly, he pulled on his wool beanie, transforming it into a ski mask.

In perfect synchrony, five more men in black ski masks surged out of an arched door next to Trecaffè Due Macelli. Like bowling balls cascading down an alley, they encircled Gemma's table. A high-pitched scream punctured the street's ambient hum, and I cut hard into a woman's clothing boutique. Peeking out the window, past a headless mannequin draped in a delicate rose chemise, I watched a grey van screech to a halt.

The man outside the BMW raised a gun to its window and fired a single shot. A scream erupted, momentarily drowned out by the gunfire. The five masked men stormed the table; three of them grabbed Gemma, roughly covering her head with a black hood and dragging her to the back of the van. The other two men, their backs turned to me, did something to Porn Guy that I couldn't see until they stepped away. I then recognized the handle of a screwdriver—or perhaps an ice pick—protruding from his ear. A second shot thundered, and Porn Guy's head jolted sideways, where it remained. I wondered briefly if the BMW driver, face obscured by the reflecting windshield, was Tadpole. Either way, he and Porn Guy were dead, the first of many to be killed.

I can't say it upset me much, but watching it was still gruesome and disturbing. Wishing them dead was easier than seeing them die.

Screams erupted from every direction. Thrashing and squealing, Gemma was swallowed up by the van, followed by all six men. The van then sped off before the doors were even shut.

The whole thing took about twenty seconds.

Shrieking customers poured out of the coffee shop and neighboring stores, scattering everywhere. The owner of the clothing shop darted past me into the street. She raised her hand to her mouth and let out a howl. Stepping out behind her, I hurried away. She never laid eyes on me.

I didn't follow Sergei's instructions. I took different streets, deliberately avoiding his driver. I didn't want to be found. I needed to be alone—to think. Things were escalating at a pace I couldn't absorb. Five days ago, I arrived in Rome imagining an amorous romp with Natalya mixed with sightseeing, fattening dinners, and exquisite wine.

I'd just abetted a woman's kidnapping in broad daylight, not to mention a dead driver and another guy wearing an ice pick in his ear.

Wars don't always begin with roaring cannons.

Sometimes, they announce themselves with just a scream.

CHAPTER THIRTY-SIX

A COUPLE OF HOURS AFTER THE ABDUCTION, I returned to Hotel Raphael, its flowing tresses of naked vines looking more and more like suspended razor wire. I'd walked the streets of Rome listening to police sirens slicing through the prosaic city noise. I got lost twice but wandered into random *paninoteche*; each time, someone was happy to put me back on the right path using broken English and a considerable amount of vigorous finger-pointing.

As soon as I arrived, Sergei, pacing in the lobby, grabbed my elbow and pulled me into the hotel manager's office. I passed Bo, who stood with Brody and a group of men, some of whom were likely the six responsible for the killings and kidnapping.

"You listen to me, you arrogant little pants-pisser," he said, breathing a lungful of Turkish tobacco into my face. "My men have come a long way to get your girlfriend back. They could die or be thrown in prison if it goes wrong. You did not wait for my driver. I called your phone many times, but no answer. We are all waiting here because you are missing. We don't know what happened. Maybe someone grabbed you. Maybe cops picked you up."

Suddenly, with a snarl, Sergei grabbed an ashtray off the office desk and hurled it toward me. The miss was deliberate; it shattered against the wall over my left shoulder. "The next time you do not follow my orders, I will kill you myself and tell Dmitry you had an accident. You understand?"

I reached into my pockets. They were empty, and for the first time I realized in my nervous preoccupation I'd left my phone in my room that morning. I had wandered the city because my brain was in a numbed trance. I'd folded myself into an insulated shroud, seeking sanctuary from the screaming. It never occurred to me that anyone was worried about me.

"I'm sorry," I said.

"*Otvali!*—Piss off!" he answered, storming out of the room, leaving the door open. I could see everyone in the lobby staring at me. I hung my head in shame, trying to hide the scarlet tide creeping up my neck.

"Jesus Christ, Marty," said Bo, walking up to me. "I thought you'd been kidnapped."

"I wasn't thinking," I said. "I'm new at this."

"So am I."

"I need a drink," I said.

He looked at his watch. "It's not even noon."

"What's your point?" I asked.

////////////////////////////////////

I learned to drink in the mornings during Vietnam—scotch was my coffee. I was stationed at Udorn, a base tucked deep in the northern jungles of Thailand. It served as the headquarters for Air America, also known as the CIA, and housed more F4 fighters than any other base in the region. The local Thais ran the Udorn NCO (Noncommissioned Officers) Club, but their alcohol sales took a hit on weekends when the base chapel offered free steak and beer after services.

Ever the savvy capitalists, the Thais countered with a cunning strategy: complimentary scotch and water every Sunday morning. This clever move kept the base crowd flowing in for the rest of the day, and by mid-morning, regular pricing was back in effect.

Lines started forming before dawn.

Beautiful, nearly naked women strolled through the packed NCO club, balancing trays of small plastic cups filled with scotch and water—more water than scotch. Airmen snatched drinks off the trays by the handful. The scotch was blended, cheap, and diluted to the color of weak urine—but it was free, and there was no limit. It took me six to eight drinks before I even felt a buzz, and I'd usually down a dozen to make it worthwhile.

The running joke on base was that if Udorn had ever been attacked on a Sunday, the insurgents would've found nothing but drunks.

///

I followed Bo to the lobby bar. We pulled out every bottle of scotch we could find, starting with the most expensive. Brody Lynch and the other men followed while Bo, acting as bartender, poured.

I glared at Brody, knowing only he could have tattled to Sergei about the "pants-pissing."

"What are you doing here, Irishman?" I asked.

"Unscrewing your screwups," Brody said, downing a shot of Macallan in a single swallow. "I manage Mr. Chernyshevsky's properties in London."

I raised my glass in a sardonic toast. "We're so proud of you." I also threw back my drink and asked, "Where'd they take Gemma?"

"Top floor," he replied. "Locked down tight. Elevator and stairs are off-limits from the fourth floor up."

Sergei entered the bar and looked pleased that his men were drinking.

"We will call the Di Lupo brother now," he said.

"It's only been a couple of hours; how do you know he even knows what happened?" asked Bo.

"They had a man follow Marty from the Spanish Steps. We let him live. Trust me; they know."

///////////////////////////////////////

"*Ucciderò la tua donna prima di uccidere te, figlio di puttana!*"

"*Angliyskiy!*—English!"

"I will kill your woman before I kill you—you son of a bitch!"

"*Togda ya ub'yu tvoyu sestru, prezhde chem ub'yu tebya, sukin syn!*"

"*Englese!*—English!"

"I will kill your sister before I kill you—you son of a bitch!"

In the silence that followed, I kept my eyes on Sergei, who stayed unnervingly calm, like a poker player holding the winning hand. The phone sat on the coffee table between us—Bo and I in the wing chairs, Brody and Sergei on the couch, and a barrel-chested man, an Italian version of Sergei, seated against the far wall, as still as a sentry.

"Who is talking?" asked the voice on the other end of the line.

"Natalya's friend," said Sergei, assured and firm.

"Do you know who I am?" demanded the other voice.

"Cosimo Di Lupo," answered Sergei.

We heard murmuring—Cosimo had his hand over the phone.

"Where are Bo Bishop and Martin Schott?" Cosimo asked.

"I don't know," Sergei answered before we could.

"*Signore* friend, why are you at this table?" Cosimo pressed.

"I told you; Natalya Danilenko is my friend."

"Spina—Gemma is my sister," Cosimo shot back, his voice cold.

"Natalya is a *very* good friend," Sergei repeated evenly.

"You are Russian," said Cosimo.

"Yes."

"Natalya is Russian," Cosimo added.

"Yes."

"But her passport is American." Cosimo was trying to solve the puzzle.

"It is a small world, yes?" Sergei remained unfazed.

"*Siamo in stallo*—we have stalemate."

"I will trade with you," Sergei offered.

There was a pause, muffled sounds. "*Tornerò da te*—I will get back to you."

"Don't take long," Sergei replied.

"*Sarà a Napoli*," Cosimo said, meaning it would happen in Naples.

"*Khorosho*," Sergei responded, and I recognized the word— *Fine*—from hearing Natalya say it so often.

The line went dead silent, and I held my breath. Then, in a low, flat voice that sounded like he was sharing a secret, Cosimo asked, "Do you know what my family can do?"

"No," Sergei said placidly.

"Perhaps you should look me up," Cosimo suggested. "I am in all the papers."

"I don't read Italian," Sergei replied, then pressed the red button, hanging up.

I inhaled deeply, feeling disturbingly smug, gratified that my team—a murderous squad of *Vory* soldiers—had left the Di Lupos scared and confused. We were bigger, badder, bloodier. It was like rooting for the zombies in a horror movie.

"We need a plan for Naples," Sergei said to the large, silent man sitting against the wall, who now tilted his massive body forward like a shifting boulder.

"I am Raffaele Casertani," he introduced himself, his eyes lingering on Bo's drubbed face.

"I've read about you. You're the one fighting with the Di Lupos. They call you *il secessionista*—the secessionist," I said.

"*Si.*" He nodded curtly. "I am at war with the Di Lupos. I intend to kill them all."

CHAPTER THIRTY-SEVEN

STEEPED IN A CLOYING MIASMA OF MENACE, the Hotel Raphael had turned into a prison dayroom. Inked thugs were everywhere. The lobby bustled with their silent threat. Bo and I nodded curtly when we passed them, as if we were all in business together. It was surreal.

Sergei and Casertani were huddled in a room somewhere when a brawny *gopnik* told us we had a friend waiting in the lobby.

Leo Giacobbe was sitting in the same Louis XIV Bergère chair Valya had occupied just the night before—a lifetime ago.

Brody stood beside him, looking bored. "Here's your *grass*," he said, passing Leo over to us. "Casertani's guy at the Michelangelo saw he was checkin' out, so I picked him up."

Leo looked like he'd aged a decade. His silver-streaked hair lay akimbo, his normally pearly eyes bloodshot and wary.

"What do you mean Casertani has a guy at the Michelangelo?" asked Bo.

Brody shrugged and began to strut off with his typical swagger. I intercepted him and quietly asked, "What's a grass?"

Brody looked back at Leo. "The guy who snitches to the bad guys."

"Who are the bad guys?" I asked.

"Whoever is on the other side."

I returned to Bo, who held his finger to his lips, signaling Leo to keep his mouth shut. The three of us walked to the hotel's restaurant, Relais Picasso, which was empty now except for one table near the door occupied by three Italian men, most likely part of Raffaele Casertani's crew.

We selected the furthest table away from them.

"We think our rooms are bugged, so this is the best place to talk," I said.

"What is going on here?" asked Leo, sweeping his hand in a wide arc.

"We can spend the rest of the day answering that question," I said. "But first, where were you going? And second, where've you been?"

"I'm flying to the States," he started in a flurry. "I want out of Rome. I've been hiding. I did my job. I recruited you to buy the Chiurazzi. I lied and informed on you. It was unethical but not criminal. We'll never be friends, and I can live with that. Now, I want to be out of here. I will visit my daughter."

"I'm afraid you're stuck like the rest of us," said Bo. "At least until we get Natalya back."

"What are you talking about?" he stammered, and I realized Leo didn't know about the kidnapping—either one. He'd gone dark since we kicked him out of Bo's room after he admitted to collaborating with the Di Lupos.

In his typical stolid voice, Bo explained almost everything. The purse containing Natalya's fingernail, our dinner with Dmitry, Sergei Sidorov's assignment to get Natalya back, the retaliatory kidnapping of Gemma, and how she was now interned on the hotel's fifth floor.

Leo listened to Bo as if he were receiving a terminal diagnosis. He stared at the tabletop like it might reveal a secret cure. "You said your Dmitry guy wasn't mobbed up."

"He's not, but he's an oligarch…so he employs them," said Bo.

"I'm going to die. Either Gemma or Natalya will kill me," he moaned.

Fair enough—he was right on both counts.

"We don't know why this Raffaele Casertani guy is here," I said.

"He wants to kill Di Lupos, but we're not sure why he's involved with us. He and Sergei are very chummy."

"The Casertanis were allied with the Di Lupos," said Leo. "They were the second most powerful clan inside the organization. When the oldest kid, Cosimo, took over from his father, he changed the organizational structure and reduced Casertani's power."

"How do you reduce a mafia clan's power?" asked Bo.

"Old man Mauro ran the empire like a franchise. He let other families control their little fiefdoms. The Casertanis controlled the business with Eastern Europe and Russia. The Di Lupos collected their percentage."

"Their *pizzo*," I said.

"Yeah, but then Cosimo demoted them to simple earners without territory power. Casertani got pissed and rebelled. He separated from the Di Lupos. Your Russian friends probably know him because he's been supplying them with drugs and counterfeit brands for years."

Brody Lynch, looking for us, laced his way through the tables. As he approached, Leo's stance stiffened with alarm.

"Gemma Di Lupo wants to speak with you," he said, pointing at me.

"That's my cue to go," said Leo, standing up. "I want no part of this."

"Not a bad idea," Bo agreed. "Let's you and I get a drink at the bar."

They left, and Brody sat down. It looked deliberate. I searched my mind for a conversation starter.

"How much is being reported on the news?" I asked.

"Only on the telly right now. The papers haven't come out yet. TV is reporting two men dead. One guy drivin' the BMW and one guy on the patio. They're holding back information about the woman."

"That makes sense. When did you start to work for Dmitry?" I asked.

"Two years ago. After Natalya told Chernyshevsky what happened in Portland. He flew me to Cyprus for an interview and offered me the job. Not the financial stuff, you understand. I'm no good at that. Just the physical stuff."

"There's a lot of physical stuff?"

"Yeah, dipshit—I shoot somebody every other Thursday. I have a quota."

I started to laugh, then pulled it back. I could never be friendly with Brody Lynch.

"Why is Casertani involved in this?" I asked.

He hesitated and looked around the empty restaurant. I realized this was why he'd sat down. "Repeat this, and I'll kill ye."

"You keep saying that; it's getting tiresome."

"Here's the thing of it." He breathed and expanded his chest. "As big as they are, the Moscow *Vory* can't fight a war in Italy. It don't make sense. They don't know the territory. They've got no allies, no base of operations, no spies; you get my point."

I nodded.

"If the Russian mafia wants to go to war in Italy, they gotta do it with other Italians. Sergei knows this. He also knows the Casertanis. They've been supplyin' the *Solntsevo Bratva* for years. When Chernyshevsky heard that Natalya'd been snatched, he called Sergei 'cause he's not just Sergei's *Krysha*—protector, he's his *Koresh*—buddy."

He lowered his voice to a stage whisper. "I think Chernyshevsky told Sergei to solve this problem, and by 'solve,' he meant forever. So, Sergei started thinkin' about how in the hell he could wipe out an entire Camorra clan."

"Wipe out the entire family? Seriously?"

"The Russian mafia is different than the Italian mafia. Over here, they fook around the edges. Kill a guy here, kill a guy there, send a warnin', spank a few of 'em, and then be done with it. In Russia, they wipe out your family, your extended family, and the neighborhood your family lived in. Italians think they're tough 'cause they'll grab a bull by its horns. The Russians don't grab at horns—they decapitate the bull and bury the head."

"Jesus!" I whispered.

"Sergei knows Casertani's got a feud brewin' with the Di Lupos. Casertani solves Sergei's problem, but only if he does it the Russian way, not the pussy Italian way. Chernyshevsky told Sergei and Casertani he'd fund the entire war against the Di Lupos: men, money, weapons, bribes, safe houses—whatever. Like cleanin' an oil spill usin' a flamethrower."

"That's nuts," I said, shaking my head. "Dmitry's strategy isn't scorched earth—it's *extinction*."

"Aye, but the operation must be a black secret—blacker than a raven's heart. Things could go tits up in a flash. If other clans find out the Di Lupos are fightin' Russians, they'll band together. Then it's not clan on clan anymore, but country on country. That gets Interpol involved, and the Russians are fightin' on foreign lands. So, Casertani gets Sergei's help and Chernyshevsky's money, but their involvement has to be buried deeper than nuclear waste. Even rumors need to choke and die."

"If you want a clandestine war, Napoli's the right city," I said.

"It ain't the war that'll be secret—it's who's doin' the wetwork."

We stood up simultaneously, and I was reminded how much bigger he was as I watched swells of muscles shift under the folds of his shirt.

"I'll cut off your dick and feed it back to ye in bite-size pieces if you repeat what I told ye. The Di Lupos—hell, the whole fooking world—must believe the Casertanis are actin' alone."

I didn't have to answer. We had enough history for our compact to be understood.

CHAPTER THIRTY-EIGHT

THE ELEVATOR TOOK ME ONLY TO THE 4TH FLOOR, so I climbed the stairs to the 5th. I passed two soldiers, one at each door. Gemma's hotel room was at the rear of the hotel corridor, facing the back alley. The same two wrestlers guarding Dmitry the night before sat in front of her door. I had no clue if they spoke English, but I said, "She wants to talk to me."

Neither of them replied. They stood and pulled their chairs away from the door. I knocked, immediately realizing it must have seemed amusing to them—it certainly was to me. When I received no welcoming reply, I opened the door and stepped inside.

Gemma's skin was as white as an altar cloth. The bold red lipstick was gone, leaving only a ghostly gloss on her thin, tightly pressed lips. Her knotted bun had come undone, with strands escaping like unraveled threads. The contours of her face resembled a smooth porcelain mask.

"*Chi cazzo sei*? Who are you?" she hissed as I shut the door behind me. "Do you have any idea how dead you're about to be?"

I looked around. The phones and TV were taken from the room. One-inch plywood was nailed over each of the two windows, and all the lights were on. Gemma's adrenaline kicked in the moment I entered. I let her pace and rant to work it off. I wondered if the two ursine enforcers outside the door could hear her. I felt no pity—not a drop. Though she was being held unharmed in a luxury hotel room, her goons had seized and brutalized Natalya in minutes, fueling a cold anger within me.

The fury on her face, expressed through the tension in her mouth, was a palpable force that pushed against me, and I leaned into it. She switched from English to Italian for peak profanity. Ironically, Americans swear more than Italians, but Italians have a virtual pantheon of swearing possibilities. She sputtered and steamed for another ten minutes before collapsing into a chair.

"I want Natalya back," I said with an even tone, proud of my control given my pounding heart and churning innards.

"She will be returned to you in several deliveries."

"Then I will throw you to the wolves." I pointed to the door.

"You can't *throw* me to the wolves, Marty," she said through a sneer. "They come when I call."

"Gemma—Spina, we can do this for hours, but it's tedious. We talked to your brother. We offered a trade."

"*Vaffanculo!*"

I headed for the door.

"Where are you going?"

"I've got better things to do than listen to you bitch about the same thing you did but worse." I took a beat and then said, "Drop dead!"

"Sit," she said, composing herself.

I avoided the bed and sat in the desk chair next to a large wall mirror, where I could see her reflection if she wanted to throw something at me.

"You won't believe me, but I'm trying to save you *and* Natalya."

I took the desk pad, wrote *The room is bugged*, and showed it to her. We stared at each other, the tension so thick it could bend light. I ripped the paper off the pad, folded it, and stuffed it into my pocket, and she sat down across from me.

"Tell me who you are," she said.

"I'm a businessman, and so is Bo. We're here to close on the

Chiurazzi Foundry in Naples. We came to Rome because Cardinal Bertolini and Angelo Caloia wanted to meet us."

"You're not *il sistema*? You're not connected to the *Casertani famiglia*?"

"Really? Look at me. Do I look like a *sistema* man to you? Do I even look Italian?"

She laughed—a subdued laugh, but still a laugh. "No. You look too soft and corporate to be Camorra. More like you spend weekends sailing, not brawling." She hesitated. "But taking me hostage is insane. I've been trying to figure it out all morning. I expected you to show up, pretend to be a tough guy, and tell me you were walking away from the Chiurazzi. I'd have had Natalya released and back in your bed before we finished breakfast. But—you kidnapped me! *Ma che cazzo*! That's not American business behavior."

I shrugged. "Is it Italian business behavior?"

"It is *sistema* behavior. That's why I want to know who you are. The men in the van spoke Russian."

She's getting there.

"Where is Ciro? Is he in another room?"

I guessed she was asking about Porn Guy. It hadn't occurred to me that she didn't know Sergei's men had jabbed an ice pick in his ear and shot her driver. She had a bag thrown over her head and was ignorant of what followed.

"I don't know," I lied.

"Natalya is Russian. Is this a *Vory* thing?"

I shrugged, avoiding a response. After Brody's warning, I didn't want to talk about Russians.

We sat in silence for a while. She felt no fear, likely because of her surroundings. Murderous kidnappers don't typically hold their victims in luxury hotel rooms, even if the windows were covered in plywood. I sensed she instinctively believed this was a quid pro quo arrangement, with her release just a matter of time.

Her breathing slowed, and she stared blankly at her hands resting in her lap. One of her nails had broken in the struggle, and she'd bitten off the loose end.

"We're in the Raphael?" she asked.

There was no point in lying; the hotel brand was everywhere. "Yes."

"Nice. Aren't you worried my family will find me?"

"No. If they do, they'd have to fight through four floors of the meanest motherfuckers you've ever seen. Your head would be tossed out the window before they reached the lobby."

She looked at me like she was staring into a dark hole. "Who the fuck are you?" she said, sighing.

We fell into another silence.

"How'd you get into our rooms at the Michelangelo that first night?"

"Ciro and Primo bribed one of the desk clerks for key cards. They told me it took a long time. Cutting clothes is not easy. But they had all day, so they enjoyed themselves."

"I'm happy we could provide some amusement to liven up their bleak little world."

Another lull hung between us.

"She's impressive," she said at last.

"Meaning?"

"Natalya. She's tough. My father would say, 'She carries the weight of invisible battles.'"

"You spent time with her?" I asked, self-consciously averting my eyes to give the question less weight.

"Yeah, she's feisty," she said, letting out a thoughtful scoff. "Ever notice how men are never described as feisty? Well, I think she's feisty."

"Like yourself," I said.

"*Si.*"

"But not like Cosimo."

"No, he's not feisty; he's just flash. My brother loves his fame.

He likes the women it buys. He's always been the pretty one in the family."

"Is he like your other brothers?" I asked. "You have plenty."

"One too few," she said mournfully.

"I heard about that."

"Cosimo is head of the family now. He is all showman—charisma has always been in short supply for my family, but what little there was, Cosimo stole all of it. It's a twisted fairy tale—Cosimo and the seven dwarfs."

"What's with your nickname?"

"I was born in the middle of my brothers. My father always said I was *la spina*—the thorn—in his garden of sons. It stuck, and I like it."

"Why'd your father retire?" I was looking for someone with influence.

"My father is a great man. He built an empire. He always gave back to the neighborhood. People said the difference between Mauro Di Lupo and a saint was that Mauro delivered the miracles faster."

"He's in hiding?"

"He's not hiding; he's in retreat. When my youngest brother, Antonio, died, my father concluded it was a message from God and he needed to make amends. He now lives in a room with peeling plaster. His only possessions are playing cards, cheap furniture, a TV, and cigarettes. When I visited him last, he was drying peppers on a newspaper for dinner."

"So, his brain is broken," I said, and she nodded in agreement.

I shifted the subject. "Why do you want the Chiurazzi?"

"I love art. I studied art. I'm never going to be head of my family. I want something of my own. I think it will give the family a new level of respect."

And then it hit me like a scream in a silent crowd.

She doesn't know about the bank account.

"Alessio Rosa works for you?" I asked.

"Not yet, but I told him he will."

"Did you follow me to the concert after-party?"

"No, I told Leo to take you there so I could meet you."

"Were you going to sleep with me?" I asked.

"Yes."

"Why?"

"Why not?"

"You're married."

"So are you."

She had me there.

"Why the hell didn't you just talk to me? Why the game?"

"It's not how things are done. *Omerta* has governed my family forever. To us, silence is discretion."

We talked sensibly for another fifteen minutes. I wanted her to understand that the Chiurazzi was out of her reach, regardless of Bo or me. I blamed Cardinal Bertolini and Angelo Caloia, carefully avoiding any mention of Natalya, Dmitry, or the Russians. I never mentioned the bank account, and neither did she. She insisted that the Di Lupos would ultimately take control, irrespective of who bought the foundry. If not from the outside, then from the inside. That was how *il sistema* worked; she'd never known a time when she didn't get what she wanted.

What she didn't realize was that each of her words were shovels of dirt on her grave. Sergei was listening, and I knew he would report to Dmitry that Spina would be a *thorn* in his side forever.

"I think I made a mistake," she said. "I took the wrong person. I wanted to take you!" She laughed, continuing, "I was going to persuade you into my car after meeting you at Rione del Fico, but you were sitting with your bodyguard, and I changed my mind."

She explained how she'd sent an older couple into the restaurant to scope it out, and they described Brody Lynch to her over the phone.

The local couple with the worn shoes.

She assumed he was the same guy who came to the rescue of Bo the night before and supposed we'd hired protection.

"Attacking Bo was a shit move," I said.

"Ciro and Primo wanted payback for Caffè Greco. I didn't tell them to assault anyone."

"You didn't tell them not to."

"Your bodyguard did a number on Ciro, and Bo broke Primo's ankle. He couldn't be at our meet this morning because his foot's in a cast."

Primo is Tadpole—and he wasn't the driver. Bo saved his life!

"You bugged our phones," I said, changing the subject.

"My *familia* owns a cellular store. We can set up a call-forwarding function. When you call someone, it first connects to our monitor before it rings the other number—but there's a little delay."

"I know."

"It's crude, and Natalya never used hers. We only heard the conversation when you called her."

"I know."

"I think you *don't* know that the bank president and the cardinal are playing you."

I didn't respond.

"Very little happens in Napoli without my family knowing about it. The VAT president, Angelo Caloia, has been looking for property buyers for some time now. He does it quietly. He can't invite investigations."

"I'm not following," I said.

"The Church owns thousands of properties in Italy and around the world. Sometimes I think it's more landlord than lord, if you get my meaning."

"I've heard that," I said.

"Cardinal Bertolini controls all the Church property. He decides what to sell. Caloia then discounts it and sells it to a private company, which the attorneys Gabriele and his son Lamberto own. Then, they flip the property for the higher market value and pocket the difference. They make millions in profits."

"OK, I'm following," I said. "But how do you know?"

"Because Caloia and his lawyer buddies can't just flip Church assets openly; someone will notice."

I cocked my head.

She took a breath and explained. "Let's say the local bishop in Milan notices the old mission that sold a year ago for three million euros sold again today for seven million euros. That would raise eyebrows, *si*?"

"But transactions are usually confidential," I pointed out.

"Yes, but Italian culture is very leaky. Caloia needs to find buyers who are as secretive as the seller. So, he comes to families like mine. Caloia offered my father a bunch of properties. That's why I don't understand why he's stopping my bid for the Chiurazzi. We were good enough to do business before, but now, suddenly, we're too dirty to shake hands."

None of those properties came with a Vatican Bank account.

The small bottles and candy wrappers in the waste basket indicated she'd already worked through the minibar. I pointed and said, "Can I get you something more substantial?"

"No, I eat when I'm stressed."

I looked at her thin frame. "You must live a blissful life."

She grinned. "You can stay with me. Keep me company."

I tilted my head. "Are you flirting with me?"

"Just because you kidnap me doesn't mean we can't be friends."

I shook my head. There was plainly something wrong with her. "Gemma—I'm curious. I heard stories about your family."

"There are so many. Most are inventions—myth-building."

"I heard that if you kiss a thorn, you could end up drinking your balls."

"No—not *a* thorn—*the* thorn." She pointed at herself and gave a mocking frown. "Yes, that one is true. My father is very protective."

She rolled her eyes in a false show of reminiscing. "I was young and told my father about the *piranhas* who held me up. For years after that, finding a date was impossible for me. No one came near me. I finally got a husband because he works for my father and asked permission to date me. He's much older."

"I also heard that your father made one of his men drink his piss."

"I've heard that story many times. I don't know if it is true. Maybe—maybe not. Supposedly, my father's *sotto capo* was rude to Cosimo, and my father tested his loyalty. But it happened behind closed doors, and my father has never spoken of it—and neither has my husband."

"Your husband?"

"*Si.*"

She gave me a full Cheshire smile.

"Does he have Natalya?"

"My husband? No, of course not. She's with a brother. I have many."

"You'll walk away from the foundry, then," I clarified.

"I will, but I can't speak for Cosimo. I don't control him, and it's now all about machismo. Cosimo wants to prove himself. He'll kill people just to make a point."

"I wouldn't worry about that," I said with a flinty stare. "I think he'll come around."

CHAPTER THIRTY-NINE

SERGEI, CASERTANI, BRODY, AND BO huddled against the connecting wall in the room next door. A small speaker rested on a side table they'd moved from another part of the room.

"Not the most sophisticated operation," I remarked.

"We are not FSB," Sergei replied.

They'd drilled a small hole in the wall behind the mirror, pushed a microphone and cable through, and attached it to a receiver. It worked fine.

"You sat where I told you. For a change, you followed instructions," Sergei said.

"Gemma's warped brain is trying to figure out how Marty and I could summon Russian *gopniks* to kidnap her on such short notice," Bo said.

"They are not *gopniks*; they are *bratki*—brothers in *Bratva*," Sergei corrected.

"Natalya was grabbed in Naples," Brody added. "Probably on her way to catch the train to Rome."

"They will tell us where to make trade an hour before. Then, they set up their men before we arrive. It is customary practice," Raffaele explained. "They do nothing until they have Gemma. Then they come for us when we leave." He paused, moving his head from side to side as if to clear cobwebs. "It's what I do."

"I want to be there," I said.

"And I want world peace," replied Sergei.

///

Bo and I looked for Leo. He'd disappeared; he wasn't in his room or answering his phone. Casertani gave Sergei and his men a full briefing in the restaurant on the Di Lupo clan and their multiple compounds. I could see that the small platoon of *bratki* operated with the proficiency of a seasoned infantry squad. Every man fulfilled his designated role—the guard, the medic, the communications guy. I perused the tattooed heavies, speculating on who did what. Who were the designated assassins? Who knew their job was to jam an ice pick into a brain, and who was assigned to drive the getaway car? They were all here to rescue Natalya, and disturbingly, I felt a sense of esprit de corps.

"Dmitry said he'd stay in touch," said Bo. "Has he called you? 'Cause he hasn't called me."

"He talks to Sergei," I said. "Dmitry knows we're just grunts. Generals talk to commanders, not to cannon fodder."

"Did you learn that in Vietnam?"

"Vietnam; Corporate America; Kindergarten."

///

We hunkered in the lobby bar. The expensive scotch was gone, so we'd moved to a lower shelf.

"We've got to find Leo," I told Bo after filling him in on Dmitry's plan to nuke the Di Lupos using Raffaele Casertani as his weapon of choice. "It's top secret. If Leo tries to contact Cosimo in some misguided attempt to deflect blame and spills that Casertani is working with Russians, he'll die."

"Why would he do something so stupid?" asked Bo.

"We're talking about Leo Giacobbe—right?"

Bo tilted his head in agreement. I redialed my regular phone and was mildly shocked when Leo answered.

"Where are you?"

"The Michelangelo. I couldn't stay in that crib of criminals. I snuck out after Bo left to listen to your tête-à-tête with Gemma."

"How? The exits are all guarded."

"All the first-floor windows open from the inside for fire safety. I found an empty room and jumped out. No one saw me."

"Don't go anywhere," I warned. "We'll come to you. It's important."

"Importance is trivial to a dying man," he groaned.

My eyes rolled. "Just stay put, Leo."

***

Bo and I found the same room Leo had jumped out of. The window was still unlocked. During the cab ride to the Michelangelo, I told Bo my theory that Natalya had not been snatched in Naples but in Rome.

"Naples doesn't feel right to me," I said. "The timing is wrong."

"These guys work fast, Marty," said Bo.

"I know, but think about it. Natalya was with her pilot, copilot, and Dante until about 11 a.m. She was supposed to catch the noon Red Arrow and come to Rome. Assume she tried to get there early for boarding; she could've only been kidnapped between 11:00 and 11:30."

Bo nodded, paying close attention.

"Her nail would have been torn off then and transported in her purse to us in Rome, arriving after 2. But remember the nail? Remember how it looked."

"I'll never forget it," said Bo with repulsion.

"It was wet and raw, and…" my face twisted into nausea, "…fresh."

"It was in a plastic bag, Marty."

"I checked on this. Blood and flesh clot and dry quickly, even inside a plastic bag. After three hours there would be clear signs of desiccation."

"Drying out," he acknowledged. He curled the fingers of both hands to beckon for more information.

"Everyone assumes Naples because it makes sense, but I think she might have been grabbed at the train station in Rome, had her nail ripped out, and delivered to us half an hour later when it was still—you know—viable."

"We've got to tell this to Sergei," said Bo.

"Sergei thinks I'm a useless idiot. I've got no credibility."

"Then I'll tell him," he said.

I blinked my surprise. "So, you're buds now?"

"Jealous?" he shot back.

"Sergei's focused on the hostage exchange. Where and when Natalya was grabbed isn't important. His priority is making a clean trade."

"And avoiding any crossfire," Bo added.

///////////////////////////////////////

We arrived at the Michelangelo as the winter sun was setting, bathing St. Peter's Dome in a pale citrine glow. In the Dome bar, Leo slumped in a booth. Night manager Vincenzo sat beside him in an uncharacteristically casual outfit—jeans, a T-shirt, and a cardigan instead of his usual black suit. Leo looked smaller and older, wearing his misery like a topcoat. Squeezing in from both sides, trapping them between us, Bo and I ordered club soda, and Leo gave us a surprised look.

"We've been drinking on and off all day; time to take a break," I said as if an explanation was required.

"I've never stopped," he lamented.

Bo looked at Vincenzo, who returned his look as if he were a doctor inspecting his patient. "You're always working," Bo said.

"Not tonight. I work too many hours this week, so I have night off."

"He works for Casertani," said Leo.

Our jaws gaped. "You're Casertani's man," I said, repeating Brody's words from that morning.

Vincenzo shook his head. "I am not Casertani's *man*. I am *Cugino,* but very far away."

"A distant cousin," translated Leo tiredly.

"I never want to be a *sistema* man," said Vincenzo. "I moved away from Naples. But I read the papers to learn what the Di Lupos and Casertanis are doing. Raffaele call me a few days ago and ask me to keep my eye on *Signore* Giacobbe. Raffaele knows I am not a *soldato*. But I saw Gemma Di Lupo visit with *Signore* Giacobbe, and then your rooms were *vandalizzato*, and *Signore* Bishop was hurt. So, when *Signore* Giacobbe check out this morning—*si*—I called Raffaele, who sent a man to pick him up. It is how things work."

"That explains a lot, Vincenzo," said Bo appreciatively. He smiled and winced, his face still healing.

"Are you keeping an eye on Leo?" I asked.

"Yes, but not for Raffaele. Maybe for *Signore* Giacobbe himself. He is not doing well."

"I wouldn't let him wander about," I said. "There's a war brewing."

"I have seen the news," said Vincenzo. "A man who was killed this morning was same man watching you in our lobby."

"He was with Gemma Di Lupo, who was kidnapped," I said.

Vincenzo may not have been a *soldato*, but he continued to absorb news with his typical unflappable demeanor.

"And you are involved?" he asked.

"Gemma kidnapped our business partner. We reciprocated," said Bo.

He looked puzzled. "Recip…?"

"We did the same thing," Bo clarified.

We continued briefing Vincenzo while Leo slumped, staring into his empty glass, stained with the ghost of an Irish coffee. Vincenzo waved at the bartender to bring him another and, with a thumb and forefinger gesture, signaled to cut the alcohol by half.

"I think we should call Sergei and tell him Natalya might be held here in Rome," said Bo after we'd summarized the situation for Vincenzo.

"She would never be held in Rome," said Vincenzo.

"Why?"

"The Di Lupo *famiglia* operates out of Naples. Their *territorio* is Scampia. That is where they live, and that is where they have *sicuro casa*—secure houses."

The bartender brought Leo's drink, and Vincenzo paused to think.

"The one brother who doesn't live in Naples has small farm by Lago Albano, near Casa Gandolfo."

"Who's that?" asked Bo.

"Franco Di Lupo, but he is never called that. He has been called *Cicciotto* since he was a boy."

Leo, who I thought wasn't listening, surprised me by interjecting, "*Cicciotto* means chubby."

"Yes, he is the brother born just before Gemma. Italians say, *Fratello del cuore*," Vincenzo continued.

"Brother of the heart," translated Leo before sipping his Irish coffee.

"I've heard of Casa Gandolfo," I said.

"It is *Il Papa*'s summer residence," said Vincenzo. "I think Cicciotto's house is about a mile away." He waved his hands and added, "It is maybe thirty minutes from here."

Feeling my heart speed up, I waved to the bartender. "Glenlivet, please." Bo threw up his hand to signal for one as well. I furrowed my brow, deep in thought.

"Gemma said she'd have Natalya back in *my* bed before I finished breakfast. Do you remember that?"

"Damn right, I do," Bo replied. "When she said it, Brody gave me his stink eye. I thought, how the hell does Gemma know about that?"

"I called Natalya on the bugged phone, and we got…personal," I said.

"Oh lord, this just keeps getting better and better," cried Leo. "You're screwing the chairman of your company, who is also the oligarch's girlfriend! I've landed in Dante's second circle of hell." Then he emptied his glass.

Bo looked at me and smirked, "Now look, you've upset him."

I ignored Bo and asked Vincenzo, "Do you know exactly where Cicciotto lives? Do you have an address?"

"No, but I can get it with a phone call." He squeezed past Bo out of the booth and walked into the lobby.

I reasoned aloud, "If Gemma had to snatch someone quickly, without a prepared plan, because, remember, she wanted to grab me instead, she'd probably call her closest brother, who lives only half an hour away. He could have taken Natalya when she got off the train in Rome. Gemma said her seven brothers don't have a full brain between them. She probably could convince Chubby to help her."

Vincenzo returned a minute later with an address scribbled on a hotel notepad. Leo announced he would be sick, and Vincenzo assisted him to the bathroom. Bo and I found a deserted corner of the lobby. I pulled out my phone, pressed speaker, and called Sergei.

"Where are you?" he asked with a surprising serenity.

"At the Michelangelo," said Bo. "We went to find Leo." Bo and I had agreed he'd talk to keep the conversation from becoming a verbal knife fight.

"How did you get past my men?"

"First-floor rooms have windows that open for fire safety. Send a man to Room 114 and have him shut and lock the window."

"You violated my orders. I cannot protect you when you play hide and seek."

"We needed to be sure Leo wouldn't spill his guts about Casertani working with you."

After a short silence, Sergei said, "OK. I agree with those actions."

I pushed air out of my lungs in relief.

"We have an idea where Natalya might be, and it's not Naples."

"I am listening."

Bo explained our theory and read the Lago Albano address to him off the notepad. After another silence, he asked, "You want my men to...look for wind in a field...you would say wild duck chase."

"Wild goose chase," I corrected, and Bo glared at me to shut up.

I sensed Sergei's simmering burn. I didn't care. I'd already made up my mind. I was going to Lago Albano, and Sergei could take his imperious attitude and stuff it up his arrogant ass.

"A hundred Di Lupo men are looking for you right now, hunting you. You understand this, yes?"

"Yes," Bo answered for both of us.

"If they find you, I will not come and save you."

"We understand," said Bo. "If we find Natalya, will you come to save *her*?"

"How will you find her, Bo? Will you knock on this Di Lupo man's door and say you are the Red Cross with a care package for the hostage?"

"We're not sitting on our asses and doing nothing," I spat out.

"You are a monkey playing with a grenade," Sergei hissed.

Bo chopped at his throat, a signal for me to stop talking. The knives we wanted to avoid were starting to be flung.

"Can you send Brody Lynch over? We could use him," Bo said.

"He doesn't work for me," answered Sergei with a petulant sigh.

"No problem, Sergei," I said. "I'll call Dmitry and get approval. He needs an update anyway."

I could almost hear the cogs in his head whirring. "I will talk to Brody," he said, and I thanked him just as Bo hung up.

"He's going to kill you, Marty," said Bo. "Why are you so eager to slap his balls?"

"He reminds me of Vasili," I blurted vehemently, and Bo looked at me with a new understanding.

CHAPTER FORTY

BRODY LYNCH SAUNTERED INTO DOME half an hour after we'd hung up with Sergei. The collar of his peacoat was raised to his ears. A black wool beanie pulled low like a helmet hid his forehead. He was unrecognizable, except for the familiar glower carved on his face.

Vincenzo had stashed Leo in an empty guest room after we warned him, under threat of death, not to talk with anyone—Italian mafia, Russian mafia, or anyone in between. Then, Bo persuaded Vincenzo to join us on our quest to locate Cicciotto Di Lupo's compound. Vincenzo may not have been a *soldato* for the Camorra, but Bo and I had bonded with him without intention or effort. I told him that when all this was over, I would hire him to work for us—to be our man in Italy. We'd also switched to coffee, flushing out the reservoir of alcohol we'd consumed all day to sober our purpose.

We explained our rationale to Brody, who listened without interruption and apparently understood the details and definition of "desiccate."

"Aye, it's fair enough," he said. "But Sergei's right. We already have an agreement to trade, so why risk a direct attack? Natalya could get killed in the scuffle."

"Let's cross that bridge if we come to it," I said. "It's just a hunch for now. We need to know if she is here or in Naples."

"Let's go then. But understand, if you're right, we call Sergei. We don't act the maggot. I'm not takin' on the Di Lupo clan with a pants-pisser, a beat-up footballer, and a waiter."

"I am not a waiter," answered Vincenzo indignantly. "I am the night manager."

"Same shade o' spuds to me, fella," said Brody as we followed him to Vincenzo's car.

"I'll drive," said Bo, holding out his hand, and Vincenzo gave him a skeptical stare. "Trust me," said Bo.

Brody and I got into the back of his old Peugeot. Bo drove, and Vincenzo navigated.

"Has Cosimo given us a meeting place yet?" I asked Brody as we struggled to keep from being thrown together by Bo's sharp steering.

"No," he answered. "I'll bet the Di Lupos haven't had to plan a hostage exchange for a long time, if ever, so they're probably fallin' over themselves. On our side, Sergei and Casertani are figurin' out the logistics of transporting the Di Lupo woman to Naples without gettin' jumped first. That's why Sergei's not sparin' any men on our little scavenger hunt. He wants to keep the lot together and hightail it to Naples when it's time."

"I'm worried that idiot Cosimo will do something stupid," said Bo, his eyes straying from the narrow, moonlit road, making Vincenzo and Brody nervous. "He thinks he's dealing with a couple of American yahoos looking to buy an art foundry."

"You *are* a couple of American yahoos lookin' to buy an art foundry," huffed Brody. "From what I've heard, that *gobshite* is in over his head—his old man shoved him out to sea too soon."

"What do you mean?" I asked.

"You know what it takes to run an outfit the size of the Di Lupo clan?"

I shook my head.

"It's at least two hundred strong—all on monthly salaries, with mouths to feed, wives, kids, and the like. It all needs management." He began counting on his fingers. "Bootleg cars, pirated scooters, untraceable weapons, strategic allies, scam suppliers, ambitious partners, warehouses, safehouses, shootin' ranges."

"That's mostly done in the trenches," said Bo.

"It still needs management," Brody replied. "Rules still got to be followed."

"Shooting ranges," I interrupted.

"After a hit, the hitters are sent to a range that records their time, so they have an alibi in case of a bang-bang test."

"You made that up, hoping to get me to say bang-bang," I responded with a grin.

"No—you eejit—it's a gun residue test. A hitter's worst nightmare 'cause it's not removable."

"Killing people just ain't what it used to be," grumbled Bo, shaking his head, and Vincenzo let out a short laugh.

///////////////////////////////////////

After several minutes of silence, I asked Brody, "Does Dmitry have a lot of assets in London?" I wondered how Brody had expanded his resume from Vasili's assistant to Dmitry's property manager.

"Aye, London's the capital for washed money." He was surprisingly chatty for a guy notoriously silent as a sphinx. Perhaps it was a coping mechanism. "New York's got flash, Paris' got style, LA's got hot women, but there's somethin' to be said for persistence. London's become a mecca for newly scrubbed, wet, slushy money, on purpose. The British want the title like they want the World Soccer trophy. They passed the most liberal non-domicile tax system on the planet."

"How'd they do that?" asked Bo.

"Anyone livin' in the UK but is a citizen of another country—they call 'em 'non-doms'—doesn't have to pay taxes on income earned outside Britain. It's called the 'golden visa,' and it's granted to anyone who invests a million quid in the country—basically, the cost of a crappy apartment in Soho. I heard over forty thousand homes in Britain are owned by Russians. Many aren't lived in. They call 'em carcass condos."

//

We'd driven out of Rome on *Via Appia Nuova*, following it past Casa Gandolfo. We were now deep in the dark embrace of skeletal cypress trees, their silhouettes stretching into our headlights. After the blinding lights of the city, the overwhelming darkness of the countryside felt intimidating. Through bare branches, flickers from scattered hillside homes winked—eerie and sparse. The road narrowed to a single lane; each sharp turn felt like a tight gamble. My fingers were crossed against the chance of oncoming traffic. It took thirty minutes, just as predicted.

Bo killed the headlights, and we coasted the last quarter mile in near-total darkness. Finally, we pulled into a dirt driveway beneath a massive stone pine, its wide black canopy swallowing the outline of the Peugeot.

"We're here," Vincenzo murmured. I wondered why he kept his voice low while we were still in the car. Whispering, he told us not to open any doors. He reached into the glovebox, took out a long screwdriver, and used it to snap off the cover of the car's dome light, removing the bulb. Then he shoved the screwdriver into his belt like a hunting knife.

Brody pulled a Beretta from his peacoat pocket, racked it, and then returned it. We exited, leaving the doors slightly ajar. The only sound that broke the silence was the nervous rasp of our own breathing.

The farmhouse was a white silhouette against a half-moon sky. Old but renovated, its white travertine walls glowed amber from the ground lighting set throughout the front yard. A six-foot wall of the same whitewashed stone enclosed the entire back acre. In the middle of the wall stood a black metal gate. We scuttled over to it, but not because it looked inviting; rather, the compound appeared so impenetrable that the gate seemed like the only feasible breach.

Brody and Bo peered through the gate from flanking sides while Vincenzo and I hugged the wall. Bo shook his head, indicating he saw nothing, and then traded places with me. Across the gloomy expanse stood a pale stone outbuilding attached to the back enclosure. Its white walls stretched for about forty feet, with a corrugated roof catching slivers of moonlight. Two weathered wooden doors, thicker than a man's fist, stood close together, their surfaces scarred and worn. One door hung open, revealing what looked like an abandoned chicken coop, while the second door was sealed and secured with a hefty plank resting in two flat metal brackets across its middle.

Everything looked quiet, almost peaceful—a small hobby farm put to bed for a long winter night. I gripped the metal bars of the gate and sighed in defeat. Cicciotto Di Lupo's home was not the villain's lair I'd hoped it would be. There were no guards, dogs, sounds, or lights. It appeared that no one was there. I glanced at Brody, and he couldn't hide his disappointment.

"Looks like we took a wrong turn," he whispered. "Let's be off."

He started to turn, ready to vanish into the deeper night and the black folds of regret when light flooded the lower quadrant of the house and back entrance. We all clung to the wall, and by luck of position, I had the clearest view. A large man in a white sleeveless undershirt, black jeans, and heavy boots came through the back screen door, its hinges screeching, balancing a plate with something on it in one hand and a crumpled jacket in the other.

Brody glared at me, held his finger to his lips, and mouthed, "Don't breathe."

My world shrank to a pinprick as I realized he was the man who'd delivered Natalya's fingernail to Bo and me in the Piazza Navona. Unfazed by the night chill, he marched across the yard to the barred door. Throwing the jacket over his shoulder, he hoisted the plank and opened it. Even in the deep murk, I could see a shifting mass of bloated flies emerge from the shed in a slow, writhing tide. The stench of excrement assaulted me from nearly fifty feet away.

The man disappeared into the black maw of the doorway, and low, unintelligible rumblings escaped from the opening, absorbed by the night. Then, Natalya's voice pierced through me, sharper than any blade. I knew the sound of her voice like my own. I didn't need to hear the words; I just needed to hear the resonant tenor of her despair.

A surge of energy coursed through me, but I clenched my jaw and took a deep breath. Brody heard her voice as well, and he cocked his head at me in a silent warning to stay quiet. Bo pressed against the wall beside me, pushing his hand against my back as if to hold me aloft.

We'd found Natalya.

Now we needed to rescue her from the scumbag holding her captive.

CHAPTER FORTY-ONE

THE CHUNKY GOON DROPPED THE PLANK back into place with a loud thump and trotted back to the house, hugging himself against the nocturnal nip. Brody ran to the car as darkness reclaimed the structure, and we followed. He was already on his phone when we caught up with him.

"What are you doing?" I whispered.

"Callin' the cavalry," he hissed back. Then, "Sergei? Yeah…we found her." He paused, cupping his hand over his mouth and phone. "Aye—even a mutt finds a bone now and again."

"Asshole," I hissed.

Brody relayed more details and handed the phone to Vincenzo, who looked increasingly uneasy. "Give him the address and directions. Get 'em here as fast as possible."

Vincenzo walked to the rear of the car, cupping his mouth and speaking softly but distinctly.

"Why wait?" asked Bo. "I can get over the fence. There's no lock on the door, just a plank."

Brody shook his head vigorously. "No guards," he whispered, almost to himself. "No lights. No locks. No barking dog. Nothing. There's no head or tail to it."

"Stop overthinking it, Brody," Bo whispered back, waving his hand dismissively. "They never had a plan. Gemma Di Lupo decided to kidnap Natalya at the last minute after failing to grab her new boyfriend." He gestured toward me, and I gave a slight bow. "She called her brother, and they snatched her somewhere between the train station and the hotel and brought her here." Even in the dark, I could tell by the glint in Brody's eyes that he tracked Bo's logic. "I'll bet her brother barely knows the details. He gets a call from his beloved sister, jumps into action, throws Natalya into what smells like a decrepit outhouse for safekeeping, and now waits for instructions."

He paused to ease the strain in his throat from all the whispering. "He doesn't have guards or backup because we're insignificant to the Di Lupos. You said it yourself—we're just a couple of yahoos from America who couldn't find their asses with both hands. He's too arrogant to worry about us and, more importantly, too clueless to anticipate anything like Sergei, Casertani, and the Russian *Vory* version of the Green Beret."

"Bo's right," I added. "We need to get in there and pull her out before that dumbass calls for backup."

"Hold your fire, soldier," Brody shushed.

Vincenzo rejoined us, gave Brody his phone back, and signaled us back into the car. We quietly closed the doors.

"If they follow my directions, press the gas to the floor, not get stopped by the *polizia*, and get past traffic, they'll be here in thirty minutes," he said.

"That's a lot of ifs," said Bo.

"Too many," I said. "We're getting her out now."

"Why is the house so dark?" asked Brody. "They're not in bed, and they're not vampires. So why is it pitch black inside?"

"I can explain," said Vincenzo, his gaze sweeping back and forth as he studied shadows in the enveloping night. "*Molto*—many—*Italia* farmhouses have big *cantinas*—how to say—basements. In old days, farmers lived underground, away from summer heat and winter cold. Many new owners fix up the downstairs and make it a big apartment. When the basement door is closed, the house looks empty."

The car was cold, and sitting, not moving, didn't help. We quivered and waited through precious minutes, our chatter and petty squabbling a thin veneer over the tension that gripped us. Then, a crunch of gravel stopped our hushed conspiring. A piercing beam of light sliced through the trees. We ducked while the light swung past our car and rested on the front of the house. It belonged to a white Opel van missing a headlight. I could see a man get out and walk to the house, which lit up again for half a minute before plunging back into black.

"Mafia biggies don't drive one-eyed vans," whispered Bo. "He's here to move Natalya…"

"To Naples," I interjected.

"*Shite!*" growled Brody. He checked his watch. "The lot of them are still fifteen minutes out if they break every traffic law in the country."

"They'll move her by then; I'm going in," I said.

"Aye," said Brody. Then, looking at Vincenzo, who'd taken the screwdriver from his belt, he said, "You stay by the gate. If anyone comes out of the house, start shoutin' and run like a scalded cat." He reached out his hand, pointing to the screwdriver. "I'll be needin' that."

We eased out of the car and returned to the gate. Brody inserted the screwdriver into the shackle of the small, cheap padlock. With him gripping the handle end and Bo pressing on the flathead, they pushed together, leveraging their strength until the shackle rod popped free from the lock bar.

Brody put a finger to his lips as if we needed reminding not to shout. He slid his arm through the gate with the precision of a bomb disposal technician, checking for alarm wires or doorbells. I exchanged an exasperated look with Bo—Brody was acting like we were breaking into Fort Knox, while I was convinced we were just raiding a simple backyard owned by a mafia thug who lived under the immunity provided by his family's power and privilege. I wanted to move faster, and Bo's eyes flared in agreement.

The half-moon emerged from behind a cloud, its light stretching the white stone wall into the eerie shape of a bony arm. Brody, Bo, and I slid along the wall's inner shadow.

My thoughts raced to Natalya and how she might react when we opened her prison. What if she screamed? The house was eerily quiet, and I imagined her voice ringing out like a gunshot in the silent night.

"I should get into her line of sight quickly so she doesn't scream," I whispered to Brody as we inched forward.

"Right you are. You're goin' in first."

"You got any kind of light? Maybe a cigarette lighter?"

"It's not a good idea. Her eyes have adjusted to the dark, and any light will blind her or scare her." He was right, and I felt a camaraderie I would never have predicted or wanted.

The door loomed before me, distorted by my anxiety into a warped, grotesque portal that felt like the entrance to some nightmare tunnel. Bo and Brody took each end of the bar beam and slowly lifted it from the corroded brackets, careful not to make a sound—not out of fear of detection but to avoid startling Natalya. We could have tried whispering to her through the door, but with no idea of her condition, we concentrated on not alarming her.

I pulled the door open quickly, its hinges letting out a classic metallic moan revealing an abysmal gap that swallowed even the drained light of night. The inside surface of the door was alive with thick clusters of glistening grey flies crawling over each other like bees in a hive. The stink that hit me was overwhelming—a putrid mix of decay and human waste.

I saw Natalya in the pale dimness that shone into the reeking cubby. She was crouched in a fetal position on the sodden earth, knees drawn up to her chest, head resting on them, her body frozen from captivity and cruelty. The sound of the door had stirred her, but she hadn't looked up. Then she heard my voice, a murmur carried on the fetid air.

"Natalya," I said softly, my heart pounding in my ears. Her head snapped up, her eyes wide with panic. I lunged forward, my hand covering her mouth before she could scream.

"Don't shout," I hissed, my voice barely audible over the stridency of our ragged breathing.

Her face was streaked with something I couldn't identify, but my hand felt the oily clamminess of her skin. I put my head so close to her that our noses touched, my lips brushing the back of my hand. I stared fiercely at her, willing her into clarity. As recognition seeped into the crevices of her wounded mind, I could see, even in the darkness, her eyes morph from anguish to relief.

I loosened my grip over her mouth, but her desperate hands, cold and slippery, clutched my fingers, pulling them back to her lips. She kissed my palm, pressing it to her face in silent salvation.

"Martin," she mumbled, kissing my palm again. "Oh, Martin."

"Marty!" hissed Bo. "We've gotta move."

"Can you stand?" I asked.

"*Da—da.*" She unfolded slowly from her crouch and clutched her wrinkled jacket for warmth. It was the same old jacket I'd seen the lumbering oaf bring her a few minutes earlier. She moved slowly. Her shoes had been taken, replaced by thin synthetic flip-flops.

"I cannot feel my feet," she whispered, her voice trembling. Her face was partially obscured in the dim moonlight, but I could see tears glistening in her eyes. She cleared the mucus trickling from her nose with a quick, self-conscious swipe, fighting to regain her composure.

"They are frozen, Martin. I cannot feel the ground."

Brody, close enough now to hear her, wrapped his arms around her waist, picked her up, and whispered to Bo and me, "Give 'em a quick rub."

Bo and I fell to our knees. We each grabbed a foot, pulled off the flip-flop, and briskly kneaded her blue skin, trying to get the blood flowing.

"Carry her," I hissed.

"Not 'til the gate," Brody hissed back. "Walkin' will get the blood circulatin', and I need to keep my hands free."

"I'll carry her," said Bo.

She waved her injured hand wrapped in a wrinkled rag and murmured, "I can walk."

We slipped Natalya's flip-flops back on, and Brody gently lowered her to the ground. She wiggled her toes and took a tentative step. We moved carefully, cloaked in the shadow of the building and the wall. I led the way, gripping Natalya's cold hand as if I were keeping her from falling off a bridge. She held her injured hand close to her chest while Bo stayed close behind to catch her if she stumbled. Brody brought up the rear, having drawn the Beretta and unlocked its safety. We snaked along the wall agonizingly slowly, as Natalya needed to steady each step over the rough, grassy ground.

Flashes of light and two loud explosions erupted from the direction of the house. Brody collided into Bo like a cascading domino, and Bo grunted as he clasped his forearm. Natalya let out a sharp gasp, and I pulled her to the ground. Out of the umbra emerged the hulking figure in the wife-beater T, moonlight and smoke glinting off the rifle's muzzle held firmly in his grip. He hesitated, pushing his head forward to study our scattered silhouettes, assessing the damage, then raised the rifle to his shoulder, ready to shoot again.

Brody, his right arm hanging like dead weight, slumped to the ground. Bo caught him and hauled him upright. In one fluid motion, he grabbed the Beretta out of Brody's slack hand, raised it toward the shooter, and fired three times. The white T made a visible target; the shooter convulsed as the bullets entered his chest, then toppled backward, his rifle hitting the ground just a second before him.

Brody let out a guttural growl of pain and rage as he fell at Bo's feet. Natalya dragged herself to him, her hands hovering over his chest, not knowing where they should land. I crawled over on my knees and ripped open his peacoat, exposing his shirt. A bloodstain was spreading across the fabric like spilled oil.

"*O Bozhe*," Natalya exclaimed in a breathless sigh. She applied the ragged cloth wrapping her right hand to Brody's chest in a useless effort to stem the blood flow.

Bo's attention wasn't on Brody. He was occupied with the man lying across the yard, whose legs kicked slowly as he tried to breathe. Without comment, Bo walked over and stared at him like an animal he'd just hit with his car. I could barely see Bo's expressionless face as he pointed the Beretta down at the man and shot him in the head.

"Bastard," Bo said impassively.

A second shot echoed sharply after the Beretta's crack, and for a second I thought Bo had pulled the trigger twice. Then I realized another gun had been fired from outside the wall. Without hesitation, Bo raced toward the gate, and I followed.

Vincenzo!

My Italian friend lay sprawled on the dry grass, a widening pool of dark, treacly blood blossoming around him. A jagged, gaping wound showed on his back, swallowing the melted wool of his jacket. Surrounding the crimson cavity was a constellation of smaller gashes, raw and angry. The air smelled metallic and burnt.

Stomping toward us from the front of the house, where the ground lighting cast a yellow glow, was a fat man pointing an over-under shotgun at us. His wild black hair and thick mustache framed a bloated face etched with menace. The lighting showed me his eyes, dark pits sunk into the pulpy folds of his flesh.

"*Getta la canna!*" he barked.

"English!" I shot back.

"Drop gun!"

"Not a chance," growled Bo.

His obese frame suggested he was Cicciotto. His face suggested he was psychotic. His drunken drawl suggested he was unstable.

"Don't do something stupid," I said, as if stupidity was a choice.

"*Casso*! Who are you?" he yelled, sweeping the rifle between us.

"We want Natalya back," I said, trying to keep it simple.

"*Secessionista*? *Uomini Casertani*."

"No, we're not secessionists. We're not Casertani's men," I said.

Bo stayed silent, likely believing he might spook the fat man since he had the gun, so I raised my hands in surrender, hoping to divert his attention.

"You try kill me," he shouted.

"No! We are here for Natalya. Nothing else."

"You steal my sister!"

"We will give her back!"

"No!" He stopped and stood twenty feet from us. "Spina first— *poi la tua troia*." He breathed, and the rifle hitched a little. "Drop gun—Ruggero will shoot your slut."

He doesn't know Bo just put three into Ruggero's chest and one in his brain—say nothing—he's nervous—drunk. Where's the van driver?

"We're not your enemy," I said.

"Spina's enemy is mine." His beady eyes glared with a feral rage.

I heard Brody moan from inside the wall, and Natalya silenced him. I imagined her blood-soaked hand gently holding his mouth closed.

"When I raise my hand, duck," Bo murmured into his shoulder, shifting his head slowly.

"No! He'll kill you," I whispered back. "Where is the van driver?" I said to Cicciotto, buying time. "He can take us to Spina, and we'll trade."

"Calling men. They be here *un minuto*."

"My arm took a bullet," continued Bo under his breath. "Blood is pooling in my hand. I'm losing my grip." He looked straight at Cicciotto. "We do this now, Marty, or the gun slips from my hand."

I opened my mouth to say no when Cicciotto's head exploded in a brume of blood and bone. Bo and I dove for cover, hitting the ground as Cicciotto's rotund body slowly toppled over like broken scaffolding.

CHAPTER FORTY-TWO

TWO YEARS AGO, when I saw a bullet go through the eye of Nico Scava, I wet myself. Then, when I killed Vasili days later, there was a splattering spray of crimson mist. But, with Cicciotto, it was different. Whatever hit him didn't enter and exit his head; it vaporized it.

Footsteps pounded through the grass behind us at an alarming speed. Bo and I rolled in the direction of the shot.

"Stay down," Bo spat, aiming the Beretta toward the approaching sounds.

"Shoot at me, and it will be your last," huffed Sergei Sidorov as he planted the barrel of his pistol at the back of Bo's neck. With adrenaline-soaked relief, Bo and I lay flat as a group of men swept past us through the gate with lethal precision. Exhausted and dazed, we stayed still as Sergei disappeared behind the wall, giving us a brusque order not to move. I heard Natalya's voice growing stronger as she communicated with the Russian men. About five minutes passed before Sergei returned, saying, "We are leaving now."

Bo and I heaved ourselves up like two old men afflicted with arthritis.

"Who is this man?" asked Sergei, pointing to Vincenzo lying several feet away.

We explained who he was and why he was with us.

"He is with Casertani?" Sergei asked.

"Not really," I said. "He is a distant cousin."

"I will leave him for Casertani to clean up."

"He's not laundry," said Bo.

"He is a side effect," replied Sergei. "Casertani will deal with it. He will be here in minutes."

"So will Di Lupo's men," I added.

"I know. It is why we will get out and let the Italians sort it out—they are fighting dogs, and we get out of their pit now, yes?"

"There's someone in the house," I said. "The van driver."

"His driving days are over," Sergei said grimly.

Six men in camouflage came through the gate carrying Brody on an evacuation stretcher. Behind them came another two men holding Natalya in a double carry, her arms around their shoulders, sitting on their clasped hands. Our eyes met briefly, and her lips flattened in an affectionate grin, her eyes glossy with unwiped tears. She and Brody vanished into the inky void of an open van.

One of Brody's bearers detached himself and approached Bo with swift, silent proficiency. Without a word, he pulled a pair of surgical scissors from his pocket and neatly snipped Bo's jacket sleeve open, revealing a seeping gash. He poured disinfectant solution from a canteen over the wound, dabbed it dry, and applied skin adhesive tape while squeezing the wound together. Finally, he wrapped it tightly in Coban. The process took less than a minute, and Bo's bruised face grimaced.

The medic, whom I recognized from the cafeteria and regretted calling a *gopnik,* handed Bo a ball of gauze, which he used to clean the blood from his palm. He had played enough football to know how to handle pain on the field. The medic then informed Sergei, who translated, that Bo's wound was a superficial graze, despite the heavy bleeding, and wouldn't require stitches. A tight bandage and a few days of healing would suffice, leaving only a faint scar.

"It will look like a bicycle accident," said Sergei.

"Like my face," Bo said dryly.

I followed the medic toward the van carrying Natalya, but Sergei pointed me and Bo to a different car.

"I'm going with Natalya," I insisted.

Sergei put the barrel of his gun against my chest. "What did I say about not following my orders?"

"You'll kill me and tell Dmitry I had an accident?"

"You want to die here?" he said. "I will tell Dmitry the fat goat shot you."

"Natalya knows I'm alive."

"Natalya knows what I tell her—now go to car."

Bo and I sat in the back of a Lancia sedan while Sergei drove. A taciturn guard in the passenger seat held a Kalashnikov 47 with a pistol grip. I wondered two things simultaneously: where did Sergei get all these vehicles, and when did I become so well-versed in weaponry?

On our way out, we passed another van that could have been dark blue or black—I couldn't tell in the night. Sergei got out, walked over, and talked to Casertani, who leaned out of the van's passenger window. At one point, Casertani slapped his forehead and let his chin fall to his chest. Sergei must have told him he'd find Vincenzo face down by the gate. Finally, they shook hands, and Sergei climbed back into our car while Casertani and his men continued toward the house.

////////////////////////////////////

Halfway back to Rome, Sergei broke the long silence. "You are not in the van with Natalya because the van is not going back to hotel. It stops at doctor, where Brody will get help, and Natalya gets tetanus and penicillin shot to stop infection."

That made sense, and I was glad the car was too dark for Sergei to see my blush.

"You could have said that instead of pointing a gun at my heart," I replied.

"Won't the doctor get the *polizia* involved?" asked Bo.

"She is a special doctor—the daughter of a *secessionist*. She has a private clinic in her *cantina*."

///////////////////////////////////////

The Hotel Raphael and its street were a charcoal sketch waiting to be colorized by morning light. I could see Sergei's men strategically placed in corners and alleys. Bo and I sat, sullied and bruised, in the lobby bar, as quiet and deserted as a mausoleum. We stared mutely at a tall rectangular bottle of Ballantine's. After a while, Sergei joined us, flopping down with a loud groan. Pouring himself a shot and sighing, he said, "*Pokhishcheniye*—kidnapping—is a young man's sport."

We regarded our glasses like old assassins, reflecting on better times.

"Are you done here?" asked Bo.

"*Da*," said Sergei. "Some of my men will go to Naples with Casertani. The rest will tourist in Rome. They will scatter and vacation, so they draw no attention."

"Like when the Navy has shore leave," said Bo, grinning uncomfortably.

Sergei's phone rang.

"It is Dmitry," he said, picked up his glass and walked away.

One of Bo's eyes was nearly back to normal, while the other still looked like a shattered ruby. His face was a muted tapestry of the assault. "Look at us," he muttered. "We're in the heart of a mob war."

"You're giving us too much credit," I said. "Dmitry is steering this ship."

"And we're letting him," he said. "I killed someone tonight. Dmitry didn't. He's on his yacht somewhere pulling strings. He buys his violence, like ordering a pizza." He looked at his hands. "For the first time, I understand what you felt when you shot Vasili. It's ugly—and exhilarating."

I stayed silent. He needed to release the words and let them out before they rooted in his chest.

"I'll never be the same, and you're the only one who'll ever know." His red eye glistened. "How in hell did we get here?"

"They kidnapped Natalya. They ripped out her fingernail and threw her in an abandoned outhouse to rot."

"What happened to 'You don't start a war over a torn fingernail?'"

"That was before I saw her face streaked in shit—before I saw what they did to her." I clenched my teeth in a quiet, seething hatred. "Before I saw Vincenzo lying face down in bloody mud."

///////////////////////////////////////

An hour later, Sergei returned to the bar to tell us he'd heard from his medic. Brody had sustained a significant injury, including a collapsed lung, but the bullet missed his other vital organs. He was going to need surgery but was expected to survive. Natalya was in the van on her way to the hotel.

"Is she OK?" I asked.

"The Di Lupos were not good hosts. My man said she is a mess."

I stood up. "What does that mean?"

"*Yebát'*, how should I know? We'll both know in a minute."

"Has anyone checked in on Gemma? Does she know?"

Sergei checked his watch. "It is three in the morning. She is probably sleeping like a princess and snoring like a bear."

The lobby started filling up with Sergei's men. A palpable spirit of grim satisfaction had settled over everyone. Bo and I went outside, where I saw the outline of a Fiat sedan approaching. As it neared, it turned off its lights, plunging the narrow street back into darkness. Five men climbed out as it stopped. Natalya was the last to emerge. Two men, with the lithe fluidity of shadows, helped her. She said nothing, so we did the same. The weight of the ordeal hung on her, pulling down her shoulders and her back. She shuffled into the lobby, and I winced as she came into the light.

Although her face had been washed and cleaned, grimy ringlets of dirt still clung to her greasy hair. Streaks of dirt covered her arms and legs. Her clothes, intact but torn, testified to her torment. A clean, fully wrapped gauze bandage had replaced the crude tourniquet on her right hand.

"I need bath—hot water—strong soap. There's still shit on me," she said quietly. Her head remained bowed, shielding her face from the intense scrutiny of the men around her. Sergei spoke to her quietly in Russian, his brief words cutting through her stupor. Slowly, she lifted her head, meeting their collective stare, and uttered a firm "*Spasibo*"—thank you.

A ripple of awkwardness passed through the small crowd as the men responded with grunts and nods. Gratitude wasn't a currency exchanged often in their line of work. She and Sergei continued to speak Russian as he put his hand on her back and guided her to the elevator.

We made eye contact, and she said softly, "Do not worry, Martin. I will be fine. I will see you once I am clean again."

CHAPTER FORTY-THREE

Rome, Wednesday, January 21st

SHE WAS BURROWED IN THE CENTER OF HER WIDE BED, swaddled in one of the hotel's white plush bathrobes. Six pillows surrounded her like a snow fort. The scent of the citrus soap clung to her robe and her damp hair. Heavy with exhaustion, her brown eyes held the certainty that she was safe and the memory of what she'd survived.

I sat on the side of the bed. I wanted to climb in but didn't, knowing her door was unlocked. Without knocking, Sergei had come in earlier to deliver a platter of food and then leave.

She took her time to tell me what happened, pausing occasionally to steady herself.

"A man at the train station had my name on paper sign. I told him I was Natalya. He said you sent him to pick me up. He told me your name and Bo's name, where you were staying, and that you meet me in Piazza Navona in an hour. It was all correct, so I was not suspicious—he had *brosat'*." She pointed to her foot.

"A cast?" I asked.

"*Da*—cast—and the station had many people, so I felt safe." She shrugged.

"My phone was bugged," I said. "They got all that information from our conversation." I'd tell her how the guy got his cast another time.

"The man gave a big smile and took my bag. I followed him—but then I saw it was a van. I said no when someone pushed me from behind into van. My head was covered immediately, and I fell to floor because van moved quickly forward. Someone grabbed my hand and pulled my finger straight. I thought I was being robbed. They pulled my ring off, and then I felt cold metal on the tip of my finger. The next second, a bomb exploded in my brain."

She stopped talking and stared at her bandaged finger, which lay on the folds of her white feather duvet. "Now I know it was not a robbery and was scared. They ripped the hood off my head and took a picture. They held my hand out. The pain, Martin. It was terrible. The van stopped once, and I heard men speak outside the driver window. I didn't understand them."

"They were giving your purse and your fingernail to someone else," I said. "They drove you to Lake Albano."

"First, I was in small building on side of house. It was empty garden—how you say *saray*?"

"Shed," I answered.

"My hands were free, but this one was on fire. A bald man took my shoes. His face had bruises. An hour later, I don't know, they took my watch, a woman and a fat man came in."

"Gemma Di Lupo and her brother Cicciotto," I contributed.

"No, she said her name was Spina."

I explained the difference.

"She was very cold. In Russia we say *Snezhnaya Koroleva*, it means *snow queen*. She asked many questions."

"Like what?"

"'Who are we? Why are we buying Chiurazzi? What are we paying? Will we go away?' I told her, *Otvali*."

I knew that meant "screw off."

"After they left, a big, ugly man took me to the back house. I walked across backyard with no shoes. My feet were frozen. Then he pushed me into toilet—*budka*. He had a rag and wiped the toilet seat. He wiped up old chicken shit and dead flies. He wiped inside of sitting hole and all around and made the cloth very dirty. He spit in it and rolled it in his hands. Then he grabbed my hair and wiped the filthy cloth over my face. He said if I screamed, he would put the rag in my mouth and tie it with a belt so all the filth will drain slowly down my throat. Then he shut the door and went away."

I shook my head in disgust and commiseration. She squeezed her eyes shut and opened them, bright with the sheen of moisture, then took a deep breath.

"The cold, Martin," she said and shuddered. "The cold was terrible. And the flies—*mukhi.* So many flies. They are lazy in cold air, so they crawl, not fly. But they sound the same. On my face, in my hair. Big and fat. They loved my warm body." Her hand swiped the air by her head. "I didn't want to sit, so I walked. Five feet forward and five feet back. The night came, and I thought I might die. Just before dark, the man came and gave me a chocolate bar and *shlepki*—shoes with just soles?"

"Flip-flops."

"Yes. Flip-flops. My feet felt frozen. I stayed up all night. I swatted flies and walked back and forth. I saw daylight through cracks in wood. The man brought a cornetto with Nutella and a water bottle. I was hungry, so I said thank you. He said again he would stick the polluted cloth in my mouth if I even whispered. As sun hit the toilet, it got warmer, and I could sit on ground and sleep, but only for an hour. Once, he brought egg salad sandwich, but I was afraid to eat it. I thought maybe he spit in it. But I was so hungry I pushed the egg off and ate the bread—it was dry. The flies liked the egg salad more than my hair. At night, another chocolate bar and bottle of water. I told him it was too cold at night, and he finally brought a jacket."

She reached out, took my hand, and started to cry. "And then I heard your voice." She kissed my hand the way she'd kissed it before. I held myself together by picturing the bastard taking three bullets to his chest and another to his brain.

"Now, Martin—*Milyy*—tell me what happened while I was gone."

I updated her as if she was my commanding officer. I told her about getting her purse delivered, the phone calls, the dinner with Dmitry and Sergei, the arrival of a small militia, Brody, and the taking of Gemma. She already knew about the mafia princess. Sergei had explained that Gemma was locked in a room one floor above her.

"Who is Raffaele Casertani?" she asked unexpectedly.

I wasn't sure how much to reveal, but figured she'd likely hear it from Dmitry, so I told her what I knew.

"And this Casertani person will go to war with the Di Lupos?"

"That's the plan," I said. "And crazy as it sounds, I think it's working."

"Who is Vincenzo? Sergei said he helped you find me."

I explained his involvement from the beginning: how his offer to help us had cost him his life and my culpability in his death. "I needed him to find you. I never thought about the consequences."

Natalya's eyes filled with a complex mix of gratitude and sorrow. "I will forever be grateful," she said.

"Me too."

We said nothing for a while.

"Dmitry came for you immediately," I said, breaking the silence. "Within hours, he delivered a regiment of Moscow *bratki* to Rome, ready to ransack the city. He's a force of nature."

She laughed softly. "That was not for me, Martin. That was for business."

"You sell yourself short."

"I never sell myself, Martin, long or short—but I know Dmitry always hits so hard, no one ever hits back."

"What happens next?"

"Dmitry said Valya will arrive by breakfast. I will buy new clothes. Then we go and sign our deal."

She caught me completely off guard, and my mouth fell open. "When did you talk to Dmitry?"

"In my bath. Dmitry called Sergei and he gave me his phone."

I cocked my head and squinted.

She smiled. "You are so American, Martin. You think Sergei has never seen a naked woman in a bathtub?"

A bitter taste crept into my mouth. It wasn't her nakedness that bothered me—nudity was natural for Natalya. When we were alone, she preferred no clothes. Meals, movies, and memories were all shared naked. So were plotting, planning, laughing, and even fighting. She liked cooking naked, though I objected, given the sharp cutlery. Once, I challenged her to play Monopoly naked—she won. We slow-danced through an entire album once without a stitch. Our hours together were a relentless pulse of skin on skin.

But this was different. I had just pulled Natalya out of a literal shithole, which sparked a strange sense of possessiveness. What unsettled me wasn't her bath privacy—it was that I was suddenly jealous of Dmitry, the unmarried boyfriend of my unmarried girlfriend. My emotions were definitely malfunctioning.

"After the deal is signed we go home." She sighed with the crushing weight of what we'd all endured.

"Why is Valya coming?"

"It is for insurance. With Brody wounded, Dmitry wants someone near me for protection."

"What about me?" I said defensively.

"Two times, Martin, you saved my life. I wish to wrap you in my gratitude." She looked me right in the eyes. "But you are not a bodyguard—and neither is Bo. Valya is a true bodyguard."

Fair point.

"By the way, we're not a secret anymore," I said.

She feigned indifference, but the look in her eyes indicated something more—relief, anger, or both, I couldn't quite tell.

"I have been locked in a toilet, so I have not talked to anyone," she said.

"Dmitry made a remark, and I had to tell Bo."

"What did Dmitry say?"

"Love is evil." I cringed.

"*Lyubov zla*—is true, but perhaps not how he meant it."

"Well, I wanted you to know in case Bo says something to you."

"Martin, he is your best friend. I thought he already knew."

"Why would you think that?"

"I don't keep secrets from Dmitry—I thought you don't keep secrets from Bo."

CHAPTER FORTY-FOUR

BO SAT IN THE HOTEL RESTAURANT, flanked by Sergei's men—a strange alliance forged by circumstance, like uncomfortable tablemates on a cruise ship. As I pulled up a chair and wedged myself into the group, Bo asked, "How is she?"

"As good as can be expected."

I tossed down a freshly delivered copy of the *International Herald Tribune*. The headline blared, *HAS THE SEASON OF KIDNAPPING RETURNED?* Bo's eyes twitched. The angry purple around one of them was fading, giving way to streaks of olive and amber. He picked up the paper and began to read. "It says the *polizia* is out in force. They've canceled all vacations, and every cop in the city is on high alert until Gemma Di Lupo is safely recovered."

"All that attention for one woman?" I asked.

"She's not just any woman," Bo replied. "It says here the authorities are trying to avoid a bloody war."

"Good luck with that," I taunted.

Sergei entered the restaurant with Casertani, silencing the room. Silverware stilled, plates stopped rattling, and every head turned. He radiated power, but I couldn't forget he still answered to Dmitry.

"I talk in English, so our hosts will understand," Sergei said, pointing to our table and then at Raffaele standing beside him.

"We are almost done with our task. *Molodtsy*—well done. The *polizia* are looking in every corner, but not in small luxury hotels like this one, so all is good for now. But too many handsome men in one hotel pulls attention." He smiled, and the room gave a throaty rumble.

"So, we all go now. Slowly. Pack and leave one at a time. Go to other hotels or fly home as you wish. Depart as you came, *prizraki*—ghosts. Our upstairs guest will be returned later, and then we will give back the hotel to the tourists. Thanks—*Spasibo*."

By "guest," he meant Gemma. I hoped "returned" wasn't a Russian euphemism for killed.

Casertani came over and shook our hands. I was conscious of the fact that his hands had probably butchered people a few hours earlier. Discreetly, I wiped my palms on my pants. Out of the corner of my eye, I caught Bo doing the same.

"Later today, I will drive Spina out of city," Casertani said.

"What will happen to her?" I asked.

Casertani hesitated and averted his eyes, and I knew he was about to lie. "She will be fine."

He saw the *Tribune* on the table, pointed to it, and said, "You will read much more in future days. I will bury many Di Lupos."

In my world, there is little to say as a response to that. I looked at Bo, and we had one of our typical nonverbal conversations:

Me: Should I wish him good luck?

Bo: Break a leg?

Me: Knock 'em dead?

Bo: May the force be with you?

We grinned awkwardly and looked down at our shoes.

I told Bo to expect Dmitri's translator, Valya, and then left him to have his breakfast. I took the elevator upstairs. I'd given Natalya enough time, and I wanted to be with her when she spoke to Gemma—*spoke* being the operative word.

Her room was empty.

Damn it, I'm too late! I thought.

I bounded up the stairs to the fifth floor. The same two Russian bears were outside Gemma's door. I tried to enter it, but they pushed me away.

"*Nyet*," one growled.

"Is Natalya in there?" I demanded.

"She say no one can go in…"

He never finished because the door to Gemma's room opened, and Natalya strolled out. She wore men's jeans rolled up over her ankles, a Hotel Raphael sweatshirt from the tiny gift shop in the lobby, and white bath sandals that came with the room. Her surprise at seeing me quickly transformed into a smile and a nod.

The air filled with Gemma's bone-chilling scream as Natalya closed the door. I heard things smashing and a loud shattering of glass. I thought of the mirror I'd sat in front of, which hid the microphone.

"You better go in," Natalya told the two bears. They moved in like bouncers breaking up a bar fight.

"What happened?" I asked.

"I told her she lost her brother," she answered. "She still wants to know who I am."

"What did you say?"

"No one important—just an art dealer." She took the stairs back to her room while I followed.

"Martin, in Russia, we say *choknutyi*. It means not right in the head. You understand?"

"Yes. You should see her brother Cosimo."

"Sergei told me about him, but I think she is the *psikh*—psycho—in that family."

/////////////////////////////////////

As quickly and silently as the company of men arrived, they vanished. Every half hour, another one disappeared—a wisp of smoke inhaled by the Eternal City. Dmitry's translator and bodyguard,

Valentin Kovalev, arrived without fanfare and attached himself to Natalya like a satellite. The two of them left, along with two of Sergei's men, to shop for clothes for her final meeting with Vatican Bank President Angelo Caloia.

After showering off the night's madness and getting back into my new suit, I sat alone in the lobby bar, drinking club soda from the bottle. In the middle of the table, the bottle of Ballantine's and an empty glass still sat.

You know my feelings about blended scotch.

The bar TV was muted—just as well since I wouldn't have understood it anyway—and the top story was about the massacre at the farmhouse. *Massacro* scrolled across the ticker at the bottom of the screen, and the helicopter footage showed stretchers loaded with body bags headed for ambulances. Raffaele Casertani and his brigade had gunned down several more Di Lupo men who'd arrived late and unprepared. Someone had even entered the house and shot Cicciotto's wife, who was found dead under the kitchen table.

I turned it off.

The two *bratki* bears guarding Gemma's room emerged from the elevator, followed closely by her and another soldier. She looked exactly as one might expect after being abducted and held prisoner in a luxury hotel room for twenty-four hours—presentable with no signs of cowering. As far as she was concerned, she was going home. What she didn't know—and would never live long enough to grasp—was that in kidnapping Natalya, she had unknowingly unleashed a shitstorm of cataclysmic consequences for her and her family.

Spotting me in the bar, she said something to one of the soldiers. He nodded, and the four of them made their way over. Gemma sat down while the soldiers remained standing at a respectful distance. Her face twisted into a mask of angry petulance, erasing her previous calm. She radiated revenge.

"Your bitch killed my favorite brother," she said viciously.

"She's not *my* bitch, Gemma, but you have certainly become *hers*."

"This is not over."

"It is for me," I said.

She paused to breathe, sedating herself, and I could see the gears of her psychosis grinding to a halt, giving way to a serene tranquility.

"May I have a drink?" she asked.

"I have only second-rate scotch," I answered.

"Second-rate scotch for a second-rate guy," she said derisively.

I didn't take the bait, instead pouring a shot into the empty glass. "Please," I said. She drank it in one slug.

"I should have grabbed you instead," she said. "I might have lost the foundry but maybe gained a lover." The spoiled brat still shone through even as she tried to suppress her defiance.

"I'm not that easy," I said and grinned.

"Of course you are," she said, returning my grin.

"You just said I'm second-rate."

"You're not very good at this, Marty." She held out the glass, and I poured another shot. "Lovers are supposed to be second-rate—that's why they're not mates."

"Did you send goons to beat up Dante in his hospital room, or was that Cosimo?"

She looked around. "Are you recording me, Marty? Are you an American secret agent?"

"No."

"I believe you—yes, it was me. My father always said bluffing is a coward's weapon, so I play to win."

"It's not a game, Gemma."

"Everything's a game, Marty. Don't you know that yet?"

I shook my head despairingly. "You need to let this one go, Gemma. Take the loss and move on."

"It's gone too far, Marty. You don't have to worry about me. Cosimo will hunt you down no matter where you are."

"I don't think Cosimo will get the chance," I said.

"Who are you?"

"Just a businessman in Italy to buy a foundry."

"I don't think you're just a businessman, Marty. I underestimated you. But don't underestimate me," she warned. "I'll tell you a secret I've never told anyone else."

I nodded.

"That story about me in the bar being held up by a group of boys—remember?"

I nodded again.

"It's not true. The truth is *I* told the boys they shouldn't leave until I picked one to blow in the bathroom. They waited for me to make my decision, and I tormented them for an hour with an old rhyme my mother taught me: 'One for sorrow, two for joy, three for a girl, four for a boy, five for silver, six for gold, seven for a secret never to be told.'" Her forefinger danced from left to right like a malicious metronome, a sneer tugging at her pale lips. "But I didn't want to tell that to my father."

Then, her expression twisted back into a smile. "And it makes a better story the other way."

She stood up, and threw the shot of Ballantine's in my face.

"That's for my brother."

The soldiers inched closer.

"*Ciao.*"

CHAPTER FORTY-FIVE

VALENTIN KOVALEV, dressed handsomely in a suit sans tie, strolled into the bar. After washing my face, I was once again the sole occupant. I'd turned the TV back on without sound, watching muted images flash across the screen. Prime Minister Berlusconi was being interviewed as he walked between government buildings. The crawl mentioned Camorra and *massacro*—a word I was becoming all too familiar with. I continued to nurse my club soda.

"Natalya's done shopping," he said. "She's changing, and we're all going to the Vatican for the document signing."

I nodded. "It's unnecessary, but she wants to show that nothing intimidates her."

"Where is everybody?"

"Bo's resting in his room. I don't know where Sergei is. Leo's being escorted from the Michelangelo. The *bratki* are dribbling out like a bar at closing time. Dmitry's on a yacht in the Mediterranean, Natalya's getting dressed, and you and I are here. Anyone else you want to know about?"

"Where's the Di Lupo woman?"

"Casertani and his men took her away—I suppose to kill her." I released a long, labored sigh, recalling how I'd watched Sergei's men place a grey pillowcase over her head before ushering her into Casertani's van. She didn't fight or struggle, believing they were just following protocol. It wouldn't dawn on her that Casertani's men

260

had replaced the Russians until they were well underway, leaving her alone and helpless in the back of the van.

Valya stared at me with silent empathy. At that moment, I understood why Dmitry kept him around. His quiet, soothing presence masked his dual role as both bodyguard and translator, allowing him to establish a subtle rapport. I felt unexpectedly at ease with him.

A faint impression caught my eye along the right side of his suit jacket. "You have a license for that?"

"Of course."

"Hard to get in Italy, I suppose."

"I am an official bodyguard for a very rich man. Even in Italy, it is recognized as a security threat. I have licenses for most countries."

While Valya explained the complexities of concealed-carry licensing, Leo Giacobbe joined us and introduced himself to Valya while slumping into a chair. He looked the worse for wear. He hadn't shaved, and his clothes seemed like they'd slept better than he did.

Then Bo came down. When he saw Leo, he said, "You look like death warmed over."

"Poor choice of words," I muttered.

"Have you seen the news?" asked Leo with a shaking voice. "A Di Lupo compound was hit last night; the war with the Casertanis has started." He ran his fingers through his tousled hair. "Gemma's locked up here on the fifth floor. Natalya's been kidnapped. I need to leave this country before I become collateral damage."

"Always nice to share a trench with you," said Bo.

"Gemma isn't here anymore," I added. Leo had no idea what had happened while he slept off his Irish coffees at the Michelangelo, but he was about to find out.

"Gentlemen," Natalya announced as she entered the bar.

Her transformation astonished me. Seven hours prior she was a daunted victim, laminated in filth and excrement, and now she looked ready to attend a gala opening. I reviewed her with the precision of a Milan fashion critic: Ferragamo leather pumps, Gucci pleated black pants, Armani cream blouse, and a Tom Ford black leather jacket, cropped at the hip.

I could only guess at the tempest raging inside of her, but from the outside, Natalya Danilenko emanated an admirable dignity. Even Bo, who rarely commented on a woman's appearance, especially Natalya's, whistled softly and whispered, "Wow."

"Thank you, Bo," she said. "Valya paid for everything because they stole my Birkin and my wallet."

"I have your Birkin, but not your wallet," I said, remembering Sergei's man had put it into my suitcase along with my torn clothes. It still held her fingernail and the photo.

"Leave it for the service staff. I will get a new one. Shall we go to meet with Angelo Caloia now?"

She looked at Leo for the first time. All the color had fled his face. His mouth gaped, his eyes bulged, and I was sure I saw his hair stiffen, but it could have been my imagination.

"Hello, Leo," she said, her voice flat and frank. "You are not looking well."

He stood and staggered a bit, putting his hand to his heart. "You were kidnapped!"

"Yes—Rome is a lovely city, but it lacks hospitality."

"The news—the compound at Lake Albano—was that about you?"

"I don't want to talk about such unpleasant things," she said. "We are all going to Vatican City to sign the Chiurazzi papers, and you will make a fat commission. I think that is a better topic, don't you?"

She's good—really good, I thought.

Sergei strolled into the bar, attired in full formal black. It seemed that Russian and Italian gangsters shared a penchant for funeral attire. He touched Natalya on the back with a gentleness that startled me. "I have cars waiting," he said.

"I called Lamberto Liuzzo and asked him to hold the closing in the Pope's Garage," she announced.

"That's a euphemism," grumbled Leo. "It's actually called the Carriage Pavilion, and it's generally not open to the public."

"I know, Leo," she said, smiling at Bo and me. "That is why I requested it. Martin and Bo wanted to see it, and I made sure they will."

We went in separate Fiats: Bo, Leo, and I in one, Sergei, Natalya, and Valya in the other. Both drivers were Sergei's men. They dropped us off at the *Viale Vaticano* entrance by the Vatican Gardens and then drove off. Sergei explained he would call them to pick us up.

The advantage of knowing the right people at the Vatican is that you get to walk past everyone who doesn't. A Vatican guide named Luigi, dressed in a light grey suit and blue tie and carrying a small cardboard sign with "Paladin" written on it, led us without delay, through a large crowd held back by makeshift barriers. We entered the giant white travertine marble portico of the Vatican Museum, its coat of arms sculpted in the pediment. As we hurried up the short steps, someone from the waiting masses pointed at us and called, "*Mafioso*."

Maybe it was our suits, maybe our privileged access, maybe both. I smiled in private amusement. I would have thought my light brown hair and blue eyes were a foolproof disclaimer against any misguided assumptions of Italian lineage. Bo had also heard the remark and said, "More like *mafioso* magnets."

We took a sharp left at the entrance, bypassing the ticketing and security checkpoints, and descended a long staircase roped off from other tourists.

The Carriage Pavilion is a long, underground warehouse—the length of two football fields—that holds a collection of carriages and vehicles used over the centuries by the papacy. We walked down a concourse filled with gilded Berlin-style carriages adorned with elaborate golden engravings and flaxen trimmings. The museum was empty except for two maintenance men pushing their janitorial carts at a respectful distance. At one point, our guide turned to Bo and asked if he wanted to step inside one of the carriages. He hesitantly agreed, and for a fleeting moment, Bo Bishop, still a bit bruised and battered, experienced a taste of the pontifical.

At the far end of the museum, bank president Angelo Caloia and attorney Lamberto Liuzzo waited, seated at a makeshift table. As we approached, Sergei, Valya, and the guide veered toward a display of ancient bridles in a choreographed move, implicitly excusing themselves from the meeting.

"You're lying bastards," declared Bo without preamble before we even sat down.

"*Ciao* to you, too," said Lamberto. Then, seeing Bo's face, "What happened to you?"

Bo waved it off.

"Do not blame the Liuzzos," said Caloia. "It is my fault. I wanted the Di Lupo *problema* kept secret."

"No kidding," snorted Leo, and Natalya glared at him to keep his mouth shut.

"I think it's more than a *problema*," said Bo.

Caloia wore the same suit he'd worn to the meeting in Bertolini's office. His sunken eyes were cordial, and his smile exposed a significant overbite. A fedora covered his bald head, with the side hair tucked neatly behind his ears, reminding me of Marlon Brando in *The Godfather*. His lips spread into a languid smile. His last four days, unlike ours, had been characteristically normal. He hadn't suffered, nor had he witnessed any suffering.

We'd all agreed not to tell Caloia and Liuzzo what happened to Natalya. She didn't want us to, and we respected her privacy. Besides, as Valya pointed out, with the mayhem about to hit, the less we were associated with it, the better.

Sharp and prickly-faced, Lamberto eyed Bo's motley eyes with suspicion, and his voice sliced through the awkward tension. "Speaking of the Di Lupo problem, have you seen what's happened in the last day?" His eyes were hard as marble. "One of the sons,

Cicciotto, his wife, his bodyguard, and others were brutally murdered in his own home, and his sister, Spina, the only daughter, has
disappeared. A war is looming."

"Sounds like it's not looming so much as it's already begun," I
replied.

"It's a sad day for Napoli," Caloia said earnestly. "The Scampia
neighborhood is like a third-world country. It's Europe's largest drug
market. If a war erupts between the ruling *dinastia* and its enemies,
the *polizia* will celebrate each new death as one less criminal to
deal with."

A heavy silence settled between us. Caloia's cynicism had long
ago suffocated any Christian piety. His stern expression then melted
away, replaced by a gentle countenance.

"His Eminence Cardinal Bertolini and I speak in one voice when
we say that Paladin has been approved to purchase the Chiurazzi
Foundry." He pushed a leather portfolio toward Natalya with the
Vatican Seal embossed on the cover.

"All necessary documents are in there. You are now the owners
of the famous Chiurazzi Foundry," said Lamberto.

"We haven't transferred any funds," said Bo.

"The bank has temporarily loaned Paladin the money to close
the deal. You can pay it back at your convenience. No interest is
charged."

Bo and I were stunned. Even Natalya was startled.

Caloia smiled, his overbite exposing his upper teeth like shingles.
"You are now part of the Vatican Bank family. We do things a little
differently than other banks."

"*Signore* Caloia," I interjected. "May I ask how you know our
largest investor, Mr. Dmitry Chernyshevsky?"

"We share real estate interests," he said mildly.

"We already know that. We're wondering if Dmitry came to
you, or you went to Dmitry with the 'real estate interests,'" said
Bo, using air quotes.

"His Eminence Cardinal Bertolini has tasked me with a great responsibility. I am to trim the Church's property portfolio. But it is a delicate matter. I need to find a buyer willing to buy directly and quietly." He looked at Natalya. "Remember our meeting in Paris at Caritas Internationalis?"

"Yes," she answered.

"I asked *Signore* Chernyshevsky if he could help us, convincing him that I could make it worth his while."

"Wonderful," proclaimed Leo, standing up. "Thank you, *Signore* Caloia and Lamberto. I do not need to be part of this conversation, nor do I want to be. We must have espresso the next time I'm in town."

Before I could tell him to shut up, Natalya said, "You may leave now—go find Sergei." She waved him off like an intrusive waiter. He slunk away, his head downcast, disappearing into the shadows of the nearby carriages.

"You're flipping Vatican properties, *Signore* Caloia," said Bo.

Lamberto put his hand up to stop further conversation. "We are getting into affairs that are not your business and of which you have a false understanding."

"Then make it clear," said Natalya firmly. I sensed the weight of her recent experience behind her words.

Caloia glanced at Lamberto, granting him silent permission.

"You need to understand our commitment to Opus Dei," said Lamberto.

"What's that got to do with anything?" I asked.

Lamberto raised his finger to stop my interruption. "*La Signora* Natalya asked, and I am explaining. Opus Dei members pursue spiritual sanctity by integrating faith into their daily lives. It operates under the prelature of the Holy Cross and emphasizes the concept of divine filiation. Followers of the prelature believe that penance and mortification reduce selfishness, allowing our love for God to grow."

"Marty's right," injected Bo. "What's this got to do with flipping Church property?"

"We believe in sacrifice."

"Like in the novel," said Bo.

He shook his head angrily. "That book is offensive. It extols blood, masochism, and degradation."

"What book?" whispered Natalya to me.

"I'll tell you later," I whispered back.

"Jesus invites all Christians to help him carry the cross," said Caloia.

"I think it's weird, but—again—what's your point?" asked Bo, his patience waning.

"Cardinal Bertolini is not an unethical man," said Lamberto, realizing he was losing his audience. "He is pious and completely obedient to *Il Papa*. What you do not know, but I will share with you, is that the Holy Father gave Cardinal Bertolini the task of supporting Opus Dei, but not directly with Church funds."

"What means 'not with Church funds?'" asked Natalya.

Angelo Caloia tapped his forefinger to his lips. "Let me try to explain. Do you remember the Polish Solidarity movement back in the early 1980s?"

Natalya shook her head no, and Bo and I nodded yes.

"Well, right after *Il Papa* ascended, he...*abbracciato*—embraced—the Polish revolution for independence. He openly supported Poland and its efforts to break from the Soviet Union, but most people don't know that he provided enormous financial backing for the movement. He funneled millions and millions of dollars into the Solidarity labor union, secretly and off the books."

"I keep repeating myself," said Bo. "What's your point?"

"The Solidarity project was not much different from the current Opus Dei project," said Caloia, and he nodded at Lamberto to continue.

"*Il Papa* awarded Opus Dei official autonomy in 1982. He

canonized the founder of Opus Dei and proclaimed him a saint. He has *affinità*—affinity—for the organization. It is important to him and all of us. In secular terms, think of it as *Il Papa*'s…what would be the right word?"

"Baby," suggested Bo.

"Precious," I said.

"*Lyubimchik*—pet,*"* added Natalya.

Lamberto nodded approvingly. "Yes. It is a priority for him. But with autonomy comes the need for sustainability. Money and time are needed to build strength. So, Cardinal Bertolini and my uncle found a creative approach. Angelo—*compro-vendo*—buys and sells Church property for a profit, which my father and I then donate to the Opus Dei. We are all supernumerary members."

"What's a supernumerary member?" asked Bo.

"I'll fill you in later," I interrupted, remembering what Gabriele had said in the bar before the concert.

"It is our method for funding the order," said Caloia, "off the books. I needed a silent and reliable buyer to make things easier. So, I offered Dmitry a Vatican Bank account along with the Chiurazzi for motivation."

"We don't burden *Il Papa* with the details, but we are sure he would approve if he knew," said Lamberto. "I think we are done here."

"Flipping Church property for personal profit is not legal," said Bo as we all stood up and raised our hands to shake. "Even if you donate it to Opus Dei."

"Robbing a bank and then giving the money to charity doesn't keep you out of jail," I added.

"The law is like salami. You slice it where you want," said Caloia, tilting his fedora lower, shading the wells of his eyes while his thin smile bore the secrets of centuries.

I briefly wondered if I was staring at a future version of myself—a haunting vision of what I might become.

CHAPTER FORTY-SIX

SERGEI, LEO, BO, AND I SQUEEZED INTO ONE FIAT while Natalya, Valya, and the two *bratki* drivers piled into another. Sergei took the wheel and drove us back from the Vatican. As we approached the hotel, he guided the car into the narrow alley beside the lobby entrance.

"Leo," he said, "stay a minute; I want to talk with you."

Bo and I climbed out, slamming the doors in unison, and trudged through the chilly shade toward the hotel's back entrance.

Two muffled thumps reached my ears—the sound of books falling—and a familiar tremor surged through my gut, tilting my world. I lost my balance and dropped to one knee.

"What the…?" Bo exclaimed as he sprinted back to the car.

Inside, Leo Giacobbe took a few agonizing seconds to die. His expression turned dumbstruck while his hands flitted to his chest as if trying to swat away a fly. Then he lowered them to his sides. His head lolled forward until his chin brushed his collarbone, and he stopped breathing.

Bo fought to yank the door open, but Sergei leveled a gun at him through the window. I lunged at the back door, trying to wrench it free, but Sergei had auto-locked all of them. Bo pounded the roof, and I smashed my elbow into the glass, only to feel the painful recoil shoot through my arm.

Sergei climbed out on his side. "Stop! You'll bring the *politsiya*!" he barked.

Two of his men charged around the corner of the hotel lobby

into the alley, quickly wrapping us in body locks. Bo, a former college wrestling champion, used his muscle memory to twist out of his attacker's grip and slam him into the car with such force that it knocked Sergei—standing opposite—into the hotel's brick wall.

I hadn't been a wrestler, but I stomped the heel of my shoe down on the toe of the man holding me. He grunted in pain and retaliated by slamming my head into the Fiat's pillar trim. The impact jolted my skull, and I saw a flash of light.

Sergei let out a muted shout. "Stop! Now! Or I'll shoot both of you!"

Bo uncoupled, and his guy fell over.

I uncoupled with my guy, and I fell over.

Bo came and helped me to my feet.

"Get inside," hissed Sergei, and we all staggered into the hotel lobby.

The alley was empty, and no one had noticed our scuffle. Sergei's pistol had a suppressor attached, and to anyone walking along *Vicola di Febo,* the shots blended seamlessly into the sounds of the street— perhaps fruit crates being unloaded.

I locked eyes with the *bratki* who'd grabbed me, recognizing him from the breakfast table next to ours the day before—thick head, nose, and neck with a gothic cross tattoo covering the nape. Sergei spoke Russian to him, and he muttered "*Da,*" several times. Sergei tossed him a blanket, and without a word he walked back out to the car, draped it over Leo, and drove away. The whole thing took less than five minutes. I never saw either of them again.

The other guy Bo had manhandled was silent, maybe embarrassed. After Sergei said something to him in Russian, he took the elevator to an upper floor. Sergei then waved his Beretta and motioned for us to sit on the grey leather couch in the lobby. The hotel had emptied of his men, leaving only a few stragglers wandering about.

"Where's Natalya?" I asked.

"Shut up," he said. "I talk now. You listen."

He clicked the safety on and laid the gun next to him. There were specks of blood on his jacket and neck. I'm not sure he knew.

"I shot Leo in his chest, not in his head, because I wanted him to know he was dying," he declared grimly, his face looking cold and pasty. "Now you understand who I am. Yes?"

We said nothing.

"Leo helped the Di Lupos. He gave information to the enemy. He died the moment Natalya was stolen. He lived two more days because I thought he might be useful. His last function was to be at the Vatican paper signing. Now, his usefulness is done. I told my man to drive him out of town, burn the car, and bury the bones deep. To leave nothing for the *politsiya* to identify."

"Where is Natalya?" I asked again.

"She is gone. Dmitry did not want her to be in Rome when I cleaned things up. Valya and Brody are flying with her to Cyprus. Brody needs repairs, and Dmitry's *dacha* has a small hospital."

"Did she know? Did she plan to leave after we met with Caloia?"

"Yes, she knew. You think Natalya gets kidnapped a second time—by Valya?"

I looked at Bo, noticing a thin skim of sweat on his forehead. "Her pilot needs time to file a flight plan. She probably called him when she was changing into her new clothes," he said.

I felt sick, but my stomach was as empty as the rest of me. I couldn't stop seeing Leo, his arms folding toward his chest as if preparing for a coffin he'd never have.

"I will go now," Sergei said. "I leave two men to clean the rooms, make sure nothing is left. The hotel people will return tomorrow and be open for business the next day."

The guy Sergei had sent upstairs emerged from the elevator carrying a backpack and a suitcase. Sergei took the backpack, shoved in the gun—suppressor still attached—and zipped it shut.

"I never want to see you again. My man will drive you to the airport. Your bags are packed and waiting in your rooms. You will not speak of these past days—to anyone." He paused as if double-checking that he'd covered everything. "Natalya told me she will go back to America after a week of rest."

Then he and his soldier exited the lobby and got into a waiting Peugeot. Through the glass, I could see the cobblestones shimmering in the late afternoon sun, buildings leaning in as if to swallow the car.

I looked at Bo.

"Don't look at me, Marty," he said. "She's your girlfriend."

CHAPTER FORTY-SEVEN

Lake Oswego, Oregon — later that winter

DO YOU KNOW THE DIFFERENCE BETWEEN FACT AND FICTION?

Fiction demands plausibility—fact does not.

Case in point—it is a fact, however implausible, that a minor skirmish between two mafia clans in Naples escalated into Italy's most violent gang war in modern memory because my silent partner, Dmitry Chernyshevsky, got his nose out of joint after his girlfriend—and mine—lost a fingernail.

But then, perhaps I'm just bitter.

///////////////////////////////////////

Bo and I caught the Delta red-eye and landed in Portland, Oregon, on Thursday at noon. We'd been gone for a week.

We didn't speak much on the way to the airport or during the flight. There wasn't much to say, and Bo preferred sleep over conversation at times like this. He reclined his chair and slept restlessly the entire trip. I couldn't stop thinking about Natalya and how she had left without a word or gesture, leaving only a nagging absence—like a phantom limb.

While waiting at baggage claim at the Portland airport, Bo said, "I'm taking a few days off. You should do the same. Spend some time with your wife and kids. Figure out your priorities."

"I'll be fine," I replied defensively. "I don't need marital advice."

He looked at me hard. His eyes were nearly back to normal, except for a slight yellow hue that resembled jaundice more than a bruise.

"Marty, you've been making a lot of bad choices lately. You're not who I thought you were. Maybe you've changed, or maybe you were always this way, and I just missed it. I can blame myself for the latter, but not the former."

A sharp, lucid warning flashed through me: I wasn't just losing Natalya. I was also on the verge of losing my best friend.

"I'll see you in a few days," he said. "Say hello to Abbie for me." With that, he walked off to his car.

///

Bo stayed away for more than a few days. He took Katherine on a month-long island-hopping vacation to Hawaii, Belize, and the Caribbean. His daughters sulked at being stuck in school, but Katherine's mother looked after them. He called me twice a week to check on things. Our exchanges, while pleasant, always felt a little forced, a little off-kilter.

I stayed dutifully in the prison I'd built for myself. I went to work, held meetings, ate dinners with my family, did the chores, smiled appropriately, frowned appropriately, and made love to Abbie when she wanted me to.

Shortly after returning to work, I received an email from Natalya that said: *Martin, forgive me for leaving Rome rudely.* I smiled and mentally replaced *rudely* with *abruptly*. It went on: *I will be on vacation in Cyprus for several weeks and will not call to work. Thank You.*

///

I scoured newspapers and news sites daily for information about mafia activity in Italy. The most informative reports came from an

American freelance journalist, Mark Snyder, who worked for *the Guardian* in the UK. His beat was Italian organized crime, and his reports on Naples were fascinating and grim.

WEEKENDS TURN BLOODY IN NAPLES MAFIA WAR:

By Mark Snyder in Naples

Thirty-Eight Killed as Battle Rages to Control Narcotics Trade:

Alessio Rosa saw them coming. Police say the 48-year-old was someone on the lower rungs of a Naples organized crime ring. In panic, he turned into the nearest shop, a delicatessen hung with hams and salamis.

Two men followed him and shot him several times in front of staff and customers. One of the bullets lodged in Rosa's skull. He died in the ambulance on the way to the hospital as a police helicopter swept low overhead, searching for the killers. Witnesses reported that the assailants escaped on a motorbike.

The murders are almost always committed on Saturdays and Sundays. Last weekend was the worst so far—ten people killed or fatally wounded. The killings began with the abduction of Gemma Di Lupo on January 20, which the police believe sparked the conflict. She has not been found since her disappearance, and the death toll so far is 162, including bystanders.

Cosimo Di Lupo, the leader of the clan that has bloodied Naples, has been arrested. The Scampia Feud is a war against the "secessionists," who police believe are battling for control of Naples's booming drug trade.

Italian President Carlo Azeglio Ciampi called for the mafia "cancer" to be cut out of Italian life during a visit to Naples. One woman asked Mr. Ciampi if he would help

her leave, but he denied her request, saying everyone must
have the strength to live in Naples.

///////////////////////////////////

After a month of silence, Natalya called.

"Hello, Martin?" she said softly with a tentative lilt that left room for a reply.

"Natalya," I responded boldly, closing any avenue to reluctance.

"I will be in Portland tomorrow," she said.

"How was your vacation?"

"It was long and relaxing. But it is time to go back to work. I am coming to Portland to visit with my stepson, and I want to catch up."

"Do you want to meet in the office?" I asked with an edge to my voice. Typically I would have met her at the airport, and we would then go straight to her hotel room.

She fully understood what I was doing and let me know in her brisk voice. "Just come to the hotel, Martin. We have some private things to talk about."

///////////////////////////////////

She was tanned, and her hair had grown out a touch.

We sat by a window in the tavern of the Heathman Hotel in downtown Portland, passing the first half hour in idle chatter, observing the gentle rain and the hurried pedestrians. How was Bo? How was Dmitry? How was she? How was I? How was Cyprus?

"Sergei came to visit us in Cyprus. He was nice," she said.

"The Sergei I met wasn't 'nice,'" I scoffed. The vision of Leo Giacobbe gulping his last breath flashed into my head.

"He had a job. He was working."

"I'm not a fan of his work," I answered. "And his social skills are for shit."

"You are wrong," she countered softly. "Blame the language. It is hard to get *Russkie* to talk in English, but in Russian, they can't stop." She smiled.

As I studied her lovely face, my lingering anger dissolved. The joy of being with her overshadowed the pain of missing her. She must have noticed the shift in my eyes because hers narrowed slightly.

I switched gears. "I've always wondered why you had the attorney, Lamberto Liuzzo, instruct Leo Giacobbe to approach Dante with the deal. Why not me?"

She took a sip of her latte and reached out to touch my hand.

"I was stupid," she confessed. "Dmitry told me he needed Paladin to buy the Chiurazzi, and I...*panika*."

"Why would you panic?"

"I don't pick companies for us to buy. It is not my specialty. I thought it would not be agreeable with you and Bo."

"You certainly worked hard to convince me," I pointed out.

The corners of her lips curled in a smile. "Yes, I remember every detail."

She took another sip of her drink. "It was an unnecessary trick. I wanted it to look like idea came from Dante, not me."

"Because 'me' implied 'Dmitry,' and 'Dante' implied blind luck."

"I think you are a little harsh, but yes."

"Why Paladin? Why not any number of companies you and Dmitry own?"

"Dmitry is not listed on any Paladin documents other than as an investor. Paladin is the only company he controls but doesn't own."

"He doesn't control it," I insisted.

She looked at me like I was a lost child.

"But he does, Martin."

CHAPTER FORTY-EIGHT

WE ORDERED LUNCH AT THE HEATHMAN and spent another hour talking, whispering, laughing, and reflecting. We shared a crème brûlée, and I retold the story of our dinner with Dmitry, Valya, and Sergei, this time embellishing the details. And then, because of my compulsion to pick at scabs, I abruptly pivoted the conversation and asked, "Did Dmitry tell Sergei to kill Leo?"

She stared into the empty ramekin, a few caramelized crumbs clinging to the sides, and her expression soured. "Martin, do you think Dmitry stands like a general in front of a big table, like in a movie, while his men move pieces around? Dmitry says nothing. Maybe he nods his head, and maybe he doesn't even do that. Leo was a spy for Gemma. That made him *predatel'*—a traitor."

"It was just a business deal," I reminded her.

"And I was kidnapped and tortured. To me, it was more than a business deal. You did not feel the pain in my hands and feet. You did not swat at flies."

"You're right. I wanted all of them dead. But not Leo. He messed up, sure—but we all do. I practically invented screwing up." I played with my fork. "A week ago, Leo's daughter Grace called. She sounded like him, polite, sincere, and a little pushy. She hadn't heard from her father in over a month and was worried about him. He'd told her he was working on a project for a company called Paladin and she wanted to know if I'd spoken to him recently."

I paused, the lump in my throat growing. "I fed her smooth, empty

278

lies—the kind that nest like ringworms, eating away at what's left of my conscience. After I hung up, I pulled out the bottle of scotch we keep for emergencies and drank until I passed out on the office couch."

She reached across the table and touched my hand. "Revenge requires two graves. It means…"

"I know what it means, Natalya," I said irritably.

She gently pulled back her hand, and I looked unflinchingly into her eyes.

"What happens now?" I said. "Are you staying?"

The following hush provided the answer.

"No, Martin," she said at last.

"Then it's over," I said.

"Yes," she answered, her tone cutting with surgical precision.

"Can we at least argue about it?"

She smiled bleakly. "I have something to tell you now, Martin, and it will hurt."

My stomach started sending signals to my brain to be on alert. I said nothing and waited for her to speak.

"You need to go home and fix your marriage," said Natalya. "Abbie is not sleeping with her boss. It is a story you inflated in your head." She paused to study my face. "I think you searched for reasons to punish yourself after you and Abbie broke your marriage. But they were false suspicions, Martin. It was—how to say—a trick for your brain. Something not true, but you want it to be true so much you convinced yourself it was—yes?" She tapped her finger on her temple. "Before me, you wanted excuses for not being a good husband. Then, after me, you wanted excuses to be with me." She reached out again and retouched my hand. "And me too—I wanted excuses to be with you."

I said nothing, staring at her blankly.

"You will be angry now," she said delicately—every word a

calculated caress. "You know I have business in Geneva. I have large storage vault in Geneva Freeport."

I remembered hearing about it two years ago. She'd kept the forged Raphael in her storage vault and then surreptitiously moved it to Dmitry's vault.

I nodded.

"I use a company in Geneva. It is called Seaclop, and it checks things for me, like backgrounds of customers and buyers. It is investigation company. I asked them to check what Abbie was doing with her boss on her trip to Geneva. They watched her in hotel and everywhere she went. She is friends with her boss, and that is all. They stay on separate hotel floors and stay in their rooms all night. The hotel has a wonderful spa, and she gets treated head-to-toe on every trip. She and her boss have dinner and drinks, but mostly with other people. When they are alone, they never touch their hands and always sit opposite each other. They laugh and like each other, but only as *kollegi*—colleagues. The investigator gave me full report."

Her words raked across my nerves like a blunt blade.

"When did you get this report?" I asked.

"Many months ago."

"Why tell me now?"

"Because Martin, we were both *uchastnik*—participants in our involvement. I liked it as much as you liked it. I didn't tell you because I didn't want you to know the truth. I wanted you to stay with me—stay involved. It is my betrayal, and I am sorry."

"Why do you want us to end now?"

"Because you made a mistake." She paused, thinking of ways to express herself. "You used your hands to pick up broken glass."

My bewildered stare told her I didn't understand.

"I will translate old Russian saying."

I rolled my eyes.

"It means you tried to fix your marriage by making it worse."

"Americans just say, 'You fucked things up.'"

"Yes. I know what Americans say. I prefer the Russian. I think it is why Russians write better books."

I exhaled.

"But I learned in Rome our involvement is not healthy anymore. Maybe it never was. It is too complicated." She withdrew her hand slowly. "Our involvement is too important to you and not important enough to me. You understand?" She said *You understand* with the finality of a dropped gavel. "We will be business partners. We will be friends," she added, and I winced at a phrase so trite it felt cruel.

"I will miss your stories," I said.

Her lips stretched into a straight line, and her eyes creased at the edges, hinting at a smile.

"Russian stories, *milyy*, never end well."

CHAPTER FORTY-NINE

WE SAID GOODBYE UNDER THE HOTEL'S ENTRANCE CANOPY by rubbing our cheeks together. I knew that in the future, the silence between us would always hold our history, and I was fine with that.

I pulled into our Lake Oswego office on my way home.

I thought about what Natalya had said about endings, and how many of them had been in my life recently. It wasn't the inevitability of endings that bothered me. It was that they were unyielding.

"You look like you lost your best friend," said Bo, strolling up as I exited my car. I hadn't seen him in over a month, and we embraced in a typical man hug with plenty of back-slapping.

"Have I?" I asked, separating from him and staring at the pavement.

"Lost your best friend?" he repeated. "Naw. Takes more than a mafia war to break us up."

"Stop it," I quipped. "You're a married man."

We entered the building and headed for the glass cage. Bo shook hands with everyone while I led the way.

"Natalya and I are done," I said as soon as the glass door shut.

"I figured," he said. "Can you still work together?"

"Probably," I said.

He smiled broadly. He looked healthy, relaxed, and as brown as a bronze sculpture.

"I've been thinking, Marty," he said. "I don't know how or when, but we're getting ourselves out of this mess."

"By mess, you mean Dmitry and Natalya."

"Yes. We will find a way to extricate ourselves from this part-nership without getting ourselves killed."

"You sound optimistic."

"I just want my life back—our life back. We can't get back what we lost, but maybe we can keep from losing any more."

We sat for a while, watching the rain wrinkle the lake's surface. A lone fisherman, bundled in wet-weather gear, bobbed in a small dinghy, a solitary silhouette against the grey expanse. I wondered what thoughts drifted through his mind as he looked like the lone-liest man on earth.

We drank from the fresh bottle of Glenlivet I'd exchanged for the one I polished off after Leo's daughter's call.

I told Bo all about it and cried for the first time.

///////////////////////////////////////

Some time ago, in one of those quiet leisure moments after our intimacy, Natalya had once said, "Martin, I hope suffering happens to you."

At the time, I was affronted, but I came to understand that, para-doxically, she was caring for me. Suffering forges resilience; people who have never suffered sometimes shatter too easily.

I took the back roads home, driving slowly, lost in thought and regrets. I thought about the tangled skein of deception woven from lies—not all mine but lies nonetheless—tightening around me.

I thought about Abbie. How badly I broke things. So much to fix. So much to atone for.

When I arrived, I didn't pull into the driveway but instead parked on the street. The rain had stopped. I turned off the engine and sat there, intently watching my house—waiting to see if a brick might move, a window warp, or the chimney collapse.

When the glass fogged up, I lowered the passenger window,

letting in the damp air, and continued my vigil, all the while considering how to unwind the past into the promise of an endless present.

AUTHOR'S NOTE

ON JANUARY 17, 2004, I attended the Papal Concert of Reconciliation hosted by Pope John Paul II at the Vatican with my friend and business partner, Roy Rose, and seven thousand other invited guests. We sat next to Luciano Pavarotti. We were in Rome because our company had purchased a license for the Vatican Library Seal. While negotiating the contract, we had a private tour of the Vatican, visited the Pope's Garage, attended a function at the Vatican Observatory, and met numerous Church officials and the American Ambassador to the Vatican. On a separate trip, we toured the historic Chiurazzi Foundry in Naples, which provided the molds for art we reproduced under license from the Vatican. We considered buying the foundry itself but were outbid by a close competitor.

My experiences in Italy were fertile ground for many good stories over the years, and so, when it was time to write book two of the Marty and Bo's thriller series, I decided to set the book there.

Coincidentally, one of the biggest mafia wars in Italy's history took place in 2004 between rival Camorra gangs—the Di Lauro clan and a secessionist group. More than a hundred and sixty people were killed. And it occurred to me that if Marty and Bo, with the Russian oligarch backing them, were ever in conflict with the Camorra over the purchase of the Chiurazzi, that might provide a fictionalized reason for the war.

The third element of my story involves the Vatican Bank, which was implicated in numerous money laundering scandals over the years. Gerald Posner's book *God's Bankers: A History of Money and Power at the Vatican* is a good source of information on this. In 2013, Pope Francis began a process of cleaning up the Vatican Bank, but back in 2004, the IOR was very much as described in my book.

Angelo Caloia is a real person. He was president of the Vatican Bank for a decade, from 1999 until 2009. In 2021, he and his personal lawyer, Gabriele Liuzzo, were sentenced to eight years in prison for money laundering and skimming profits from the sale of Vatican properties. Lamberto Liuzzo, Gabriele's son, was also found guilty of his role in the scheme, which took place during the period in which my story is set. I used their real names in the story but invented their involvement in the plot to provide my fictional Russian oligarch access to a Vatican Bank account.

Cardinal Rautan and Cardinal Bertolini are fictional characters loosely based on the real prelates who headed the Vatican Library and the Bureau of Economic Affairs for the Holy See in that period. There is no evidence that the actual cardinals who held these positions collaborated in Angelo Caloia's unsavory schemes, so I've invented some characters who might have. All the other characters in *The Vatican Deal* are fictional.

I borrowed liberally from old newspaper articles, notably *The Guardian*, from which I crafted the articles in the book. Should you find similarities in the newspaper articles and parts of the book, it is intentional.

I also borrowed and refigured some unique phrases and thoughts from others, specifically: Bertrand Russell – "The hardest thing to learn in life is which bridge to cross and which to burn." Mark Twain – "Truth is stranger than fiction, but it is because Fiction is obliged to stick to possibilities; Truth isn't." Tom Clancy – "The difference between fiction and reality? Fiction has to make sense." And Alan Watts – "The present moment is the only time that exists, and it is an endless present."

I want to credit Roberto Saviano and Sovietologist Mark Galeotti, whose writings and speeches greatly informed my research. Some of their phrases or anecdotes found their way into this book.

I sincerely thank everyone who helped make my second book a reality. The biggest thanks go out to everyone who read and loved my debut novel, *Chasing Money*. I am thrilled whenever I hear from someone who is a fan of my writing and wants to read more about Marty and Bo's adventures. That inspires me to go to work every day at my favorite coffee shop in Charlevoix, Harwood Gold, where I plug away at my writing. Thanks to my four friends who often share my table and let me work: John, Steve, Ted, and, of course, Larry, who is always full of suggestions.

Thanks to my publisher, Doug Weaver, and the entire team at Mission Point Press. My editor, Susanne Dunlap, provided invaluable feedback, as did my beta readers, Tom Barnes, Valerie Snyder, Warren Anderson, and Greg Calfin.

Special thanks to my best friend, Roy Rose, who shared more adventures in Italy with me than I could squeeze into these pages. In plotting out the story, he was often my memory and advisor.

And finally, my wife Suzanne, to whom I dedicate this book. She is not just the love of my life but just about everything else as well—my confidant, my conscience, my mentor, my support, my cheerleader, my drill sergeant, my editor, my advisor, my promoter, my agent, and most importantly the mother of our two great children, Andrew and Ali. I have tried to imagine my life without her and can't because it would have been dark and bleak, and I am grateful every day that she agreed to spend her life with me.

For more information on the background of this story and updates on upcoming books in the Marty and Bo thriller series, please visit my website at mbalter.com.

MICHAEL BALTER is an award-winning author and a talented and witty storyteller. His debut novel, *Chasing Money*, won multiple awards including the 2023 Best Indie Book Award for Crime Thrillers, the 2024 Feathered Quill Award for Best Mystery/Thriller/Suspense Novel, and the 2024 Crime Thriller of the Year Award from BestThrillers.com. Born in Berlin, Michael grew up in a bombed-out building with bars on the windows and bullet holes in the walls. When the Berlin Wall went up, his family fled to Ottawa and then moved to Detroit at the height of the 1967 riots. During the Vietnam War, Michael served as an air traffic controller at the Udorn Air Force base in Thailand. After graduating college with an aerospace engineering degree, Michael joined Intel Corporation, entering Silicon Valley on the ground floor and building a successful career in sales and marketing. In 1998, Michael was bitten by the entrepreneurial bug and joined a voice recognition startup. Over the next 20 years, he became a serial entrepreneur, helping to create and launch new business ventures in Oregon, ranging from a Renaissance art company to a private equity firm. One of his business partners was kidnapped by a Russian mobster, which inspired a portion of the plot of *Chasing Money*. Michael now lives in Charlevoix, Michigan, and is writing his next Marty and Bo thriller. Learn more at mbalter.com.